Her Lessons in Persuasion

"Tell me why you kissed me that night," Bram asked.

He heard her inhale sharply, then spin toward him again. Still holding his hand.

"Why not?" she replied simply. She released his hand, but then placed her now-free hand onto his chest. Could she feel his heart? It felt as though it was beating harder now.

"Why not?" he repeated, placing his hand on top of hers.

This time, he knew what to expect. This time, he lowered his head so she wouldn't have to be all the way up on her tiptoes.

This time, he met her gaze, keeping his eyes locked on hers as she rose up, her lips slightly parted.

This time, like the last time, he let her kiss him.

By Megan Frampton

School for Scoundrels
HER LESSONS IN PERSUASION

The Hazards of Dukes
FOUR WEEKS OF SCANDAL
GENTLEMAN SEEKS BRIDE
A WICKED BARGAIN FOR THE DUKE
TALL, DUKE, AND DANGEROUS
NEVER KISS A DUKE

The Duke's Daughters
THE EARL'S CHRISTMAS PEARL (novella)
NEVER A BRIDE
THE LADY IS DARING
LADY BE RECKLESS
LADY BE BAD

Dukes Behaving Badly
MY FAIR DUCHESS
WHY DO DUKES FALL IN LOVE?
ONE-EYED DUKES ARE WILD
NO GROOM AT THE INN (novella)
PUT UP YOUR DUKE
WHEN GOOD EARLS GO BAD (novella)
THE DUKE'S GUIDE TO CORRECT BEHAVIOR

MEGAN FRAMPTON

HER LESSONS *in* PERSUASION

A School for Scoundrels Novel

AVONBOOKS

An Imprint of HarperCollinsPublishers

Excerpt from *His Study in Scandal* copyright © 2023 by Megan Frampton.

HER LESSONS IN PERSUASION. Copyright © 2023 by Megan Frampton. All rights reserved. Printed in the United States of America. No part of this book may be used or reproduced in any manner whatsoever without written permission except in the case of brief quotations embodied in critical articles and reviews. For information, address HarperCollins Publishers, 195 Broadway, New York, NY 10007.

First Avon Books mass market printing: January 2023

Print Edition ISBN: 978-0-06-322418-6
Digital Edition ISBN: 978-0-06-322419-3

Cover design by Amy Halperin
Cover illustration by Victor Gadino
Cover image © Sean Pavone | Dreamstime.com

FIRST EDITION

23 24 25 26 27 BVGM 10 9 8 7 6 5 4 3 2 1

To Liz. You're dynamite.

HER
LESSONS
in
PERSUASION

Men I Do Not Wish to Marry: A Not at All Comprehensive List by Lady Wilhelmina Bettesford

A man who believes he knows better than any woman in any situation, regardless of her expertise. The type of man who would explain what a rhyme scheme is to a poet. Who tells a cook she's not stirring the pot enough, even though he's never cooked anything in his life. Who insists a woman will be happy if she stays at home while he goes out in the world, even though he hasn't asked her what she wants, from how she takes her tea to how she wishes to live her life.

Chapter One

London 1850

London in the evening was a dangerous place if you had money in your pocket.

It was already dark by the time Bram Townsend left his office, clapping his hat onto his head as he shut the door behind himself. An ordinary man with coins jingling in his pockets would, perhaps, hail a hackney cab to take him from where he was in the depths of The City to the fine streets of Mayfair. Far safer than walking.

That he *did* have money, despite his ignominious birth, made him far from ordinary. Unusual, even. *Distinctive.*

Bram didn't take his good fortune for granted. He'd worked hard to become a barrister, making sure justice prevailed in England's courts of law. He had ambitions of becoming a judge to serve justice even more widely.

He had no time for anything save his profession and his friends—four fellow orphans who'd also been at the Devenaugh Home for Destitute Boys, more famously known as the School for Scoundrels.

That was why he was walking on foot, despite the danger. His long stride and quick pace would get him to where he was going far faster than a hackney would. This evening he was on his way to meet his friends for their monthly meeting, where they discussed books and their respective lives. They'd be debating Elizabeth Gaskell's *Mary Barton* tonight, and he was already preparing his arguments. Which were numerous.

Bram didn't spend any time heeding the calls of certain women to come find his pleasure with them as he walked. He also ignored the lively chatter that spilled into the streets from pubs catering to all sorts of people—even, he knew, gentlemen who had the audacity to work for their livings as he did.

Not only would it make him later, it wouldn't be proper. And since he already had the black mark of illegitimacy tied to his name, he took care to keep his behavior proper at all times.

"Was Gaskell using the murder to illustrate the plight of the Bartons?" he muttered. It felt, while reading *Mary Barton*, that he had suffered along with Mary as her life took precarious turns.

The night was cool, the temperate warmth of the early spring day having ebbed as the sun set. Bram liked how it felt to be a bit chilled—his offices and the courts could get swelteringly hot, all the bodies, both washed and unwashed, pressing together in search of justice.

His path took him across the Blackfriars Bridge, the wind a bit colder when there were no buildings to shield him from it. He dug his hands farther into his pockets and lowered his head, making it so he almost didn't see the altogether inexplicable figure of a woman perched on the parapet, her long cloak flapping in the wind. She wore no hat, and her hair streamed behind her, the moonlight limning her silhouette.

For a moment, his fanciful part—which until that moment he hadn't realized he even *had*—wondered if she was an angel come to earth, or some other sort of otherworldly creature. A fairy, a goddess. A water sprite.

But first of all, he didn't believe in any of that nonsense, and second of all, why would an otherworldly creature choose to alight on Blackfriars Bridge?

And then she wobbled, and he knew she was a mere mortal who was in very great danger of falling off said bridge into the cold depths of the Thames. A mere mortal who was courting great danger, and even greater notoriety.

"Stop," he roared, rushing forward to wrap his arm just below her knees, jerking her backward as she yelped in surprise. She tumbled off, the fabric of her cloak clinging to him as she pitched backward.

She landed on top of him while he landed right on the hard surface of the bridge.

"Mmfargh," she said as he made an equally inarticulate groan.

They both lay there still for a moment, him already cataloguing what hurt: everything.

She scrambled off him, hitting a few tender places with her elbows and knees, then rolled so she was on her knees, flinging her cloak over her shoulder.

"What," she began, "did you *do*? How dare you?"

"Stop," he said again, grabbing her ankle. "I can't—"

"Let go of me, you ruffian!" she replied, wriggling her foot. He held on tight, clasping her ankle with his other hand as well.

"I will not," he said, his tone low and intense. "I cannot let you do this—"

"*Let* me?" she said in a squeak. "Who are you to have anything to say about what I do?"

He looked up at her. "Surely it's not worth it," he said, groaning as he shifted onto his side. "I am certain we can find you some help. If it's money you need, I can give you some now, and perhaps try to find you employment. If it's something else," he said, thinking of his own illegitimate birth, "there are resources there, too."

He couldn't see her face since the moon was behind her. Was she mortified someone had seen her? Aghast she hadn't been able to do what she'd originally intended? Relieved she'd been saved?

"Help?" she said, her tone outraged. Neither mortified, aghast, nor relieved, then. "You think I needed help? *Employment?*" She twisted around to punch him hard on the arm, almost making him fall onto his back again. It had the added bonus of getting him to release her ankle. "I do not need *help*, you interfering baboon."

He blinked up at her. "You—?" he began.

"No!" she interrupted. Her speech was that of a lady's, which was even more surprising. No lady would venture into either of the two neighborhoods the bridge served, and certainly not alone. That wasn't even taking into account the whole "standing on a narrow piece of stone that would hurl you into the River Thames if you misstepped" thing.

"I was *not* trying to harm myself," she said, sounding exasperated. "Which you would have known if you had simply inquired."

His lips twitched. "So you wished me to ask if you were planning on ending your life before I saved you? What if the answer was yes, should I have said, 'Please proceed'?" He continued speaking. "And if the answer was no, then I should have saved you? But what if in the course of answering the question your footing grew more unsteady, and you ended up falling in? You would certainly have drowned, even though I had inquired, and you had told me 'no.'" He paused. "In that case, my intention would have been noble and appropriate, certainly, but it would have had disastrous results. I far prefer my method."

He rolled onto his knees, wincing at the pain he felt in his back. He took a breath, then rose all the way up onto his feet, holding his hand out to the lady, who still knelt on the ground.

"I don't want your help," she said, and he didn't need to see her face to know she was frowning at his hand.

"Nevertheless, I must insist you take it," he replied, grasping her forearm and hauling her up before she realized it. "You must know it is dangerous to be out here this late at night, especially for someone like you."

She slapped his hand away. "Dangerous because strange men might assault me?" she asked pointedly, and he winced, shoving his hand deep into his pocket.

The moonlight shone on her face, revealing her more clearly than before. Her hair tumbled around her shoulders in gentle waves, though he couldn't determine its exact color. Her eyebrows were dark wings over her narrowed eyes, and her mouth was generous, looking as though she liked to laugh. Even though her lips were currently pressed together in a thin line.

"I didn't—I was not—" he sputtered, and she crossed her arms over her chest, giving him a fierce glare.

"You have proven that this bridge is dangerous, thank you so much," she said, her tone dripping with sarcasm. Making him twitch with the desire to argue with her faulty supposition. "The help you gave nearly pitched me into the water!" she added.

She uncrossed her arms to withdraw a cloth from her pocket and, before he realized it, she was dabbing at his face. He was so startled he just allowed it, but of course not so startled he couldn't continue to argue.

"Which you proved by standing on a parapet," he said dryly, instinctively holding his head still so she could continue her ministrations. "Yes, I can see that."

She growled in response, at which he held his hands up in a gesture of surrender. "I promise, I have no plans to assault you. I am merely pointing out the obvious flaw in your logic."

"Are you always this infuriating?" she asked, now frowning at his face as she continued to dab. He had to admit it felt pleasant—albeit unusual—to be taken care of like this. "Or is it just me?"

Bram chuckled in amusement. "I'm fairly certain it is not just you." If his friends were here, they would most definitely agree.

She was likely beautiful when she wasn't glowering, he realized.

She was glowering now.

Her head reached to the middle of his chest, which made her of medium height for a woman. She was young, but not so young to make him believe this was some sort of wayward misbehavior of youth. She looked close to his own age of thirty, and he had to wonder what kind of woman reached her age without having somebody responsible for her. *The kind of woman you should stay away from,* a voice said inside his head.

Not that he had plans to go near any women at all—he had no time for them. Even though a part of him wanted to know precisely who she was and what she was doing.

The curse of being someone whose job was ferreting out information.

"Well, you've saved my life, so why don't you be on your way?" She shoved the cloth she'd been using into his hand, then made a shooing motion.

"I cannot leave you here," he bristled. "What if you try it again?"

"Thank you, Mr. Helpful." That sarcastic tone again. "I have already told you that was not my intention. If it was, you would have to spend the rest of your life with me to prevent that. It is not as though—if that was my intention I would be deterred forever because some strange man tackled me."

"I did not tackle you," he replied stiffly. This woman was clearly far more outspoken than any lady he'd encountered before, and he did not like it. At all. "I believed you were in danger—in fact, I *know* that you were in danger—and I merely removed you from it."

"By tackling me," she finished, the tone of her voice making it sound as though she'd landed a hit.

He flung his hands up in exasperation. "Fine. I tackled you. Can you please allow me to escort you from the bridge so I can ensure your safety?" He could not believe he was having this discussion with someone whose judgment was so faulty she would get herself up onto a bridge for a reason other than self-harm. Someone who would do something so untoward that might bring unwanted attention to herself.

"If you had just left me up there, I would be perfectly safe and not sore for having fallen," she remonstrated. Apparently nearly as unwilling to give up a point of contention as he was.

So they had something in common.

Even if it was an infuriating thing.

"And what were you doing there anyway, if not—?" he asked.

"I was," she said haughtily, "merely trying to get a better look at the Pleiades."

Bram frowned in puzzlement. "What in God's name are those? That? It?"

"Pleiades," she repeated. "Sometimes known as the Seven Sisters. It's a constellation. I am an astronomer," she said proudly. If also derisively.

A lady scientist who saw fit to ascend to treacherous heights for her academic hobby. Definitely a person to stay away from. "Ah, a *constellation*," he said in an exaggeratedly understanding tone.

"I can see you would have a much better vantage point a few feet above the bridge. Not at all a surprise that you clambered on top to stand precariously atop it."

"You are mocking me," she said reprovingly. And also accurately. "I do not wish to be mocked. Or to stand here arguing with you anymore. I will be on my way—thank you so much for yanking me off the bridge and making me fall."

"*You* fell on *me*," he pointed out. "I was the one who bore the impact." He gave her a challenging look. "There is no possibility of my allowing you to continue unescorted." He paused, letting the words hang in the air. "I will not leave you, since we have established I have no plans to assault you, and I cannot assert that about anyone else you might encounter out here. Where do you wish me to take you?"

He never wished to see her again, nor anybody at all like her, but he would not break his own standards by not seeing her home safely. It was the proper thing to do.

WILHELMINA SQUINTED UP at him, wishing he wasn't quite so tall and, to be honest, formidable.

Not to mention aggravating, stubborn, and pedantic.

Words that had been lobbed her way as well, she had to admit.

She hadn't *planned* on hoisting herself up onto the parapet, but the clouds had scudded by the moon for just a few minutes, and she wanted to get as good a look at the Pleiades as she could. It made sense at the time for her to get as high as possible.

Even though of course she wouldn't see much more five feet higher. But it *felt* different.

For one thing, she'd felt wobbly once she'd gotten up there. Not the feeling she'd wanted when she began to climb, she had to admit. Sometimes her impetuous nature had her do things without entirely thinking them through. If she was being honest, most times her impetuous nature had her do things she hadn't quite thought through.

And then he had grabbed her, making her topple backward, landing her body onto his. And then she had withdrawn a handkerchief to tend to the cuts on his face. What in God's name was she thinking? Assisting the man who'd thwarted her plans?

It would have been far worse if she had landed directly on the stone. But if he hadn't interfered in the first place, she would not have fallen. Though she'd still feel wobbly.

So she had to conclude that the whole situation was worse because of his interference.

"Where do you wish me to take you?" he said again. Sounding impatient. "Miss?" he prompted.

"Lady," she corrected automatically, then cursed herself. She didn't want this meddling gentleman to know any more about her than he already did.

Which was that she liked to clamber up on bridges and would argue with anyone who tried to alter that situation. And now he also knew she had a title.

If she wasn't so sore from having tumbled on top of him, she'd go get up on the bridge and try it again. The moon still shone brightly, and the Pleiades were just up there, and she never got enough of staring at the stars. It was easier to focus when the sky was all she saw. It was easier just to do what she wanted rather than what she should.

It wasn't even what she was working on for her paper, but it was nearly impossible to see the nebulae she wished to without a telescope. Which she had, but it wasn't nearly powerful enough. Frustrating, since her father would never sanction the purchase of a better one, and she was entirely dependent on him for—well, for *everything*.

But if she could present her theories in a paper that would be read by other astronomers, perhaps she would be invited to study with the Earl of Rosse in Ireland. His brand-new telescope was strong enough to see nearly everything she wished to.

She sighed in dreamy contemplation of that possibility, forgetting entirely about where she was right now.

"My lady, then." The man's tone was amused, snapping her out of her reverie. He spoke in a cultured tone, and she wondered just what a gentleman was doing walking the streets of London at night.

Apparently the same question he had about her. Did they share a fear of wheeled transportation? Well, no, since she did not have that fear, so that was both asked and answered.

"Allow me to phrase my question more appropriately. Where will I take you? Since I will be taking you somewhere, I assure you, my lady." He said the last in an exaggeratedly cordial tone, one that was designed to ruffle her feathers.

Which were ruffled. Aggravating man.

"It's a good thing you have a jaw like Adonis, since your disposition is so deficient," she muttered.

"Jaw like Adonis?" Apparently his hearing was not nearly as poor as his personality.

She huffed out a breath, now annoyed at both of them, leaning her head to the side to peer past him in hopes of spying an escape. Drat. Only a few slow-moving wagons, likely carrying goods that hadn't sold at the market. One single horseman galloping far too fast for the road, and a lumbering private carriage that possibly belonged to someone she knew, which meant she could not risk waving it down.

And then she saw it. Its harness jingled as it approached, the two horses keeping up a steady pace, the driver perched on top. A hackney cab, something she knew could be hailed, even though she had never done so herself.

She bit her lip and considered how to manage it, then decided to just do it. The worst outcome was that he would tackle her again, only this time he would have no defense for his behavior, so she would feel justified in screaming. Screaming would attract attention, attention she certainly did not want, but it was unlikely this random man who misguidedly thought he was saving her from self-harm would stick around for the constable.

It was a risk, since if her father found out—she shuddered to think of his reaction.

If the gentleman didn't tackle her, he might chase after her when she was in the cab; he was quite tall, and long-legged, and she didn't doubt that he could keep up for a while.

But why would he? she reasoned.

Once she was in a hackney, she was no longer his responsibility, regardless of what he himself might think.

There. The cab was now about three yards away. She'd have to act now, or she would have to allow him to escort her somewhere as though she was unable to take care of herself, and she didn't want any of that.

She was Lady Wilhelmina Bettesford, infamous for her nonconformity, not to mention her impulsivity, and she refused to have to allow anyone to do anything for her.

And with that thought, she pushed past him, rushing to the edge of the street and raising her hand, waving it in the air so she could attract the driver's attention. "Halllooo!" she called.

She sounded ridiculous. Why hadn't she thought to practice this before?

Perhaps because hailing a hackney cab was not one of the skills a young wellborn lady was supposed to have.

Not that she could paint a watercolor, speak more than fragmented French, or do anything but stab her finger with a needle in the course of doing needlepoint.

If she were to advise young ladies on what they should learn, she'd suggest hackney cab hailing. Along with how to decline an offer of marriage, discreetly take an extra biscuit at tea, and scratch an itch in an awkward place when one was in company. She'd had to learn all those things on her own.

The hackney cab appeared as though it was going to drive right past her, even though she halloooed again, and then the man standing beside her let loose a piercing whistle beside her, and the cab stopped with a sudden jerk, the driver lurching in his seat.

She felt a hand at her elbow and wrinkled her nose. Drat. Of course the man was able to summon a hackney. Likely *he* had gotten hackney-summoning lessons.

"If you had wished me to escort you home in a hackney, you could have just said," the gentleman said, still sounding amused.

She made a harrumphing noise, but got into the carriage, watching as he slid gracefully behind her, sitting on the opposite seat.

"Well?" he said at last.

"Well, what?"

"Your address." He tilted his head toward her. "The driver will need to know where to go. Unless you wish to stay on this bridge a bit longer?"

"Fine," she muttered. "Tell him 55 Grover Street."

He repeated the address in a louder voice to the driver, and the cab sprung forward, making her fall toward him.

Again.

He caught her arm, steadying her.

And then he snatched it away, likely aware she had already accused him of groping her. But honestly, what else was she to think when he'd manhandled her so?

She still couldn't see him that well, but what she saw made her grateful she wasn't a flibbertigibbet. Because he was remarkably and astoundingly handsome.

If one cared about such things. Flibbertigibbets did; Wilhelmina did not.

Still.

In addition to that jaw, his hair was quite dark, likely near black, swept away from his face in severe lines. His cheekbones were sharp and well-defined, while his Roman nose sat commandingly over a surprisingly sensual pair of lips.

His eyebrows were strong and dark, but it was his eyes that were the most remarkably handsome thing about him—in the dark of the cab they gleamed, and then a lamp shone suddenly in, revealing them to be a light, piercing blue.

Oh dear. Ridiculously good-looking, in fact.

"Why *were* you by yourself?" he asked, interrupting her assessment of him. "It is not customary—"

"No, of course not," she interrupted. She knew she was being abrupt and quite possibly very rude. She wished she could stop herself, but when she found herself in uncomfortable situations—such as being unexpectedly hauled off a bridge—she resorted to a brusque hauteur that masked whatever painful awkwardness she felt.

Which right now was quite a lot. And he'd just sounded so . . . stuffy. Like all the people she'd ever met who had somehow figured out that being a conventional lady was the last thing she wished for. Who had judged her with a sniff and a tone.

It also explained why she'd received so few marriage proposals, despite coming from a good family with a large dowry. A relief, to be honest. She didn't want to spend the rest of her life in painful awkwardness. Or, more precisely, she could do that more efficiently and comfortably if she remained unmarried, as she intended to do.

She imagined husbands would not much appreciate a woman who'd rather be peering through a telescope than admiring her spouse's greatness.

And from what she'd seen firsthand, admiring a spouse's greatness was approximately forty percent of a spouse's duties. The remainder included raising children, purchasing knickknacks, and drinking copious amounts of tea.

Not the life she wanted. Though she did appreciate a good cup of tea.

"You should have just left me alone," she said, biting her lip after she spoke.

"I couldn't." He spoke firmly, as if he was expressing a simple truth. "I cannot stand by while I see an injustice occurring. And I presumed—which you have been very clear I was wrong in—that you were on the verge of committing an injustice toward yourself."

"Oh," she said, wishing she didn't feel quite so uncomfortable. "I suppose I should thank you." Now that she'd had time to think about it, she could see why he had leapt to that conclusion.

"Not if you don't wish to." He didn't sound argumentative now; instead, he sounded as though he actually meant what he was saying.

"I do wish to." To her surprise. "Thank you for rescuing me, even if it wasn't necessary. I can see where you might have misapprehended the situation," she said in a halting tone. She wasn't accustomed to apologizing, much less to a man as handsome as he was.

You are not a flibbertigibbet, she reminded herself.

"You are welcome." He paused as he cleared his throat. "And I am sorry if I acted too hastily after making my assumption."

He sounded as unused to apologizing as she did. Another thing they had in common.

"Well," she said after a moment, "it seems we have reached an agreement of sorts."

"Indeed." At least now he sounded less disapproving. "Allow me to introd—"

"No, stop," she interrupted, flinging her hand up. "If you introduce yourself, then I'll know who you are—"

"That is how introductions work," he said dryly.

"—and then we will be obliged to know one another, and we both know that this whole situation is inappropriate, and neither one of us wants to be forced into anything—"

"Good God, no," he said, more forcefully than was complimentary.

Well. At least they agreed on that as well. Even if his quick response stung.

"So for now you are Mr. Helpful, and I am—"

"You are Lady Luminous," he supplied easily, as though he hadn't just thought of it. "It is a pleasure to meet you, my lady," he added, holding his hand out toward her.

She took it, noting his firm grip and intense gaze. "A pleasure to meet you as well, Mr. Helpful," she said, offering him a wry smile. *Lady Luminous.* She had to admit she liked that.

He released her, sitting back against the seat cushions, his hands clasped loosely between his knees. He looked completely comfortable, his appearance so at odds with how she was feeling it was unnerving.

Perhaps he did this all the time—rescued young ladies perching on bridges. Perhaps he was a perpetual rescuer, and if it hadn't been her, it would have been someone else.

Perhaps this line of thinking should stop, because she absolutely should not be wondering anything about him. This interlude would be over as soon as she alighted from the carriage.

She should be relieved for it to be over, honestly.

So why wasn't she?

Men I Do Not Wish to Marry:
A Not at All Comprehensive List by
Lady Wilhelmina Bettesford

Edward Oxford.

Edward Oxford attempted to assassinate Queen Victoria in 1840. Thankfully he was unsuccessful, but if he had such intentions toward a member of the Royal Family, imagine what he might feel toward a mere wife?

Chapter Two

$\mathcal{B}$ram hopped down from the cab, holding his hand out to assist the woman—Lady Luminous—down.

She ignored his hand, instead gripping the frame of the door and leaping down, tossing her cloak over her shoulder when she was on the ground.

Clearly a very independent person, not even acceding to Societal conventions. The kind of person who didn't have to worry about their reputation because of their social status.

Her gown was plain and high necked, what he presumed a lady scientist would don to go constellation viewing. He could tell, however, that it was of fine quality, even though he didn't know enough about ladies' clothing to identify how he knew that. Likely something about the fabric or the fit or whatever.

Now they were in better light, he could see her face more clearly. Her nose was a tiny button, underneath which her wide mouth and full lips looked even more of a contrast. Her eyes were dark, brown if he had to guess, and her hair was also brown. It tumbled about her shoulders in dishevelment.

"Thank you, Mr. Helpful," she said, the words

sounding stilted. "I hope we do not meet again." She dipped her head to him, then bit her lip as she glanced over his shoulder. "Wait," she said in a much lower voice. "Don't move."

She pressed close to him, pulling the edges of the cloak to his side, ducking her head toward his chest.

"My lady?" he said in surprise. Feeling completely at a loss on what she was doing, and why. True since he'd first encountered her, to be honest.

"Just wait, I don't want anyone to see me," she hissed.

"Ah," he replied.

She wrapped her arms around him, and he started in surprise before doing the same to her, drawing her close as the hackney cab pulled away. "How long do we have to stay like this?" he asked, feeling as though he was committing a great sin. Even though she felt good pressed against him—warm, and soft, and smelling of some sort of flower.

"Until they—" she said, tilting her head to look past him. "Drat!" she exclaimed, quickly returning to her position against his chest.

"Do you want to leave?" he asked. "Though I'm not certain how we'd manage that. We could attempt walk—"

"Shh!" she interrupted, her nose buried against his sternum.

He looked down at the top of her head. "I don't think you're in any position to dictate anything," he said, though he kept his voice low.

"Just for a few minutes," she said in a fierce whisper. "They'll go back inside eventually."

"Who?" he asked.

"My aunt and Dipper," she replied.

"Dipper?"

"My dog."

"Not Orion? Or Betelgeuse?" he replied.

"He's *named* after the *Big Dipper*," she explained in a low, pedantic tone.

"Yes, I figured that," Bram said, amusement lacing his voice. "Given your fierce appreciation of the stars."

"Oh, thank goodness," she said after peering around him again. "They're gone." She pulled herself away from him as she drew the hood of her cloak over her head. She lifted her face to his, biting her lip again. He had to admit he found it disconcerting. "Thank you. Again." And then she leaned up and placed a soft kiss on his mouth.

Before he could reply, before he could do anything but stand there, she scurried past him and he heard the sound of a door closing.

Completely and entirely inappropriate.

He put his fingers to his mouth. Touching where she'd touched. A part of him wanted to go after her, to demand her name and why she'd—she'd *kissed* him, for God's sake, after squabbling with him on tackling versus not tackling. After trying to escape via hackney, very reluctantly accepting his help.

But then he shrugged, glancing around the street. It was a moment in time, something that would only mean more if he let it. He didn't have room in his life for a complication, even a complication as lovely as a kiss—a soft, gentle kiss, pressed on him by soft, gentle lips.

In fact, he didn't have room in his life for anything that wasn't already there.

And more than that, he did not have time for a person who would flout common courteous behavior with such aplomb.

The street she lived on was not so far from the club where he was to meet his friends—only thirty minutes late, and he'd still probably beat Fenton, who often got so engrossed in what he was working on that he neglected to eat, sleep, and other things most people found essential.

He should be turning his mind back to *Mary Barton*, and what Gaskell was saying about class differences, and who loved whom, but he just couldn't. Not quite yet.

He looked up at her house. It obviously belonged to an aristocratic family, and one with means. Lights blazed in most of the windows, and he heard voices emerging from one of the open windows on the ground floor. Her voice, and then another female's. And then the yip of an excited dog. Dipper, he imagined.

A smile curled his mouth as he started to walk toward the club. He certainly had not expected the evening to unfold like this, but he had to admit he had found the whole experience invigorating. If also unsettling. Though he'd feel the pain of her falling on him tomorrow morning, that was for certain. And the impact of that soft kiss for a lot longer than that, he imagined.

WILHELMINA SHUT THE door behind her, leaning back against it as she glanced around the foyer. Thank goodness Aunt Flora had already made her way to the kitchen, her habit after taking Dipper out for his business.

The footmen who usually stood waiting for whichever family member might need help with either their departures or arrivals were also in the kitchen, since now was when the staff had their meal. Something she'd counted on when she'd snuck out of the house a few hours ago.

And kissed a gentleman just outside her door. Why had she done that?

She could not answer that, even in the most private depths of her soul. She could just chalk it up to the same impulsivity that had gotten her up onto that bridge in the first place. She was grateful to him, and he was undoubtedly the most handsome gentleman she had ever seen, so why not kiss him?

It wasn't as though she was planning on kissing anyone in general. She might as well give herself the experience at least once in her life. Pleased at her logic, she tucked the topic away.

"Thank goodness no one saw me," she murmured, aware of how close she'd just come. She thought herself too old for a chaperone, but of course, her father, her aunt, and all of Society disagreed.

A few times she'd been caught, but she'd been able to persuade whoever had caught her that there was a very good reason for her to have been out. That should be added to a young ladies' course of instruction: being able to talk oneself out of trouble, even if one had gotten into trouble in the first place. Perhaps even ahead of the hackney-hailing lessons.

Her father, the Earl of Croyde, was away on business, and Aunt Flora wasn't quite as determined as her brother that Wilhelmina behave as it seemed a proper lady ought to. Apparently Wilhelmina herself wasn't quite as determined about that either, given that she'd just kissed a stranger.

Albeit a handsome stranger with eyes the color of the newly discovered planet Neptune.

So much for tucking the topic away, she thought, grimacing.

"There you are," Aunt Flora said as she walked into the foyer. "I thought you might be in the garden, but Dipper and I went, and you weren't there. But you knew that already," she continued.

Aunt Flora tended to speak whatever was in her mind at the time. Rather like her niece.

For the time being, both Wilhelmina and Aunt Flora were dependent on the earl's goodwill in offering them a home—Flora's dowry had been given to her late husband, who had wasted all of it before a conveniently early death. Conveniently early for Aunt Flora, that is, since her husband was a wastrel.

It was one of the many reasons Wilhelmina herself didn't want to get married. Aunt Flora, while vague, had revealed enough gruesome details to convince Wilhelmina that marriage only benefited the gentleman in the equation. Aunt Flora was flighty about most things but was surprisingly adamant that Wilhelmina never allow herself to become subservient to a man.

Wilhelmina wouldn't have access to the money her mother had left her for another seven months, at which point she and Aunt Flora had agreed to move in together, anywhere that Wilhelmina could see the stars and Aunt Flora could find people who shared her interests: gardening, gossip, and games.

Until then, they were both dependent on Wilhelmina's father.

She'd had a come-out when she was eighteen, which had been disastrous—she'd spilled wine over several dance partners, reprimanded a few other gentlemen on their general ignorance, and wasn't comfortable with most of the other debutantes.

"And then I didn't want him to do anything in the garden," Aunt Flora continued, giving an oblique reference to Dipper's bodily necessities, "so I took him out the front."

Dipper scampered in, running up to Wilhelmina and uttering a few yips that managed to combine "welcome home!" and "I am gravely disappointed you left without taking me" in a remarkable display of dog communication.

She bent down to scratch his ears, and then he circled around her legs before running off to investigate a particularly fascinating corner of the room.

"I was occupied," Wilhelmina returned vaguely. *Kissing someone I haven't officially met.* "I must have just missed you." Both of which statements were true, if also misleading.

"Never mind," Aunt Flora said, waving her hand in dismissal. "I've had a note from your father—he is returning early. Tonight, he says."

Wilhelmina blinked. Her father never did anything different from what he'd planned—it was one of the things he and his sister, Flora, did not have in common. *He* certainly would not go about spontaneously kissing people.

His lack of spontaneity might have been one of the reasons Wilhelmina tended to prefer her aunt to her actual parent.

"You're certain?" she said. Because Flora was also prone to misunderstanding things. For a moment, the thought crossed her mind that he might have discovered her adventures this evening—sneaking out, parapetting, and then kissing a stranger—but that couldn't possibly be true. But it did make her breath hitch to even think about it.

Her father was not an accommodating sort.

"Absolutely. I asked Mrs. Windham to read it also, just to be certain I understood."

Mrs. Windham was their housekeeper, a remarkably staid woman who was absolutely precise in everything. As befit a good housekeeper.

That she also aided Wilhelmina in her frequent unconventional behavior was something Wilhelmina knew was at odds with the housekeeper's fairly rigid views, but she wasn't going to question it, not when it meant she could escape the house with some regularity. It might have had something to do with Mrs. Windham's own past, which was shrouded in mystery, but seemed to have included some misadventures.

Wilhelmina wanted to discover those secrets as urgently as she wished to discover the secrets of the stars, but the latter were far easier to penetrate.

"Ah, my lady," Mrs. Windham said, emerging from the hall that led to the kitchen. "I didn't realize you had finished what you were doing. I understand your father is arriving home soon—shall I set something up in the drawing room?"

Wilhelmina nodded. "Please do. He is likely to require refreshments after his trip. Where was he again?" she asked, turning to Aunt Flora.

"The Derbyshire estate, I believe," Mrs. Windham supplied.

"Yes, that's it. He needed to hire a new steward."

Wilhelmina's father was the sixth earl, and had inherited his title when his brother had died unexpectedly thirty years earlier. Her father had not been raised to understand the intricacies of what the title entailed, and he was scrupulously correct in everything, so he took it upon himself to be as engaged with the business of his properties and financial management as possible.

"I wonder why he cut his visit short, though," Wilhelmina mused, taking Aunt Flora's arm as they walked slowly to the drawing room, Dipper following behind. "He was supposed to be away for another week."

Her father found travel difficult, and therefore required additional time to ensure his comfort. It wasn't practical for him to take a week to get somewhere only to leave a few days later, so his trips were usually lengthy.

Wilhelmina was grateful for his long absences, though felt guilty her gratitude was at the cost of her father's discomfort. But his being away meant it was easier for her to live her life as she wished to, not having to answer to a mindful parent.

That she was twenty-four years old and well past the age where most women were running their own households was something she had pointed out with some frequency to her father, who had rejoined that those ladies had husbands, and Wilhelmina only had a dog.

Wilhelmina had no reply to that, though once she had suggested she just marry Dipper, if her marital state was that much of a problem.

Her father was not amused.

She and Aunt Flora sat down in the drawing room, a comfortable space that had been decorated a decade or so ago by Wilhelmina's mother, who had never met a furbelow she didn't like. Consequently, the room was done up in shades of pink and pale green, the drapes fussy things with several rows of ruffles, tables outfitted with matching skirts to hide their legs, and an enormous rug on the floor. The rug was mostly obscured by the sheer number of chairs, tables, and small sofas that were in the room.

Wilhelmina had considered asking her father if she could at least reduce the number of things in the room, but he disliked change, even if it made their lives more comfortable. He also refused to change anything his late wife, and Wilhelmina's mother, had touched.

Lady Croyde had died when Wilhelmina was sixteen. It had been a sudden cold that had turned worse, leaving Wilhelmina and her father stricken with grief. It was only later that Wilhelmina had realized that while her father had adored her mother, her mother had often felt stifled by her husband's attention. It was from her mother that Wilhelmina got her inquisitive mind and love of books.

Wilhelmina had turned to her mother's true love, books, as a refuge after her mother's death, particularly scientific tomes, while her father had become more meticulous, if such a thing was possible. As if his doing everything correctly could ensure that there were no more surprises in his life. Even if it meant that there were no highs as well as no lows.

Mrs. Windham entered with a tray, her normal expression shifting briefly to annoyance when she surveyed the room. She'd gone so far as to rearrange some of the furniture a few years ago, but Wilhelmina's father had moved it all back.

"Just put it there, Mrs. Windham," Wilhelmina said, gesturing to the low table in front of where she and Aunt Flora were seated.

They all turned as they heard a commotion at the door, Wilhelmina leaping up in response. "Father," she said, then paused. Her father did not like to be greeted right away after a journey; he generally required a few minutes as his valet, Hickins, fussed around him.

She sat back down, clasping her hands in her lap.

"Shall I?" Aunt Flora said, nodding to the tray.

"I'll leave you," Mrs. Windham said.

"No, stay," they heard Lord Croyde say. "You'll want to be here for this."

They all turned to look in his direction, Wilhelmina's eyes widening as she saw her father was not alone.

He was accompanied by a young woman who appeared younger than Wilhelmina. She was beautiful, with shining gold hair and delicate features. She glanced over at Lord Croyde, offering him a shy smile, before ducking her head. Her gown was the height of fashion, layers of lace over a shining light blue fabric. At her neck was a string of pearls, while pearls swung from her ears.

Wilhelmina had never seen her before.

Lord Croyde curled the woman's arm in his as they advanced into the room. "Allow me to introduce my wife. This is Alethea, Lady Croyde."

BRAM REACHED THE club twenty minutes later. The Peckham Club was one of London's newer establishments, and its admittance policy accommodated men of unconfirmed heritage. It had gained the nickname the Orphans' Club because it was home to men who were not customarily welcomed elsewhere, but who had the means and the leisure time to join a club.

That he and his orphaned friends met there was not only a sign of how well they'd each done in their lives, but also how important one's antecedents were to being accepted in Society.

The club's members ranged from members of Parliament to successful businessmen, artists, performers, and solicitors, judges, and barristers such as himself.

He greeted the doorman, slipping him a coin, then strode quickly down the hall to where his friends were likely already gathered.

He and the four others—Theo, Fenton, Simeon, and Benedict—had met at the Devenaugh Home, also known as the School for Scoundrels, all five of them having arrived within the same six-month period when they were each about three months old.

He'd been born, or so he was told, the illegitimate child of a housekeeper and an Italian tenor who'd performed in the village, though nobody had been able to tell him which village it was, so he could go look for her. The housekeeper's employers had been kindly enough not to let her go when her condition was discovered, but not so kindly that they allowed her to keep her baby. Bram believed that while he inherited his father's dark looks, as evidenced by his black hair and hawklike nose, he must have gotten his blue eyes and his powers of persuasion from his mother—she had to have been extraordinary for her employers to overlook such a misstep.

Shortly after his birth, Bram had been hastily brought to the Home, which had been established by a mysterious benefactor the same year Bram arrived—the benefactor was a gentleman who wanted to ensure his child grew up well cared for, even if the gentleman could not acknowledge him. The school was therefore far more comfortable than other places they might have ended up. They were given excellent educations, taught how to behave as gentlemen—even though they were not—and were placed into homes that had been carefully investigated.

As Bram and the other boys in the Home grew, they speculated as to which one of them might secretly have an aristocrat or even royalty as their father. Fenton, the most mathematical of them, had made calculations based on what they knew of their birthdays and their possible resemblance to a variety of aristocrats, but had been unable to come up with a satisfactory answer.

They'd each been twelve years old when they'd left the Home to be placed with different families. Bram had gotten placed with an older couple who had always wanted children but hadn't had any of their own. The father, Mr. Townsend, was a respected judge, and it was from him Bram had gotten his rigid sense of right and wrong. As well as his last name.

The uncanny ability to argue with anyone over any point was his own talent, so his choice of profession was clear.

"And then the window slammed shut!" he heard Benedict exclaim.

Laughter spilled out as he opened the door. He stepped inside, glancing to see who was there as he secured the door behind himself.

Theo Osbourne and Benedict Quintrell sat on either side of the fireplace, which was lit, casting a warm glow in the room. Simeon Jones perched on the edge of a table that held refreshments, while Fenton Ash was surprisingly there as well, pouring a glass of whisky.

"You're late," Benedict remarked. "And you're injured," he continued, beginning to rise.

"Don't get up. It's nothing," he said, gesturing for Benedict to remain where he was.

"We were just about to give you up and begin without you," Theo said, a wicked gleam of mischief in his eye.

"And let you discuss *Mary Barton* without me? I should say not." Bram walked to the table, grabbing a glass and pouring himself a splash of whisky. It wouldn't taste as sweet as her mouth, he thought, before shoving the thought away and taking a quick sip, which burned on the way down.

"Of course you liked it," Simeon groaned. "It's all about the courts and justice." He rolled his eyes. "If Mary had spoken her mind from the start, none of it would have happened."

"Naturally you blame the woman," Theo said. He

turned to the other men in the room. "Did he tell you he's had his heart broken—again?"

"Let's not discuss that," Simeon said hastily. "Why were you late, Bram? And why does your face look like that?"

"I was trying to be a Good Samaritan, only it turned out my help was not needed."

"The person wanted to go to jail?" Benedict asked, his brow furrowed.

"Was the person a feline?" Theo asked, following that up with a "Meow."

"Nothing like that," Bram said. "She didn't want my help dismounting from the bridge upon which she stood."

"Did she—?" Fenton said, his eyes wide.

"No, she is fine," Bram reassured him quickly. *Fine enough to kiss me, at least.* "She hadn't intended to do anything to harm herself, you see. She just wanted to see the stars more closely. Some constellation or another." Bram shrugged. "But she was by herself, and she was a lady, so I insisted—much to her dismay—that I escort her home."

"Did you know her? Who was she?" Theo asked interestedly.

"She wouldn't give me her name."

"Mysterious," Theo observed, waggling his eyebrows. "Would you recognize her again?"

Dark, wavy hair. Her wide, sensuous mouth. Her figure, which he had felt as she pressed against him in front of her house. Soft warmth. An argumentative demeanor.

That kiss.

"Yes," he said tersely. "I would." He also knew where she lived, of course, but even if he hadn't, he would know her.

"Oh, Bram sounds annoyed," Simeon said in a gleeful tone. Simeon liked to stir up trouble wherever he went, even if it was trouble he was stirring for his best friends. His mercurial temperament was well-suited for his artistic career—he'd already had paintings hung in the Royal Academy, a far cry from his humble beginnings. Making him even more insufferable, his friends reminded him, at which Simeon just smirked.

"I'm not *annoyed*, it's just that I got sidetracked by rescuing her, when it seemed she didn't need rescuing at all."

"Annoyed," the four other men said in unison.

"Fine," Bram replied, exhaling an admittedly annoyed breath. "I was annoyed. Can we move on to talking about books?"

"Yes, because neither you nor Simeon wish to discuss actual living women," Theo observed.

"There is nothing to discuss." Bram took another sip of his whisky. "It is the reason I am late, that is all." Even to himself, his tone didn't sound convincing.

"Somehow I don't believe you," Simeon said. He popped a piece of cheese from the table behind him into his mouth. "But since you don't know the lady's name, and you don't travel in those circles, you're unlikely to see her again." He shrugged, dismissing the topic. "Shall we move on to discussing Elizabeth Gaskell's writing? I appreciate how gently she brings up the important issues in her works, sneaking in her revolutionary ideas within her delicate prose."

The conversation about the book began to flow, but for once Bram wasn't in the fray. It was difficult to pay attention to the discussion when his thoughts were swirling with what had just happened.

He wished the thought of never seeing her again didn't bother him. He would like to see her again, if only to see if she argued as vehemently when there wasn't a constellation sighting involved. If only to teach her how to hail a hackney cab.

If only to reciprocate the kiss she had bestowed on him so suddenly.

Men I Do Not Wish to Marry:
A Not at All Comprehensive List by
Lady Wilhelmina Bettesford

John William Bean.

Mr. Bean, like Mr. Oxford, made an attempt on Queen Victoria's life. According to the reports, he wasn't serious about wanting to assassinate the ruler of the British Empire. But if he wasn't serious about such a monumental and terrible decision, how would he approach every other aspect of his life?

Chapter Three

"Your *wife*?" Wilhelmina said, her voice strained. Aunt Flora made a gasping wheeze, while Mrs. Windham stood frozen, her bearing rigid.

"Yes, that's what I said," her father replied, sounding irritated. As he always did when someone did not immediately grasp his meaning. "Allow me to settle you, Alethea," he continued in an entirely different tone. One that sounded almost besotted.

He escorted the young woman to one of the sofas, treating her as though she was a precious figurine made of the most delicate china, like the ones littering every surface in the room. Definitely besotted.

Wilhelmina recovered herself, taking a deep breath as she nodded to the newcomer. "It is a pleasure to make your acquaintance, my lady," she said, dipping her head.

"Please," her father's new wife said in a breathless voice, "call me Alethea. I was going to suggest you call me Mama, but you're at least ten years older than I am, and wouldn't that be odd?"

She spoke in a guileless tone, but Wilhelmina felt the sting of her words nonetheless. *Yes, I am here, an unmarried woman who might be ten years older than a married woman.*

Why must all females be judged on whether or not they'd made pledges they had no intention of keeping? Not the faithful part, mind you—just the part where you promised to love one another until the end of time. How would that even work? Wouldn't someone grow incredibly tired of another person after so long?

"Not ten years, Alethea," her father corrected. At least his need to always be right hadn't changed, even if his marital status had. "My daughter is twenty-four, just five years older than you."

The lady's eyebrows rose in surprise. "Oh goodness! I would have thought—oh, but never mind," she said in a sweet voice, shaking her head. "And this is your sister, Charles?" She offered a beaming smile toward Aunt Flora, who still seemed to be having difficulty catching her breath. "You just stay right there, we will get you something to drink." She turned to regard Mrs. Windham. "Could you fetch something more restorative for Lady Flora?"

Mrs. Windham curtseyed briefly, then fled. Wilhelmina wished she could join her, if only to process the news by herself.

Her father sat next to his bride, taking her hand in his and laying both on his leg. "Alethea is the daughter of my new steward, Mr. St. Cliffe," he explained, not taking his eyes off the woman. She preened under his regard. "We met, and it was like lightning struck both of us at the same time. Before I knew it, I was kissing her. I begged her to marry me the same day." He finally looked at Wilhelmina. "She has made me the happiest man in the world," he said, sounding as though he was offering a challenge.

"I see," Wilhelmina replied. Even though she did not. And she was mistaken, apparently, that her father would never kiss anyone unexpectedly. Because here he'd just admitted it! Perhaps she and her father had more in common than she thought.

The door opened again, and Mrs. Windham appeared with one of the lower maids, who bore a tray with a pitcher and glasses.

"Just there, please," the lady ordered, gesturing to a small side table to the right of where Aunt Flora sat.

Wilhelmina suddenly realized she was still standing, and immediately dropped into a chair.

"I have been to London only a few times," Lady Croyde said, glancing between the ladies. "My Charles has offered to take me everywhere. Perhaps you could join us, if you wanted some fresh air, Wilhelmina. You look as though you might need it." She put her gloved fingers to her mouth. "Oh! You don't mind if I call you Wilhelmina, do you? Since we are to be family."

Wilhelmina shook her head. "No, I—that is, of course." She spread her lips into what she hoped looked like a smile. "Please do."

"I hardly think Wilhelmina will want to traipse around London with us, my dear," Lord Croyde said. "We will be shopping, and eating ices, and going to plays and the opera. Wilhelmina doesn't care for such things."

Wilhelmina bristled, but then realized that no, she did not generally care for such things. Or rather, there were always more interesting things to do than go shopping for yet another hat or listen to some woman screech in a foreign language for a few hours.

Hmm. Was she as judgmental as that sounded?

She had to admit she likely was.

She just didn't enjoy the same things it seemed others did. That was another reason she avoided Society—she just didn't understand other people, even ladies her own age. She would much prefer to spend time with Dipper and Aunt Flora, if not alone with her books.

"Then we will attend some events that she will enjoy," Alethea said firmly.

Please, no, Wilhelmina thought to herself. The idea of being the third with a newly married couple— one of whom was her father—was enough to make her want to leap off that bridge she'd been standing on an hour ago.

That her father likely agreed that she shouldn't be there as well was something she would ignore.

"I wish I could," she said in a regretful tone, relieved she could lie so easily. Though that made her character suspect, didn't it?

But if it was for the greater good?

She'd wrestle with that moral dilemma later. Right now she needed to find a way out of this situation.

"But I need to assist the—the Devenaugh Home for Destitute Boys."

The truth was that she volunteered there once a week for two hours, sorting linens and doling out soup, but she could exaggerate the importance of her work, couldn't she? And she *had* been meaning to offer more time, so now was the ideal opportunity.

"Oh, that is too bad," Alethea said. "Isn't that too bad, my dear?" she asked Wilhelmina's father.

That gentleman didn't even look at Wilhelmina, too busy staring at his wife to spare his daughter a glance.

Wilhelmina wished she didn't have a strong feeling of dread in the pit of her stomach. But she did, and she knew it wasn't because she'd missed supper.

Was it too late to make an honest dog out of Dipper by marrying him?

WILHELMINA STARTED AS she heard the knock at the door. "Who is it?" she called.

It was the day after her father's announcement, and about half an hour before dinner. The first dinner where her new stepmother would preside as the hostess, a position Wilhelmina had held since her mother had died. Not that she regretted losing those duties, but it added to the general odd feeling. As though she belonged in her own house even less now.

"It's Aunt Flora," her aunt said, her tone no doubt trying to be discreet, but loud enough to make Dipper sit up and stare at the door.

Wilhelmina got up and strode to the door, flinging it open to reveal her aunt.

"May I?" her aunt said, speaking in the same stage whisper.

"Please," Wilhelmina replied, gesturing for her aunt to enter.

Wilhelmina's room—the one she'd had since she was born—was the only room that hadn't suffered from her mother's overwrought taste. It was simple, and elegant, and a pleasant refuge from Society and her father's picayune concerns and even Aunt Flora's fussing.

Wilhelmina limited her untidiness to a desk that was placed in the corner, piles of books and papers and maps of the constellations spread across it like a whirlwind had deposited everything and then left in a rush.

Aunt Flora went to sit in her usual seat, a chair in front of the fireplace, though the fireplace wasn't lit. It was too warm for a fire, and in fact Wilhelmina had opened all the windows, even though she could hear the shouts from the street and smell the strong odors of London life wafting in on the breeze.

"What do you think of her?" Aunt Flora asked after a moment.

Wilhelmina didn't pretend not to know who she was speaking of.

"I don't know—she is certainly very pretty," she said cautiously.

They heard a knock at the door, and then Mrs. Windham's face appeared. "May I?" she said, gesturing to the room. "I was wondering if you—" She broke off as she entered the room, shaking her head. "No, I wasn't wondering anything. I wanted to discuss the new Lady Croyde."

"Exactly what we were talking about," Aunt Flora enthused. "This affects all of us—you've been with us so long, Mrs. Windham. I hope the new Lady Croyde isn't causing a problem?"

Mrs. Windham shook her head. "No, she seems quite knowledgeable about running a household. I just hope . . ." Her voice trailed off, leaving Wilhelmina to wonder what was in the housekeeper's mind.

"I know your father is a good man—" Aunt Flora continued.

"What with being your brother and all," Wilhelmina murmured.

"But I cannot help but be concerned that such a lovely young woman has married a man old enough to be her father," Aunt Flora said, wringing her hands. "And she has no recourse! What if something happens?"

This was Aunt Flora's frequent refrain—she had married young as well, to a man she thought she'd loved, but who'd turned out to be a complete and absolute scoundrel. His death, when Aunt Flora was approaching forty years of age, had been a relief, and one that Aunt Flora wasn't shy about mentioning.

It was one of the many reasons Wilhelmina had decided early on that marriage was not for her—how could you possibly know that the person you fell in love with at age twenty-four was going to be the same person you'd be in love with at age fifty?

Gentlemen had all the rights in marriage, as Aunt Flora reminded her often. Wilhelmina would lose her autonomy, what little she had, any money that was hers would belong to him, and he could do whatever he wanted simply because he was a gentleman.

The thought of another person having that much control over her was enough to send her heart racing and cause her breathing to quicken, a feeling of panic making her throat close over.

Even someone she loved, like her father, had suppressed her mother's interests because they didn't fit easily into his life. Her mother had borne it well, but it was clear, even to a young Wilhelmina, that the bonds of marriage chafed her.

"I imagine," Wilhelmina said, willing herself to calm, "that my father's bride," she said, stumbling over the unfamiliar phrase, "knows precisely what she is doing. She seems very—" *Clever*, she wanted to say, but that sounded pejorative in this context. She shouldn't judge without getting to know the woman, after all, even though she was sorely tempted to. Even though that was what she usually did.

"She seems very young," Aunt Flora finished, sounding worried.

"Youth doesn't mean you don't know your own mind," Mrs. Windham said quickly. "Falling in love can happen at any time."

"Father is not like your late husband," Wilhelmina assured her aunt. "At the very worst, he will be annoyed she is not precisely on time, since she is not ten minutes early."

"Promise me you won't get married," Aunt Flora said, casting an anguished glance at her niece. Dipper picked his head up again, his ears twitching. "It can only end in heartbreak."

Wilhelmina nodded gravely, meeting Mrs. Windham's equally concerned gaze. "I have no intention of it," she assured her aunt.

"You want me to do what?" Bram said.

"It's for charity," Benedict explained. "For the Home?"

It was the week following the Bridge Incident, and Bram hadn't been able to get the lady out of his mind—her coolly dismissive tone at odds with her heated argument. That kiss, right at the end, followed by her darting into her house.

It was all so unexpected, and he normally didn't like unexpected things—he required order, and compliance, and adhering to common behaviors. It was likely why Simeon and Theo could get a rise out of him so easily, because he was, as Simeon had mentioned innumerable times, a stuffy pedant.

Bram didn't like the sobriquet, but had to agree that he appreciated a good rule. Or ten.

"Charity, Bram?" Benedict prompted impatiently.

Ah. Apparently he had remained in contemplation for too long.

The two sat in a pub near Bram's office drinking ale. It wasn't unusual for one of his friends to drop by unannounced, but it was unusual for Benedict, who had been taken in at age twelve by the Quintrell family, the men of which all worked for Her Majesty's government, which Benedict had done himself as soon as he was old enough.

Benedict's intelligence and generally commanding manner had brought him quickly to the top of his department, so he was usually too busy with his duties to do something as frivolous as stop by Bram's office. That was why they had instituted the monthly book club that gathered at the Peckham—they had all found escape of one sort or another through books, and they wanted to stay in touch, regardless of how complicated and busy their lives got otherwise. Plus it meant Bram got to argue more, since his friends usually had different opinions on the books they read than he did.

The most vociferous and memorable argument had centered around Mary Wollstonecraft's *A Vin-*

dication of the Rights of Women. Bram was mildly
appalled it had ended in blows between him and
Fenton. But also somewhat proud.

"You are asking me if I wish to stand up in front
of a group of strangers and put myself on a virtual
auction block? It is virtual, correct?"

Benedict nodded, already looking aggrieved.
Good, that meant his obfuscation was working.

"And you're suggesting that someone would want
to pay money to have me take them somewhere?
That seems—"

"Far-fetched, I know, since I can't imagine anyone
wanting to go anywhere with *you*," Benedict said.

"Ha," Bram said. "What does that say about you,
given that you go places with me?"

Benedict just rolled his eyes.

"Can't I just give money like always?" Bram
groaned. Going to an event meant leaving his office
at a reasonable time, wearing uncomfortable clothing, and pretending he cared an iota for anybody
he met.

The only people he cared about were the four
other orphans he'd met in the Home and his staff.
Most people, he found, were too involved with their
own picayune interests to be worth cultivating as
friends.

Did that make him a righteous recluse? A stuffy
pedant? Perhaps, but he was much happier this
way. And he was happy as he was, he told himself
firmly. He should be banishing stray thoughts of
impulsive young ladies out of his mind, in order to
maintain his calm mien. In order to remain true to
himself and his rules of behavior.

"No, you cannot," Benedict replied.

"And where do I have to go with this mysterious bidder?"

"It's for an evening at the opera. The tickets are part of the charity fee—all you have to do is show up."

"But why would anyone want to bid on another person to go to the opera with?" Bram asked in horror. Because spending time with a person he didn't know—and likely would not want to know—was only surpassed by the thought of being at the opera with that same person.

All that howling and screeching. All that melodrama, as though love was something worth fussing over for three hours.

"I promised the proprietress of the Home that there would be at least ten eligible gentlemen there. And since you are my closest friend—"

"Please tell me you're forcing the others into this, too," Bram said with a groan, accepting his fate.

"Of course. I couldn't disappoint the proprietress, after all. She is—well, she is difficult to say no to."

Interesting. Someone who made even Benedict agree to something? Bram wanted to know who this woman was, if she could make his forceful friend succumb.

But no. He didn't want to know who she was. He didn't want to know who anybody was.

Except for the mysterious bridge lady.

And he did not want to know who she was either, he reminded himself. She was far too impetuous for his taste. And for his peace of mind.

"Fine. I'll do it. But you knew I'd have to say yes, didn't you?"

Benedict's mouth curled into an easy grin. "Of course I knew that. I just like seeing you make a fuss about it," he muttered, taking a drink from his ale.

"The opera," Bram said, sounding pained.

**Men I Do Not Wish to Marry:
A Not at All Comprehensive List by
Lady Wilhelmina Bettesford**

A gentleman who complains about the crick in his neck when he stares up at the stars.

Chapter Four

And this is for charity?" Alethea asked, gazing at Wilhelmina in the glass.

They were in Alethea's dressing room, Alethea getting dressed for the evening as Wilhelmina waited. Because apparently it took hours for Alethea to achieve her pristine perfection, while Wilhelmina just tossed on an evening gown, let Jones, her maid, do something with her hair, and was on her way.

How was it possible for a woman who started out as beautiful as Alethea to spend hours on her toilette? How much more beautiful could a woman be?

Wilhelmina had to admit, as she regarded her stepmother, that Alethea was undeniably one of the most beautiful women she'd ever seen. Even more beautiful than when she'd started preparing for the evening, which answered Wilhelmina's question.

She looked like a fairy, all slender limbs and shining hair. And like a fairy, she kept trying to grant wishes, but Wilhelmina didn't want anything Alethea tried to offer.

Wouldn't you want a new morning gown, Mina?

I will just introduce you to that gentleman. I have heard he is desperate for a wife.

Let me remove some of those books from your room. You're going to damage your eyes with all that reading.

She didn't like being called Mina, she didn't like the implication that only a desperate man would want her—even if it was true—and her books were her only refuge.

Well, besides taking Dipper out on longer and longer walks, but she had to take a footman and her ladies' maid with her when she went—it wasn't possible any longer for her to sneak out.

Her stepmother somehow managed to know where everyone was at any time, so Wilhelmina was caught at least half a dozen times a few steps from the door. From freedom.

Which was why she had thrown herself into helping organize the Devenaugh Home for Destitute Boys charity auction, because at least it meant she had something to do with her days that didn't involve trailing after her father and stepmother as they saw the sights. And it meant she wasn't lying when she said she was too busy to accompany them, though she'd been forced into it more times than she'd hoped for. Which was zero times.

She had not been able to work on her paper either, which was endlessly frustrating. It was impossible to concentrate on things like space dust when the people in the household intruded endlessly on one's own space.

And then there was Aunt Flora, who'd taken to accosting Wilhelmina whenever she saw her to give her dire warnings about what might happen with a new countess in residence.

"It is for charity, yes," Wilhelmina replied. "The Devenaugh Home for Destitute Boys helps boys who have no family to help them."

"Unlike a lady such as yourself, who has such a large dowry," Alethea observed, sounding slightly peevish.

This wasn't the first time her stepmother had mentioned money; in fact, it was the topic she seemed to be the most enthusiastic about, except for asking others if she looked presentable, and beaming when they paid her effusive compliments. She'd taken careful note of just how much of a dowry Wilhelmina had, and Wilhelmina suspected she'd shared the information with all the eligible gentlemen she'd met thus far as Lord Croyde's wife.

Wilhelmina strongly suspected that Alethea wished that Wilhelmina would go off and get married so she could have the house, and Wilhelmina's father, to herself. The large dowry Alethea referenced was separate from Wilhelmina's inheritance, which would be her own regardless of her marital status, though she couldn't touch it for another seven months.

If she could just make it seven more months.

"Well," Alethea said in a self-satisfied voice, "how do I look?"

She might not be able to make it seven more days.

It wasn't that Alethea was mean, or cruel, or dismissive; it was just that they were such different types of people. Wilhelmina hadn't realized before how fortunate she was not to have had any siblings, nor for her father to have married before this. She'd taken what freedom she'd had for granted, and always wanted more.

Now she just wished she was able even to *see* a bridge on her own, much less stand up on top of it to view the stars.

Tonight was the charity auction, the event that Wilhelmina had been planning and working on for weeks. After tonight she'd have to figure out some other approved way to leave the house, because otherwise she was going to smite herself in the head with her telescope.

The presence of which Alethea had already objected to, since it cluttered up the balcony.

She had missed the last Stars Above Society meeting because Alethea had thrown a dinner party that night. She was determined not to miss the next one, even if it meant faking an illness and sneaking out the window.

From her second-floor bedroom. If only there was a strong, warm body she could fall onto. But no. She should not be thinking of that. Nor of that either. Put the topic away, she reminded herself, not for the first time.

There had been many more changes besides not having freedom of movement since Alethea arrived. There were parties, social calls, milliners' and dressmakers' visits, as well as a complete overhaul of the interior; Alethea had stripped the house down to its elements, ruthlessly removing all the furbelows, knickknacks, and geegaws that had so enchanted Wilhelmina's mother.

She'd replaced most of the furniture with new pieces, choosing a subtle color palette that was markedly different from the vibrant pastels that had dominated the rooms before.

It did look better now, Wilhelmina had to admit, but she pined for the fussiness she used to deplore.

"Well?" Alethea said again, an edge in her voice now. "How do I look?" she repeated. One thing that Wilhelmina knew about her stepmother was that the woman took her appearance very seriously. She'd risen, and was holding her skirts out wide, her little pointed chin tilted just so, a warmly gentle smile on her face.

"You look lovely," Wilhelmina replied honestly. Alethea wore a soft rose-pink gown trimmed in lace, a matching necklace and bracelet in pink diamonds gracing her neck and wrist. Her hair was twisted up into some elaborate style, a few tiny diamonds winking out from the blond strands.

"Thank you," Alethea said in satisfaction. "I wish I could have persuaded you to wear one of my gowns, Mina," she said. "You are not showing to your best advantage," she continued, sounding chiding. As though it was Wilhelmina's fault.

Which she supposed it was, since she usually didn't take many pains with her appearance.

Wilhelmina peered into the glass, wondering if she did look terrible, as Alethea implied.

Her gown was simple and elegant, made of a moss-green satin that picked up the green and gold highlights in her hazel eyes. Her hair was dressed simply, but the style made her neck look long and her shoulders look shapely.

If she wasn't standing next to a spectacularly beautiful woman she might even look presentable.

But she was, so she wasn't.

She shrugged. "I might have to work during the event, so I didn't want to wear anything that would be difficult to maneuver in." It was an excuse, but she had no desire to be done up like a porcelain figurine like Alethea. She had never wanted that, even when she'd been an eighteen-year-old debutante forced to enter Society.

She'd known ever since she was small that she did not want the life most women ended up with. Instead, she'd looked to the stars, and her books, and the few friends she'd made who shared her interests. It could have been lonely, but Wilhelmina found companionship with her aunt, her dog, and herself. Her friends were long gone, lost to marriage and children, but Wilhelmina was content with what she had.

In seven months, it would be all she would require. It would be all she had. And that would be enough.

"Should we go see if your father is ready? He hinted he had a surprise for me tonight," Alethea said in a fond tone. "That man, he never tires of spoiling me."

Wilhelmina nodded, following her stepmother out of the room and down to the foyer, where they found her father waiting for them, a large velvet box clasped in his hand.

He beamed when he saw his wife, and his smile faltered when he saw Wilhelmina. Of course she knew her father loved her, but she was also painfully aware that he had always wanted her to get married, and now he more strongly shared his wife's wish that his daughter would find a husband, and therefore another place to live. It would have been so much easier if she had agreed with them.

But the thought of that was even more stifling

than staying here with two people desperately in love with one another.

"Let's be on our way," Wilhelmina said brightly, trying to quash the unfamiliar feelings of loneliness. She'd never felt as though she belonged anywhere but in her own mind, so the feeling was familiar, but she had never expected to feel so out of place in her own home.

Which wasn't her home any longer. It was her father and Alethea's home now, and she was just a resident of the house.

"I HAVE MADE it this long without owning a tail-coat," Bram said through gritted teeth.

Simeon gave him a disgusted look as he adjusted Bram's lapels. "All gentlemen, even ones like you, should own a tailcoat."

Bram scowled. "What do you mean, 'ones like you'?" As though he didn't know the litany of complaints his friends had about him—that he was too set in his ways, that he was too quick to argue with anyone about anything, and, oh yes, that he had never fallen in love, or ever been tempted.

The two were in Finneas's Fine Establishment, a haberdashery that Simeon patronized. The shop was about to close, so they were the only two customers. Mr. Finneas himself was in the back preparing to shut the shop—he had known Simeon for years through the artistic community, and had dressed Simeon for nearly as long.

Bram could never hope to achieve Simeon's casually elegant look—nor, he had vociferously declared on several occasions, did he want to.

Simeon gave him an appraising look as he stepped

back to survey his friend. "Look, we all know you would much rather be out righting wrongs than exchanging idle chatter with people you don't respect, but this is important."

"You didn't answer the question," Bram said. "'Even ones like you'?" he prompted.

He peered over Simeon's shoulder to look at himself in the glass, his scowl deepening at what he saw.

He looked like a true gentleman, one of the men who made it a habit to inform him he didn't belong. Men who knew who both their married parents were. Men who didn't have to claw and scrape for whatever respectability they had.

Though that was doing his foster parents a disservice—his father, the man who'd raised him, had given him a considerable leg up by teaching him his profession, and he and his wife, whom Bram had called Mother, had lent him funds to set up his own office. It had taken a while, but Bram had paid them back a year before Mr. Townsend died. It was why Bram was allowing himself to think beyond his current career. If a bastard such as he could achieve an even higher status—being a judge, or a magistrate, or even becoming an Honorable—it would validate the Townsends' faith in him. Even though neither of them were alive to see it. It was something his friend Benedict had been urging him to do for some time.

Simeon had taken his comb to Bram's hair and chosen his clothing, insisting he wear unrelieved black, save a white waistcoat. Bram looked superbly polished, as though his only thought was how splendid he would appear when out on the town.

He returned his gaze to Simeon, whose evening wear was similar to Bram's, but he had added a wildly patterned waistcoat, making him look like the artist he was. His trousers were cut slimmer than Bram's, no doubt doing something to make him look even more long-legged.

Whatever. Bram didn't care about any of those concerns, much to Simeon's dismay.

"And we have to go to the opera?" Bram asked, likely for the hundredth time.

Simeon glared at Bram. "Yes. Charity. Good cause and all that?"

"Fine." Bram exhaled, wishing the evening was over and he was back in his comfortable set of rooms near his office. At least the opera event wasn't this evening; tonight there would just be the bidding aspect, which would be horrifying enough.

But all he truly wished to do this evening was go home.

He had wandered into a bookstore during a rare couple of hours, finding himself purchasing a copy of *Views of the Architecture of the Heavens* by a Scottish astronomer, John Pringle Nichol. He couldn't—or didn't want to—answer just why he had bought the book, but it was a fascinating read, and what he wanted most was to return to it, not to stand up in front of a group of wealthy opera-going ninnies.

Not that he was judging.

Even though he was absolutely judging.

"You're going to need to smile," Simeon said. "Unless you want people to bid on *not* having you take them to the opera?"

"I wish that was possible," Bram said fervently.

"You know I am friends with many of the performers," Simeon replied, giving Bram a withering look. "Just because you can't appreciate their genius—"

Bram growled.

"Fine!" Simeon said, holding his hands up in surrender. "You can keep being the hardworking no-enjoyment-having barrister who will die alone, surrounded by his dusty tomes. *I* plan on earning the most for the charity tonight."

Bram looked at his friend, assessing his appearance. All of the orphans were presentable, which had helped them get placement in their respective homes, but Simeon had a particular raffish appearance that appealed to people of all ages—grandmothers fussed over him, feeding him biscuits and sherry, children wanted him to join their games (which he often did), and ladies their age frequently fell in love with him. And he frequently fell in love back.

"I imagine you will," Bram replied in a mild tone.

"Oh?" Simeon said. "You're not going to argue with me? Not try to prove why I am wrong?" he taunted.

Bram shoved Simeon on the shoulder. Not hard, but enough to make the strands of hair falling over Simeon's eye move. "Stop trying to start an argument to distract me from this unpleasantness. I appreciate it, but I can get through it. I'm not so childish as to sulk all evening."

"Oh good," Simeon said, sounding relieved. "Benedict made me promise you'd behave yourself, and I couldn't think of any other way."

"Then to get me to debate you?" Bram shook his head. "You two have an odd impression of me."

"Odd but true," Simeon stated.

Bram opened his mouth to object, then realized his friends were right. He did like debating more than most anything.

"All right, let's go," he grumbled, reaching for the top hat Simeon had insisted on and slamming it down on his head.

"Careful, don't ruin my artistry," Simeon chided, at which Bram rolled his eyes.

Men I Do Not Wish to Marry: A Not at All Comprehensive List by Lady Wilhelmina Bettesford

Napoleon Bonaparte.

Not only did he think he was the best choice to rule France after toppling the regime, he also thought it a splendid idea to bring back the monarchy, only make it *more* monarchical, crowning himself emperor as opposed to merely a king. Imagine how conceited a gentleman like that had to be, and imagine how unpleasant it would be to disagree with him.

Chapter Five

Wilhelmina's eyes darted around the room as she, her father, and Alethea walked in. Aunt Flora didn't go out in Society, so she was staying home with Dipper.

The charity auction was taking place in a local dance hall—a far cry from the places her father preferred. She got confirmation of that when he gave a grunt of displeasure.

"Do they expect people who matter to show up here?" he said, his mouth pulled into a moue of distaste.

The room was spacious, but showed its wear. A small stage was at the front of the room, edged with curtains, which were currently closed. Tables lined the room holding a variety of auction items, while a small booth in the far right corner was where beverages and snacks were being sold.

Alethea glanced over at Wilhelmina, then at her husband. "My people would be the ones who show up here, dear," she said gently. "Are you saying I do not matter?"

Wilhelmina blinked in surprise. She wouldn't have expected Alethea to exhibit a backbone when it came to her father's pomposity about class and rank, which was well established.

He'd been born an earl's second son, with no expectation of inheriting, but had married Wilhelmina's mother, a marquess's daughter, and had adopted his late wife's family heritage as his own, disdaining anyone who was below him. And then after the unfortunate early demise of his older brother he had inherited his title, which had made him rise even further in his own estimation.

In other words, he was a snob.

"You do matter, of course," her father said gruffly, patting her hand. "I spoke without thinking."

Wilhelmina's eyes got even wider. Her father apologizing?

Perhaps this marriage would make him unbend from some of his rigid ways. In which case, she couldn't begrudge it. If Alethea made him happy, and made him more pleasant to be around, then it was all a good thing, wasn't it?

That she had very little in common with either of them was just bad luck. And something she would have to contemplate. Not that she was suddenly going to start being concerned with being on time, adhering to fashion, or knowing the right people, but perhaps there was something she could figure out that would make her life at home more tolerable. Because the alternative was even worse.

Not to mention if Alethea bore her father children. That was something she hadn't dared to even think about. But it had to be a real possibility.

"Lady Wilhelmina!"

She turned as she heard her name, smiling as she saw the proprietress of the Devenaugh Home,

Miss Maude Chalmers. Miss Chalmers was a few years older than Wilhelmina, a force of nature who brooked very little argument. Thankfully, she also was good at accepting help when she needed it, and she and Wilhelmina had planned and organized the entire event. Wilhelmina liked Maude more than she'd ever liked anyone not related to her—or who was a dog—and she discovered she was enjoying herself far more than she'd anticipated when she'd announced she was needed elsewhere.

Maude had handled the logistics, whereas Wilhelmina had used her name and title to secure the donations. Not only was the auction offering opera-going gentlemen, but the Stars Above Society had donated an evening's worth of stargazing with an expert, several copies of various scholarly papers on a variety of star subjects, and a telescope.

It was the last item that Wilhelmina longed for. She had a telescope, the one that Alethea was already lobbying to remove from the house, but the telescope donated to the auction was far superior, made for a professional astronomer rather than an amateur one.

If she owned a telescope such as that one, other astronomers—other male astronomers—would have to take her more seriously. She would be able to substantiate her theories and observe more in the sky that would inspire new astronomical questions.

It was all she wanted: to stare up at the stars without feeling as though she was doing something wrong. As though, in fact, she was doing something *right*. To be respected for her opinions, not the size of her dowry or her bloodlines or any number of things over which she had no control.

If she had a better telescope, she'd be far less likely to have to clamber up on bridges, for example, to get a better look.

And also less likely to fall onto remarkably handsome men with blue eyes.

"Good evening, Miss Chalmers," Wilhelmina replied, pushing thoughts of argumentative strangers out of her head. "How is it going?" She nodded toward the crowd, most of whom were examining the various items up for auction—the nonliving items, that is—placed on the tables against the walls.

Maude's lips twisted into a wry smile. "Well, William and Anthony decided they wanted to help, so they rearranged all the items, but didn't change the placards. So that took a while." William and Anthony were the two youngest, and the most rambunctious, of the boys at the Devenaugh Home.

Everyone adored them.

Despite its humble antecedents, the room was lavishly decorated, all of the older boys having pitched in to help decorate, while the many benefactors had offered materials, money, and the loaning of staff for the evening.

Swag in several bright colors hung from the walls, while the tables holding the auction items were covered in black satin. The enormous chandelier in the middle of the ceiling held at least fifty candles, their flickering light giving the room a golden glow. Wilhelmina had found the chandelier in the storage room, one of the many items Alethea had banished in the midst of her redecorating purge.

Chairs had been placed in rows in front of a small stage where the gentlemen would appear when it was time for that portion of the evening.

Wilhelmina had been nervous that nobody would wish to bid, but Maude had assured her—with a knowing grin—that there had already been several inquiries from various wealthy ladies about specific gentlemen.

Wilhelmina herself couldn't imagine actually paying money to go to an opera with a stranger—it sounded like the worst kind of torture—but she recognized that very few people, if any, shared her antipathy both to the opera and to strangers.

"Mina, we're going to get a seat," Alethea said, offering a smile to Maude. "I'll save one for you."

"No need," Wilhelmina replied, feeling the heat come to her cheeks. She knew she'd feel awkward even sitting in the audience; she'd already planned to begin packing up the nonhuman auction items while the opera and companion auction was taking place. "I'll be busy during that time."

"Oh, what a shame," Alethea replied, her expression exaggeratedly disappointed. "I was so hoping you might see something you liked." She accompanied her words with a wink, while Wilhelmina felt her face heat again.

"You've made Mina blush!" her father exclaimed in delight.

Her father had never called her anything but her actual full name until recently.

There were so many changes to her life now. And, she discovered, she did not like change.

At least not these changes.

"I have!" Alethea said, sounding gleeful. "I knew there must be something that would stir her emotions."

Apparently she hadn't been paying attention

when Wilhelmina had been studying the stars at night, playing with Dipper, or reading. *Those* things stirred her emotions; that she wasn't stirred by beautiful clothing or the opportunity to be married wasn't anything to be ashamed about.

Except most of the world, at least her world, seemed to think it was.

BRAM PACED IN the small room the auction had allocated for the auction participants. Not only were Benedict, Simeon, Fenton, and Theo there, but there were at least another half dozen or so gentlemen there as well, all of them dressed in fine evening wear and milling about talking about their relative importance.

Or at least it seemed that way to Bram.

"I assume I'll fetch the highest price," one of the men said. Bram looked at him with a critical eye; he supposed the man was handsome, if one liked the bland good looks of a typical English gentleman. Blond, blue-eyed, and bewhiskered. "My father has a box, and it is well-known that only the best people sit in it," he continued.

Ah, that changed the offering, didn't it? Not only did the stranger have a father, but he had a father who was prosperous enough to have a box at the opera.

"You don't have an opera box, do you?" he said in a low voice to Simeon, who was busy flicking invisible specks of dust off his sleeve.

"No." Simeon gave a level gaze at Blond Whiskers. "I don't need one." He spoke in a louder tone, one meant to be heard.

"What's that?" Whiskers said. Two other men

came to stand at either elbow, all of them looking belligerent.

Oh good, Bram thought. A fight. He hadn't expected there would be fisticuffs this evening. Perhaps things were looking up. He felt his hands curl into fists at his sides.

"I said I don't need the addition of my father's opera box to endear me to the bidders," Simeon said, instantly quieting the conversation in the room.

Benedict sighed, folding his arms over his chest in resignation.

Theo grinned, while Fenton didn't seem to notice, bent over a pad of paper he was scratching on furiously. Probably creating a new mathematical theorem that would gain him another fortune on the stock market.

Whiskers walked up to Simeon, a swagger in his step. "Do you care to make a wager on it? Who'll end up with the highest bid?"

Couldn't we just settle this with a good old-fashioned brawl? Bram wanted to ask, but he knew Benedict would shoot him a look, and then not only would they not end up in a fight, but Benedict would remind him of it for at least the next month. Benedict was very good at making his friends feel bad for their actions. It was his least endearing quality.

"I'll take those odds," Fenton said unexpectedly, what with not having seemed to pay attention for anything up to now.

"There are no odds. This is a simple wager," Whiskers said in exasperation. "You and me," he said, jerking his chin toward Simeon. "Ten pounds says I will get the highest bid."

Simeon shrugged. "Twenty says I will."

Whiskers stuck his hand out. "Done. Twenty pounds."

To his own surprise, Bram found himself speaking. "Thirty pounds says I will."

Where had that come from? How could he possibly think to compete against Simeon the Charming Artist and Blond Whiskers and His Opera Box?

But if he wasn't going to be able to punch someone, he'd like to win some money. Besides, his friends were always saying how staid and predictable he was. And normally he agreed. But betting on himself in a charity auction was hardly predictable.

Perhaps next he'd see what it was like to kiss a stranger.

Before she kissed him.

"I'm backing Bram," Fenton said.

"As am I," Theo added, shooting a mischievous glance toward Simeon, who scowled.

"And I," Benedict added, his commanding tone making everyone in the room stop their chattering.

"Some best friends you are," Simeon grumbled. "Fine. I'm in. Thirty on Bram, twenty on me." He grinned his easy smile. "That way I am bound to win, because there is no possibility of either of us," he said, pointing between himself and Bram, "losing to any of you."

"What if I win?" Fenton asked.

Everyone in the room looked at him.

"You won't," everyone said. At least everyone agreed on that.

WILHELMINA SCURRIED OUT of sight as the first gentlemen began to go onstage. She was mortified by proxy, worried that either nobody would bid or that everyone would bid and there would be animosity among the audience members.

Alethea and her father had seated themselves in the front row, an empty seat to the right of Alethea, but Wilhelmina had declined to take it, claiming she had something very urgent to take care of.

That urgent something was her hiding away, but her father and Alethea didn't have to know that.

She was in one of the small rooms to the side of the main room where the bidding was taking place when she heard a murmuring of the crowd, stronger and louder than she'd heard before. As though there was something untoward happening, and everyone had to comment on it.

She debated briefly between herself and herself whether to continue to hide here—thus avoiding the embarrassment—or finding out what the hubbub was, which would satisfy her curiosity.

She decided on the latter. Good to know she could still win an argument. Even if it was only with herself.

She ventured out of the room, glancing up and down the hallway. Nobody there. Of course not, she reasoned; all unawkward people were in the main room already making noise, which was why she had come out in the first place.

She shook her head at her own ridiculousness and kept walking to the door that led back to the main room.

As she opened the door, the noise of the crowd increased, and she stood for a moment on the threshold, her eyes taking in what was happening.

A gentleman was onstage, arms folded over an impressive chest, a top hat on his black hair. One eyebrow was raised as if in challenge, and his legs were set in a wide-legged stance, as though he was bracing himself for a fight. A fight where he might be knocked down, or more likely, knock others down. Like a game of skittles, only he'd be the destructive force.

She frowned as she gazed at him, prickles of something skittering along her spine until it came to her in sharp realization.

Dear God.

This was her rescuer. Mr. Helpful himself, being bid on as though he was a prize cow. Or a bull, if she was being gender-specific.

She hadn't remembered quite how tall and handsome he was. Or she had, but she had assumed her mind was playing tricks on her—surely one gentleman could not be so tall and so handsome?

And yet here he was. Or rather, *there* he was, since he was at the opposite end of the room.

No wonder she had kissed him that night. How could she not?

"Seventy-five," she heard a voice call. A voice suspiciously like her stepmother's. She felt her spine tense. Why was Alethea bidding on him? Why was she bidding at all? What must Wilhelmina's father think, to have his wife bidding for a gentleman to take her to the opera? And yet he wasn't getting up and stomping out in fury.

"Eighty," another voice chimed in quickly. "And I'll feed him first. He looks as though he has a healthy appetite." Wilhelmina spotted the woman who was speaking: an older woman with an enormous hat perched on her gray hair, another woman who appeared to be the lady's companion seated at her side laughing into a handkerchief.

This was nothing to laugh about, Wilhelmina thought in indignation.

"Eighty-five," Alethea said.

"Ninety," the older woman replied. "But that's as high as I can go. Even for shoulders that broad," she said in a rueful tone. The audience members chuckled in response.

"One hundred," Alethea said, sounding triumphant.

"Going once," the auctioneer said, "going twice, and sold to the lady in the front row."

The room burst out into applause, and Wilhelmina found herself clapping as well, then stopped immediately as soon as she realized what she was doing.

A group of men to the side cheered, congratulating Mr. Helpful, who looked very pleased with himself.

"I hadn't expected that, had you?" Maude said, coming to stand at Wilhelmina's elbow. "That is the highest bid this evening, and the highest we'll get, I expect. I'd thought that the most we would get would be fifty pounds." She turned to look at Wilhelmina, admiration in her gaze. "You did well, finding the people who would be able to bid so high. The boys will be very appreciative."

"Mina!" she heard Alethea say. And then there was a bustle of pink satin, a flurry of gentlemen bowing as her stepmother passed them, and then she was standing in front of Wilhelmina, a triumphant expression on her face. "Did you see?" She gave a disapproving nod. "I was so hoping you would choose yourself, but you had things to do, so I had to choose for you."

"Choose?" Wilhelmina said in confusion.

Alethea rolled her eyes. "Choose. Yes, of course. You don't think I was bidding on that gentleman to take *me* to the opera?" She slid her arm through Wilhelmina's father's. "I already have a fine gentleman—the best gentleman—to take me, should I wish it." She gazed adoringly at him, and Wilhelmina was momentarily distracted by how much it felt like she was intruding when Alethea and her father interacted with one another.

"But—choose?" Wilhelmina repeated, a feeling of dread uncurling in her stomach.

"Yes, your father agreed with me. It's his money, after all," Alethea added, more sharply. She nodded toward the stage, where another gentleman now stood. "I reviewed each of the items, and that one seemed the most appropriate for you."

"Not that we wish you to marry him," her father hastened to add. "He is not your equal, of course." The earl leaned forward to speak in a lowered tone. "His parentage is unknown."

Alethea nodded her agreement at her husband's words, then added, "But it is my belief that when you are seen in a gentleman's company, other gentlemen will notice."

"So you are sending me to the opera with a strange gentleman as a sort of marital decoy?" Wilhelmina asked, unable to keep the note of horror from her voice. This wasn't close to a telescope. "So that someone else will think," she said, deepening her voice to imitate the imaginary suitor, "'Well, he found her tolerable enough to spend a few hours with, perhaps I should have a go'?"

Maude put her hand on Wilhelmina's arm in sympathy.

"Not so crudely, no," Alethea replied, color heightening in her cheeks. "Speak to her, Charles," she commanded. "Or don't—the gentleman himself is coming this way," she hissed.

Wilhelmina turned to face him, taking a deep breath as she met his gaze.

BRAM STOPPED SHORT as he saw her. At first he wasn't certain it was her—he had wondered if his imagination had distorted his recollection of that night. If her face wasn't lovely, and distinctive, marked by her striking eyebrows, sweetly meek nose, and those mobile, expressive lips. If he had dreamt up how she stirred him with her appearance and her forceful personality. Not to mention that kiss.

But then he met her gaze, and he knew. It was her. His Bridge Lady. Lady Luminous of the Dipper.

"Good evening, sir." The woman to the right of the Bridge Lady spoke as he and the Bridge Lady locked eyes, neither seemingly able to look away. "I am Lady Croyde, and this is my husband, Lord Croyde. And our daughter, Lady Wilhelmina Bettesford. My stepdaughter, that is," she added with an arch look.

Lady Croyde was young, blonde, and beautiful, Bram supposed. But he couldn't pay attention to her, not when Lady Luminous—Lady Wilhelmina, it appeared—was there. He'd been thinking about their encounter, he realized, since it occurred. Not all the time, but he'd been wondering about her ever since.

"It is a pleasure to meet you," Bram said, extending his hand. "Officially, I mean," he added in a low voice.

Her eyes widened at that, and then narrowed, as though she wished to scold him. But she couldn't, not without revealing the circumstances of their first meeting.

"A pleasure, sir," she said, making it sound as if it was anything but.

"You and Wilhelmina have much in common," Lady Croyde enthused. "The auctioneer mentioned you enjoyed books, and she does also."

"And long walks over bridges," Bram added.

"Pardon?"

"Nothing, Alethea," Lady Wilhelmina said hastily, shooting him daggers. She made an obvious effort to curl her mouth into a smile. "What types of books do you enjoy, Mr.—"

"Townsend," Bram replied. "Fiction, mostly. My friends and I meet regularly to discuss books each month. It is a rare opportunity for us to get together and talk about things other than our professions. Last month we discussed Elizabeth Gaskell's *Mary Barton*. We agreed that Mary should have spoken the truth," he added, seeing the color come to her cheeks as he spoke.

Now why had he offered those facts about his life? Talking even about a specific book he'd enjoyed? It wasn't as though his new acquaintance would care. She hadn't even wanted to know his name in the first place, for goodness' sake.

That he had spent weeks wondering if she was

all right, looking up at the stars and thinking she might be doing the same, when she was probably just going about her life, perhaps hopping up onto other parapets, maybe even kissing other strange men—well, it was all rather lowering.

Bram wasn't like Simeon, or Theo, falling in love every few months. He didn't have time for any of that, even if he had ever met anybody he thought would keep him interested for more than a week or two, much less a lifetime.

He had never thought so much about a woman as he had this woman, and here she was. In front of him, regarding him with a—well, with a decidedly displeased expression.

"Fiction," she repeated, sounding unenthused. "I like to read books about *useful* things."

He couldn't help the low growl he let out.

"Books!" Lady Croyde exclaimed, clapping her hands together. "So much in common! I haven't any use for the things myself. I am always urging Mina—Wilhelmina, you understand, she is not my actual daughter since I am so much younger," she said, uttering a little titter as she spoke.

"Only five years," Lady Wilhelmina said under her breath.

"To give some away, or just keep the attractive-looking volumes," Lady Croyde continued.

"The opera," Lord Croyde said in a chiding voice. As though he was reminding all of them of the topic at hand.

Lady Wilhelmina looked pained.

"Yes, the opera!" Lady Croyde repeated. "You two are going together. I believe the event is in a week." She darted glances between the two of them, her pink lips curved into a delighted smile. "I am so glad you brought me to the auction, Mina." Her expression grew sly. "It's a good thing we are able to get you out in Society more. And with such a handsome accompaniment."

Bram smothered a laugh as Lady Wilhelmina looked as though she was pondering how to talk her stepmother up onto a parapet.

"The opera," Bram said, sweeping into a deep bow. "What a pleasure, and to be combined with such a good cause will make it doubly enjoyable."

She grimaced, and he caught her eye, winking at her.

This was going to be more enjoyable than he'd anticipated.

Men I Do Not Wish to Marry:
A Not at All Comprehensive List by
Lady Wilhelmina Bettesford

A man who makes an assumption about something without ever having tried it.

(Yes, I know that makes me a hypocrite, given my previous attitude toward the opera. I didn't say my list is reasonable.)

Chapter Six

"Why did it have to be *him*?"

Wilhelmina paced the floor of her bedroom, a few hours before she was supposed to go out for the dreaded evening.

She'd spent the past week doing everything she could to get out of it—she'd asked Maude to swap the bid out with the gray-haired lady, she'd tried standing in the rain to give herself a cold, she'd told Alethea she didn't want her father spending all that money on her. None of it worked, though the last had made Alethea consider it, at least for a few moments.

But then Alethea had shaken her head and insisted the Home needed the money more than they did. Wilhelmina wished her stepmother was a bit more grasping than she already seemed to be.

"If it had been another gentleman, any other gentleman," Wilhelmina continued, still pacing. *Instead of the one you kissed like an impulsive flibbertigibbet.*

She spoke to Dipper, who was sitting on the floor, tilting his head with a quizzical expression on his face. Or so she imagined.

He was probably just thinking about his dinner.

She usually didn't mind she had so few friends, but she could use another lady her own age to talk all of this out with—neither Dipper nor Aunt Flora were likely to be helpful. If Maude Chalmers, the woman who ran the Home, wasn't too busy with her own work Wilhelmina might be able to speak to her about it.

But what would she say? "My stepmother bid on a gentleman to take me to the opera, and it's the same gentleman I fell on and then kissed, so you can see how awkward it is?"

Ridiculous.

"Though if it was anybody else I'd probably still be dreading it," she continued. Dipper's expression did not change. "I have to admit that because it is him I might be looking forward to it more than I would have otherwise."

She twisted her mouth into an expression of distaste. At herself, for being so shallow. "I am not a flibbertigibbet," she said firmly. "But he is really stupidly good-looking. I have no business going to the opera with such a man." She took a deep breath. "I definitely have no business kissing him."

She marched over to her glass, determined to prove herself right.

But, unfortunately, she could not. She was attractive; it was just that she usually didn't want to admit it. Because to admit it would be to admit that someone else—someone who was not her, someone who might want to spend the rest of his life with her—might think the same thing. Which she most definitely did not want. Not if she wanted to maintain her independence, though that life would lack certain . . . amenities, if she were being honest. If

amenities meant a tall, handsome, wickedly intelligent man who challenged her.

Her face had pleasant features, her eyes were
large and expressive, and her mouth—though a
trifle wide—was pleasing.

Drat.

"He reads *fiction*," she said to Dipper in a disapproving tone. "And he is a barrister, so he spends
his days telling everyone else they are wrong."

Which wasn't that far from what she did in her
head. The unfair part of that was that he got to do
it out loud, and get paid for it. Whereas she wasn't
supposed to do it at all, much less admit to it.

No wonder he was so quick to argue with her that
night on the bridge—he was a professional arguer.

Though it would be fun to best him in an argument,
wouldn't it?

No. She couldn't think anything about this evening
would be fun. It would be the *opera* with a *man* she
was already irked by because of his *high-handedness*
and his *handsomeness*. A very tangible reminder that
she could, indeed, behave like a foolish ninny.

"Drat," she said aloud. Dipper rested his nose on
his paws and went to sleep, apparently tired of her
complaints.

"Well," she said at last, putting her hands on her
hips as she glared down at her dog. "If I can't get out
of it, I am going to have to make him wish he had."

"I THOUGHT YOU would have been trying your hard-
est to get out of it. And yet here you are getting
yourself dressed up like—and I quote—'a penguin
with a top hat.'" Fenton regarded Bram with an expression he normally reserved for his most compli-

cated of equations. "Though why a penguin would wear a top hat, I have no idea. If they would wear a top hat, does that mean they are considered naked otherwise? And what would a fully dressed penguin look like? Surely clothing would be redundant, if the penguin was going out for the evening. He's already wearing black and white."

"A gibus, if you please," Simeon said haughtily. He stepped forward to flick a piece of lint from Bram's lapel. "If you are going to talk about it at such length, please use the proper word."

"Is the gibus the penguin or the top hat?" Fenton asked in a mild tone.

They were all crowded into Bram's rooms, Fenton sitting on his bed, while Simeon darted from wardrobe to Bram, who stood in the middle of the room, and back again.

"A gibus is a collapsible hat some Frenchman invented. So men could attend the opera without worrying they are going to ruin their headwear. It's named after him," Simeon replied.

"Thank God for Monsieur Gibus," Bram offered in a dry tone. "I do not have to cancel my attendance at the opera out of concern for my hat." He accompanied his words with a roll of his eyes.

"There's the Bram we know," Fenton said, sounding relieved. "First you're rescuing random women off bridges, then you're willing to go to the opera. I was worried you had hit your head."

"Not with my gibus on, I won't," Bram said with a wink toward Simeon. Who sighed gustily in response.

"And she's not a random woman," Bram continued. "She is Lady Wilhelmina Bettesford. The daughter—or stepdaughter—of the lady who actually bid on me."

She is twenty-four years old, unmarried, with a dog named Dipper and a fascination with astronomy. She belongs to the Stars Above Society, which meets every fortnight at the Royal Institute. She disdains fiction, being helped off of bridges, and off of him.

She does not know how to hail a hackney cab.

He couldn't seem to stop thinking about her. He wanted to know more about her. He wanted to persuade her to read a work of fiction that she would actually like. He wanted to persuade her to actually like *him*.

He wanted to kiss her again. Or more accurately, he wanted to kiss her rather than having her kiss him and then run away.

"The one who annoyed you?" Fenton asked, ever inquisitive.

"The same," Simeon replied.

"I have to admit to being annoyed, yes," Bram said. Knowing the truth would come out anyway, he might as well get ahead of it. "But also intrigued." He turned to look at his friends, both of whom were staring at him. "I've never met another person—besides you lot—who seemed as though she wished to argue with me. It was," he began, sifting through the memory of the night, "refreshing." He would not, he decided, mention the kiss. They would make far more of it than it actually meant, even though he had been doing the same since he'd met her.

Simeon's brows rose. "Refreshing?" He circled around Bram, eerily similar to how Bram moved around an antagonistic witness. "I don't think you've ever called anybody refreshing before."

He gave Bram an assessing look. "And if you did, it would sound like an insult, since you don't like new things or people who are a bit different from the norm."

"Well, don't make too big a thing of it," Bram said, folding his arms over his chest and assuming his most assertive posture. "Besides, I—" But then he stopped, because Simeon was accurate in how Bram had always thought before.

His stance did nothing to intimidate Simeon, unfortunately. They'd known each other too long.

"So you're taking her to the opera," Simeon continued, "which you loathe—and you're willingly dressing up in evening wear, which you also loathe. *Interesting.*"

"Don't say 'interesting' in that meaningful way," Bram said. "I'm merely fulfilling a promise to Benedict with as much good humor as I can muster."

"You'll have to tell us all about it at the next book club meeting," Fenton said. "And we can tell you about our respective opera evenings. I am to go with the lady who tried to win you, Bram. An older woman, quite delightful, if not refreshing."

He spoke with such perfect sincerity Bram knew he wasn't being pointed. He was just being Fenton.

"And I am going with the manager of the Home, a Miss Maude Chalmers."

"Does Benedict know?" Bram asked, reminded of Benedict's reaction to the lady.

Simeon shrugged. "Perhaps. It doesn't matter— our opera nights aren't for some time. You're the first to go."

Bram swallowed. *You're the first to go.* It sounded ominous, as though there was something that might happen tonight that would irrevocably change his life.

Or had that thing already happened?

"You look beautiful!" Alethea enthused, dancing around Wilhelmina.

I do, Wilhelmina thought grumpily.

The two were in Wilhelmina's bedroom with Alethea helping her stepdaughter get dressed. Which basically meant that Alethea dictated what should go where, and Wilhelmina's lady's maid, Jones, was scurrying around obeying her orders.

Wilhelmina was going to have to give Jones a raise in pay.

Alethea had insisted they go to Regent Street to purchase a new gown for the opera, and had forced Wilhelmina to choose one that had looked entirely stunning on her.

It was made of a soft gold material, supple and shimmering, bringing out the gold highlights in Wilhelmina's hazel eyes and making her skin glow. *Lady Luminous*, she thought.

The gown was cut low in the front, with tiny sleeves that were so slight as to be merely a suggestion. The waist was tight, with skirts cascading out from it in a billow of gold, like sunlight streaming from the sky at midday.

Her gloves were white and went up to her elbow, while Alethea had piled on a stack of gold bracelets onto one arm, leaving the other bare. Making her look like one of the women in a painting of ancient Greece or something—like Cleopatra or Zenobia.

"Not Greece, then," she muttered in disgust.

"Egypt or Palmyra. Honestly, Wilhelmina, have you forgotten everything?"

"What did you say, Mina?" Alethea asked in a bright chirp.

"Nothing," Wilhelmina replied, trying to sound as though she hadn't been pondering ancient queens who'd conquered lands and men in equal measure.

Neither of *them* would have demurred at attending the opera.

She should be more like them. Except for the whole conquering lands and men part; she didn't want to do either of those things.

"Dipper, what do you think?" Alethea said, addressing the dog who lay in his bed to the right of Wilhelmina's bed.

All three of them—Wilhelmina, Alethea, and Jones—regarded Dipper, who continued to snooze.

"Well, you do look beautiful. Though I think your hair needs just a touch—" Alethea said, stepping forward to make some adjustment to Wilhelmina's coiffure.

Again, Alethea had dictated how Jones was to dress Wilhelmina's hair, demanding a far more complicated style than either Wilhelmina or Jones was comfortable with.

Several hairpins later, and Wilhelmina's chestnut hair was swept up into a classical style, matching the gown's elegant draping. It hurt when she moved her head a certain way since her hair was so heavy, but Alethea had responded to every one of Wilhelmina's complaints with a forceful denial that Wilhelmina couldn't help but envy.

Wilhelmina froze as she heard the knock on the door downstairs.

"There he is!" Alethea exclaimed. She took hold of Wilhelmina's arm and pulled her from the room, Dipper following them, his tail wagging excitedly.

Downstairs, they heard Wilhelmina's father's voice and that of another gentleman, lower than Lord Croyde's and more commanding.

Alethea flew down the stairs with Wilhelmina following more slowly.

Alethea and Lord Croyde were going to the opera as well, not so much to watch over Wilhelmina, since neither of them thought she would cause any scandal—much to Wilhelmina's dismay, though she admitted it was true—but because Society demanded someone like Wilhelmina be chaperoned regardless of the circumstances.

It was apparently fine for a person to bid on another person but not fine for a young lady nearing an unmarriageable age to attend an event with a gentleman one had bid on.

The randomness of Societal protocol made Wilhelmina's head hurt. And it wasn't just the hairpins.

"Good evening, Lady Wilhelmina."

He was bowing, his enormous top hat in one hand, his other making an elegant gesture toward her.

She wondered if he'd suffered any bruising when she'd fallen on him.

And then he straightened, and she wondered if *she'd* suffered any bruising when she'd met him.

Because she found she had difficulty breathing, and her chest felt oddly tight.

He wore elegant evening wear, but his height and appearance eclipsed the impact of any other gentleman she'd ever seen in the same clothing before.

To be fair, however, she'd seldom paid much attention to a gentleman's appearance, being far too concerned with making certain she didn't get accidentally engaged to anyone. Or step on their feet. On the few occasions she had remarked on a gentleman's looks, it was a gentleman who was in a painting or a sculpture.

She wondered what he would look like as a sculpture—all that bone structure displayed in marble.

Not to mention the rest of him.

"Say 'good evening' to Mr. Townsend, Mina," Alethea prompted.

"Good evening," Wilhelmina said, hearing her voice hitch. Why had it done that? What was happening to her?

"Are we ready to go? They are performing Rossini's *Semiramide*."

"Ah," Wilhelmina replied, as though that information meant something to her.

"It's based on a work by Voltaire. Which you likely have not read, what with it being fiction and all," he said dryly. "Shall we?"

He held his arm out for her, and she took it, immediately conscious of how much larger he was than her.

No wonder so many misguided theorists believed that men and women should live in separate spheres, separated by their respective roles, if the difference between male and female could be so stark. *He* wouldn't have to climb up onto a bridge to see the stars more closely; he could just look up.

Even so, she could not agree with the idea of separate spheres. It seemed to her that that theory was just a way for men to continue to control women, and she did not want to be controlled. That was the whole point of avoiding marriage, after all.

"The carriage is waiting just outside," her father said, sounding impatient. He hated keeping anyone or anything waiting.

They made their way outside, Wilhelmina going into the carriage first, followed by Alethea, then her father, and finally Mr. Townsend.

She and Mr. Townsend sat beside one another, and she was intensely conscious of his body just there beside hers.

He had removed his hat, and he held it in his lap, his head nearly brushing the top of the carriage anyway, due to his height.

"You mentioned knowing the opera," Alethea began in a light, conversational tone. The carriage lurched forward, and Wilhelmina flung an arm out to brace herself.

"I just know its name, and that it is a tragedy involving a queen."

"I wonder that Queen Victoria would allow it to be performed," Wilhelmina's father said stuffily.

"I would hope our queen would be secure enough to allow for such a thing to be performed," Wilhelmina replied, her tone heated. "Her example is a remarkable one. Imagine being sole monarch, and married to someone who is not your equal, at least in terms of government."

"You are quite vehement on the subject," Mr. Townsend remarked.

Wilhelmina felt stung by the criticism. She turned

to face him, everything forgotten as she argued her point. "I don't think it's out of line to want a woman to be able to do the same thing as a man. It isn't as though our past monarchs, even if they were male, were any better than she is. She is far more capable, for example, than that King George, who was more interested in spending money on art and buildings than he was on improving people's situations."

"Not a fan of art and buildings either, then," Mr. Townsend replied. He held his hands up in surrender as she opened her mouth to object. "I agree with you, for the record. I just find it interesting that you hold so little regard for fiction and art, two areas where women have been better able to find a place for themselves in our world." He raised a challenging eyebrow. "I could recommend some books, if you'd like to confront some of your misconceptions."

"I do not understand a thing you are saying," Alethea said airily before Wilhelmina could sputter a reply. "But I suppose that just means you have things in common that you do not share with us," she continued, snuggling closer to Wilhelmina's father.

"I do not have misconceptions," Wilhelmina said in a low tone, wondering just how she had lost control of the conversation. "I have not found anything I like."

"So you have just dismissed those subjects entirely." He nudged her shoulder. "I'd say that is remarkably like a man, but you would doubtless argue with that as well."

She made another sputtering noise, wishing they were alone so she could argue at will. Aware that even though she was completely and entirely annoyed, she was also similarly intrigued.

She'd never met anyone as defiant and willful as herself. And yet here he was, and he was a tall, handsome gentleman on top of all that.

It really wasn't surprising she had kissed him that first time; what was more surprising was that she hadn't kidnapped him so they could debate ideologies for the rest of time. Preferably on an island filled with books of all sorts as well as an enormous telescope.

And food. She wouldn't want to starve, after all. One had to be practical.

Men I Do Not Wish to Marry:
A Not at All Comprehensive List by
Lady Wilhelmina Bettesford

Bluebeard.
  For obvious reasons.

Chapter Seven

$\mathscr{B}$ram had hoped, but not expected, to have a good time this evening, despite it being the opera and with a woman who apparently found him obnoxious.

Though that was part of the good time, wasn't it?

He had never met anyone, besides his friends, who was willing to go toe-to-toe with him before. And even his friends surrendered when he had just barely started.

But her—she looked as though she was ready to go a full twelve rounds with him, and it was exhilarating.

They hadn't even arrived yet, and he was already having the best evening of his life, save for the book club evenings. And his book club evenings didn't include the tantalizing prospect of needling an attractive woman so much that she just gave up and kissed him.

He was acutely aware of her sitting beside him on the plush carriage seat; her full skirts flowed over his legs, swirling around him, just as her scent—something floral—lingered in his nose. He'd have to ask her what flower scent she wore, just to get an image of it in his mind. Perhaps buy her a bouquet of the same flowers to annoy her further.

She took a deep breath beside him, folding her gloved hands in her lap. One arm was stacked with gold bracelets, and he imagined, for a moment, removing them one by one until he could peel off her glove to feel the soft skin of her hand. Making the respective points of his argument as he kissed each of her fingers.

He felt his cock react to the thought, and he shifted. He had never been so stimulated on so many levels before—intellectually, physically, and philosophically. Though the former was nearly the first, wasn't it?

Perhaps they could debate that as well.

"Tell me," she began suddenly, "if you were on a desert island, what items would you require?"

"We're here!" Lady Croyde exclaimed brightly, the carriage coming to a halting stop. Bram glanced out the window to see the Royal Opera House in full splendor.

It had just been renovated, and lights shone from every one of the five domed enormous windows, casting a bright light on the attendees entering the building. Four columns stood in front of them, casting long shadows. They had to wait a few minutes as other guests disembarked from their respective carriages, and Bram was able to see some of the people's faces. All of them wore expressions of excitement, and he wondered what they were looking forward to that he didn't understand.

He got out first, holding his hand out to assist Lady Croyde and then Lady Wilhelmina. Lord Croyde got out last, speaking a few instructions to

the driver and then turning his attention toward
the group.

"Well, here we are," Lord Croyde proclaimed. In
case they weren't all aware or as though his wife
hadn't just said the same thing.

Lord Croyde extracted sheafs of paper from his
waistcoat, his eyebrows drawing together as he
looked at them. "We're not seated together," he said.
He looked up at his daughter. "You can sit with
Alethea, and Mr. Townsend and I can sit together.
There are two box seats, thanks to Lord Robens, and
two floor seats from the auction."

"Oh, I wouldn't want to separate you two newly-
weds," Lady Wilhelmina said quickly in reply. "Mr.
Townsend and I will be perfectly safe on the floor."
She kept her gaze steady on her father, as though
willing him to agree through the force of her stare.

"Fine," Lord Croyde said after a moment. Apparently the stare worked. Or he just preferred to be
with his wife, and not a stranger of dubious parentage.

"We'll meet in the lobby at intermission." He
thrust two tickets toward Bram, who took them and
pocketed them quickly in his evening coat.

"You go ahead and get Alethea seated," Lady
Wilhelmina urged. "She's never been to the opera
before."

"No, I haven't," Lady Croyde said with a simper.

Bram supposed some might prefer Lady Croyde's
fragile beauty to Lady Wilhelmina's more unique
features. But not him; he couldn't stop looking at
her, whether sneaking glances while they were
driving over in the carriage, or watching her face
down her father in a silent battle of wills.

And if the silent battle had become a vocal one, with her arguing the various points with her father, he'd bet on her to win there also.

"It's decided, then," Lord Croyde said, taking his wife's arm. Speaking as if it was he, and not his daughter, that had decided. "We will see you later."

Bram and Lady Wilhelmina watched the pair walk up the stairs to the entrance of the opera house, others streaming in alongside them.

"Goodness, that was difficult," Lady Wilhelmina said on an exhale of relief. "I am so grateful I don't have to sit with Alethea." And then she winced, looking contrite. "That is, I know she is pleasant enough—" she began.

"Only she is not your type of person," Bram finished, taking her by the elbow and beginning to guide her up the stairs. She accepted his touch, to his surprise, and that mysterious floral scent tickled his nostrils again. He needed to ask her what it was.

"No, and it is my firm belief that nobody is my type of person," she admitted. "I like my dog, my aunt, and our housekeeper. Miss Chalmers from the Home. A few astronomers I've met at the Stars Above Society. That is it. I don't like anybody else. I don't see how so many people keep finding ways to pair up."

He blinked in surprise at her confidence, and then followed her logic all the way to the end. "Does that mean you have no desire to get married?" he asked as they entered the hall.

It was sumptuous, and made him catch his breath, even though he knew that was precisely the effect the designer had wanted to achieve, which made him conversely not want to react.

But it was lovely inside.

The ceilings were huge, with several large chandeliers providing a surprising amount of light. A lavish carpet was spread on the floor, gleaming wood showing at the edges of the room. Another small flight of stairs led to double-wide doors that opened into where the performance would be.

"No." Her tone was flat.

No? Oh, right, the marriage question. He'd nearly forgotten he'd asked, so struck by the beauty inside.

"Neither do I. Another thing we have in common, my lady," he said with a grin. He still held her arm, and he began to move, escorting her through the crowd of people who were all heading to the stairs to go inside.

"Thank goodness," she said. "Do you know, my stepmother thinks that if gentlemen see me with you they will be clamoring to wed me? Merely because another gentleman has seen fit to keep company with me?" She sounded outraged.

He considered it. "I suppose it is the natural inclination to want what someone else has."

"I don't have that inclination," she said. She made a dismissive gesture with the hand not resting on his arm. "Let them have what they want, just leave me to my things and my happiness."

"And what is—oh yes, here they are," Bram said as an usher greeted them beyond the doors.

They were led to seats in the middle of the floor and in the middle of the row so that it would be impossible for them to leave discreetly if they wished to.

Once they were seated, people came in on either side to sit in the same row. The room was filled with the general chatter of people conversing and saying "excuse me" and the other sorts of things people would talk about before a performance—not that Bram knew what those things were, since he generally avoided evenings like this.

He heard her take a deep breath, as though bracing herself.

"So tell me," he said, needing to know, "what are your things? Your happiness?"

WILHELMINA HADN'T EXPECTED the Royal Opera House to be so grand, despite knowing it had been recently renovated and that Society people actually enjoyed attending. The reality of it nearly made her gasp in appreciation, only then she remembered who she was with and her general feeling toward such things, so she stopped herself right before she made some sort of silly observation such as "Oh my goodness, will you look at that!" or even worse, "Crikey, that's a high ceiling."

But she couldn't keep silent forever, not when he was asking her something so personal. Or perhaps she could try, because it *was* so personal, but she didn't think she'd succeed for very long. Nobody had ever asked her such a question before.

Was that because she had so few friends? Or because people didn't generally go about asking such things?

She didn't know.

If Dipper could speak, perhaps he would have asked such a thing. Or more likely he would have asked where his dinner was. And why wasn't it available all the time.

"If you don't want to reply, that is fine," he said, sounding resigned. As though if she didn't, she'd be disappointing him.

She didn't want to disappoint him, for no reason she could ascertain.

"My things, which are closely tied to my happiness, are my dog, my telescope, my books, and astronomy."

"You don't mention parties, clothing, dances, or sweets," he observed. Without judgment, she'd have to admit. She appreciated that, albeit grudgingly.

"No, because I don't value those things, even though that is the expectation."

He gestured toward the stage. "So what about the opera?"

"Yowling in a foreign language," she blurted out before she realized what she'd done. She clapped a hand over her mouth and met his gaze. He was laughing, which made her laugh, and then they were both doubled over in their seats.

When it seemed as though their laughter was subsiding, one would look at the other, and it would start all over again until Wilhelmina could feel her stomach muscles start to get sore because she was laughing so hard. He looked different when he laughed; his eyes crinkled up at the corners, and the harsh lines of his face seemed to soften.

The orchestra in the pit in front of the stage was warming up, disguising their laughter, and then a hush settled on the crowd just as they were both finally able to stop, though a few giggles came from each one of them. She took a few deep, calming breaths, carefully not looking at him, because she knew if she did, she'd be set off into laughter again.

Instead, she cleared her throat and tried to settle herself, wishing the evening was over and she and Dipper were tucked into bed.

Though she didn't honestly wish that, because then that would mean her evening with him was over. And there was something entirely compelling about him, from the forceful way he spoke, to how insightful he seemed to be, asking her questions nobody had ever thought to ask before.

The orchestra struck up, and the overture began. At first, Wilhelmina was impatient, wanting the curtains to open and the actual opera to begin.

But as she sat there, in the dark, his solid warmth beside her, she began to relax, the music flowing through her, making her think more and faster—about the stars, about science, about what happiness might mean.

All of it making her feel exhilarated and terrified at the same time.

She jumped when she heard a low voice in her ear. "Are you all right, my lady?" He took her hand, threading her fingers through his. "We could leave before the yowling begins, if you like."

She gave her head a violent shake. "No," she whispered back. "I think I like this."

"Oh!" he said in surprise, leaning back against his chair again.

But he didn't let go of her hand.

BRAM DIDN'T LET go of her hand, even though he knew it was the polite and proper thing to do.

Perhaps that's why he didn't—because he knew

the rest of his life would be lived properly, by the rules, so breaking them to hold her hand felt almost transgressive.

The curtains rose, revealing an elaborate set that seemed to indicate it took place in the distant past— ancient times when people sat on stone slabs and such. Rows of greenery were interspersed with low walls made of some sort of material, and there were performers on either side of the stage, probably all part of the chorus.

A woman, dressed in draped robes with a simple gold crown on her head, strode forward to the middle of the stage and opened her mouth as the orchestra began to play.

Bram resigned himself to hearing screeching misery for the next few hours, broken up by an intermission during which they'd have to converse politely with people he didn't know and likely didn't like.

And then the woman began to sing.

Lady Wilhelmina clutched his hand tighter as the various arias continued, the rising action and drama played out on the stage perfectly, comprehensibly, even though the songs were in Italian.

He glanced over at her during the performance— her expression was rapt, her wide mouth parted as she stared at the stage. At one point, she took her other hand and placed it on her heart, then turned to look at him, her eyes sparkling with unshed tears.

He didn't find enjoyment in it as directly as it seemed she did, but he appreciated it through her— following her sighs and starts, her gasps and sharp inhalations, as the story unfolded.

And then it was the intermission, and his fingers were numb from her clasping them so hard. She dropped his hand suddenly, clapping as the curtains closed and the various chandeliers were lit again.

"That was—" she began, staring at him starry-eyed. "Tremendous." She rose, and he followed, waiting as the people on either side of them began to file out from their seats. "I only knew that there was singing, and often by people with very high voices, and it sounded so unpleasant."

"What sounded unpleasant? The idea of high voices singing or the singing itself?"

"The former," she said. "I've never actually been to the opera."

His lips twitched with humor. "So you decided it was yowling based on—?" he asked.

"Shh!" she ordered as they shuffled their way to the aisle. "I assumed it was unpleasant because most other people enjoy it."

"That seems like an unusual way to approach life," he said. Though he had to admit it was a practice he himself engaged in.

"I am not most people," she replied simply. He already knew that about her, which made her far more dangerous to his state of mind than any young lady he'd met before. She would never fit into his future plans of respectability. She spoke her mind too much, she wasn't concerned with propriety. She didn't have to be, having been born into her status. A status Bram could never achieve, no matter how hard he worked or how proper he was.

This was a temporary interest, that was all. It

couldn't be any more than that, not just because her father would not allow it, but because Bram himself would not.

She took his arm, leading the way through to the lobby. "My stepmother has never been to the opera either," she said as they scanned the crowd for her father and his wife. "I wonder if we will have had the same impression after seeing it for the first time."

"We'll have our answer soon," Bram said, nodding as they spotted the couple.

"Well, here we are," Lord Croyde pronounced.

Bram wondered briefly if the earl had secret hopes of being a map, what with announcing their location so frequently.

"What did you think?" Bram asked Lady Croyde. "I believe this is your first time?"

Lady Croyde's lips turned pouting. "I thought I would be able to understand it. There was just such a lot of singing."

That is what opera is, Bram thought. *A lot of singing. You have summed it up succinctly, Lady Croyde.*

But of course he couldn't say that.

"I thought it was splendid," Lady Wilhelmina gushed. "The way the characters interacted, the way I felt transported to—where do you suppose it takes place, Mr. Townsend?" she said, turning to him.

"I believe those were supposed to be the Hanging Gardens of Babylon," Bram replied. "So . . . Babylon, I presume?"

"Not Egypt or Palmyra," Lady Wilhelmina said, completely befuddling him.

"No," he agreed, rather than demand to know what she was talking about.

"I know it is a tragedy, but I do so hope there is something good that happens at the end," she said, her tone holding a note of apprehension.

"I am getting a headache," Lady Croyde said suddenly. She turned to her husband. "Can you take me home? I am in need of a warm compress and some tea."

"Of course, but—"

"I'll ensure Lady Wilhelmina gets home safely, my lord," Bram said.

Lady Croyde gave him a warm smile. "Thank you. I know nothing untoward will occur, because Mina—" she said, her words trailing off as her hands fluttered toward her stepdaughter.

Bram saw rather than felt Lady Wilhelmina's discomfort at her stepmother's words.

"Do be on your way, then," Lady Wilhelmina said, making a shooing motion. "The intermission will be over soon, and I want to see the rest." Her eyes widened. "And of course I want you not to have a headache," she added hastily.

"Goodbye," Lady Croyde said, giving a slight wave that still managed to be elegant and charming.

"Goodbye," he and Lady Wilhelmina said as Lord Croyde wrapped his arm around his wife's shoulders and led her outside.

"Well," she said with a half smile, "since I won't do anything untoward, let's go back inside."

He nodded his agreement, but promised himself that if she wanted to do something untoward he would absolutely support her. Just as long as it was as harmless as holding another person's hand.

Not just because she continued to annoy and intrigue him, but because he knew how it felt to be told one couldn't do something simply because of what one was.

**Men I Do Not Wish to Marry:
A Not at All Comprehensive List by
Lady Wilhelmina Bettesford**

Richard Temple-Nugent-Brydges-Chandos-Grenville, First Duke of Buckingham and Chandos.
   With such a lengthy name, how could there be room for another person?

Chapter Eight

Wilhelmina felt as though everything was brighter.

Even though it was fully dark.

The moon hung high in the sky, only a few clouds obstructing the view.

She stopped on the pavement after they descended the steps from the Royal Opera House. Somehow—she hadn't even noticed when—she'd looped her arm through his, and was leaning against him, her full skirts making a shushing noise against his trouser-clad legs.

"Look there," she said, pointing straight up. "It's Canis Major."

He tilted his head back obligingly. "I have no idea what I'm looking at," he said, his low voice tinged with humor.

She laughed, aligning her arm with his, holding his hand in hers and guiding it up toward the constellation. "There. It's that very bright star that will anchor you. That one is Sirius, the dog star."

He gripped her hand in his when she would have pulled away. "Show me," he said. And something fluttered inside, as though he was asking for more than just to be shown her second-favorite constellation.

"There," she said again.

"Lady Wilhelmina!" a voice called, and she frowned, turning to face the speaker.

It was a young gentleman, but she had no idea who he was. He was of medium height and build, his pleasant features lit up with a warm smile.

He bowed when he reached her. "I did not realize you patronized the opera. Wasn't it wonderful?"

It was, but she didn't want to admit that to a stranger. Even one who knew her, though that made him not a stranger, didn't it? Nevertheless, it felt like a secret that she'd been so moved, and she didn't want anyone besides Mr. Townsend to know about it.

"Yes," she said, sounding awkward. Something she hadn't sounded for the past few hours. Not just because she was silently absorbing the opera, but because it felt comfortable to speak with him, even when they were disagreeing.

"May I introduce Mr. Townsend," she said suddenly, gesturing toward him. "And this is—" she said, faltering.

"Lord Paskins," the gentleman said, holding his hand out eagerly. "A pleasure, sir."

Mr. Townsend made some sort of polite noncommittal noise that Wilhelmina found oddly reassuring as he shook the other man's hand.

"I saw your parents earlier," Lord Paskins said, returning his attention to Wilhelmina, "and your mother—"

"Stepmother," she and Mr. Townsend murmured.

"—said I should be certain to find you to say hello.

I'm meeting some friends at my club, so I cannot tarry, but it was a pleasure to see you here. Nice to meet you, sir," Lord Paskins added.

Wilhelmina dipped her head as the gentleman turned back to rejoin his group, mostly made up of gentlemen who looked like him.

"I have no idea who that was," she said in wonder. "I must have met him during one of Alethea's dinners." She snorted. "They've only been married a month or so, and they've already entertained more than my father and I ever did." Making her miss the most recent meeting of the Stars Above Society, for example.

"He knew who you were, though," Mr. Townsend said, his voice stern. For some reason, that sent a tiny thrill zinging through Wilhelmina's spine. "And he saw you with me. Perhaps your stepmother is correct about gentlemen wanting to know what another gentleman is doing."

"Or my stepmother ensured he would find me," she said. Because it was every woman's desire to be safely and well-married. At least according to women like Alethea.

They walked slowly, arm in arm, Wilhelmina thinking of everything and nothing—how the opera had made her feel as though she was truly alive, how comfortable she was with him while also keenly aware of every movement he made. How it felt as though she were in a dream, one she did not wish to wake from.

"Oh dear," she exclaimed, stopping short.

"What is it?" he asked.

They had walked out of the crowd leaving the opera, past the line of carriages waiting to take the guests home, onto a narrow sidewalk. It was late enough that there weren't very many people out, except for the postopera people, most of whom were going in the other direction. They were nearly alone, or at least as much alone as one could be in London.

"Shouldn't we be—you know—going home?" She gave a frantic wave between them. "And here I am just walking with you as though you don't have a place to be, and as if we'd discussed and—"

He closed his hand over hers. "It's fine, Wilhelmina," he said in a low voice.

He'd called her by her first name. She didn't even know his.

"I don't have anywhere to be but here," he replied. "Unless you have to go home to walk Dipper?"

He'd even remembered her dog's name. That warmed her heart.

"No, Aunt Flora will take care of that," she said. "But do you want to hire a hackney?"

"Not unless you are in a rush," he said, meeting her gaze in the moonlight. "Or you need to practice how to hail one," he added with a wink.

"I'm not in a rush," she said baldly, ignoring his second comment. "I want to talk to you about the opera. I don't know if I can explain how it made me feel. I just—it was just magical. It was wonderful."

"And here I thought it was all yowling screeches," he said in a dry tone of voice.

"I never said screeches!" she said indignantly.

He laughed. "No, but I did." He began to walk again, holding her arm close to his body. It felt warm—both her arm and his body—and Wilhelmina felt herself drawn back into the dreamy postopera haze she'd been in before.

"What do you think now?" she asked.

"I think that I would like to hear what you think."

A prevarication, but one she was happy to accommodate.

"Fine. I will tell you, but you have to tell me something."

"What is it?"

"Your first name."

"BRAM."

She repeated it. "Bram. Where does it come from?"

"You mean where do I come from? I don't know."

She gripped his arm tight as she turned to face him. "What do you mean you don't know?"

"I'm an orphan. My mother was a housekeeper, I was told. My father was Italian, a singer who was traveling through town. That I know that much is a miracle."

"You never met your mother?" Her tone was sorrowful.

He let out a short bark of laughter. One lacking humor. "No. I was raised in the Devenaugh Home for Destitute Boys, brought there when I was a babe."

"Oh my goodness!" she exclaimed. "Well, that explains why you were taking part in the auction."

Her shock made him feel like even more of an outsider—here he'd been feeling comfortable with her, as comfortable as he was with anyone who wasn't one of his four friends, and she had just snatched that comfort away with one startled phrase.

Of course it wasn't fair to pin it on her, but it hurt nonetheless.

"That bothers you," she observed.

"What? That I don't have parents?" he said in a bitter voice. "Should I not be bothered?"

"No. How I reacted." She squeezed his hand. "I'm sorry." She paused, taking a deep breath. "I can't know what it's like, of course. I lost my mother when I was sixteen, and as you can tell, I still have my father. Somewhat," she added ruefully.

"That must be difficult."

"Don't change the subject," she ordered. "Tell me about you. About your friends, the ones you discuss books with."

He was silent for a moment. They continued to walk, goodness knew where, and he felt something stir in his chest. Something vaguely like emotion. An emotion he wasn't familiar with.

He shoved it away, forcing something else to take its place. *Why are you uncomfortable, Bram?* a voice said inside his head. He didn't want to answer the voice, much less debate its premise.

"Tell me why you kissed me that night," Bram asked.

He heard her inhale sharply, then spin toward him again. Still holding his hand.

"Why not?" she replied simply. She released his hand, but then placed hers onto his chest. Could she feel his heart? It felt as though it was beating harder now.

"Why not?" he repeated, placing his hand on top of hers.

This time, he knew what to expect. This time, he lowered his head so she wouldn't have to be all the way up on her tiptoes.

This time, he met her gaze, keeping his eyes locked on hers as she rose up, her lips slightly parted.

This time, like the last time, he let her kiss him.

OH. WILHELMINA HADN'T intended to kiss him. But she hadn't *not* intended to kiss him. If she had thought about it—which she had not—she would have told herself to remain open to the possibility, since it seemed he was slightly more intriguing than he was annoying.

Her eyelids fluttered closed as her mouth reached its destination, her lips pressing softly against his.

She'd never kissed anyone before, so she wasn't certain if she was doing it right. But it *felt* right, so that had to mean something.

His mouth was soft, and he'd tilted his head somewhat so his nose pressed against her cheek. Clever of him, especially since his nose was larger than the average.

He must have kissed someone before to know about the nose thing.

Her hand was still pressed against his chest, and she spread her fingers wider, clutching the fabric, feeling the strength and hardness of his body underneath.

And then she blinked her eyes wide open as she felt something slide along her mouth. Gentle, probing, and oddly scintillating.

She exhaled through her nose, letting her mouth open to his tongue. Because of course it was his tongue—she'd seen people kiss before, albeit from a distance and without understanding quite what was happening. But now that it was happening to her, her scientific mind could theorize that when she'd seen those people with their faces pressed together they had had their tongues in one another's mouths.

It sounded odd, but it felt—well, it felt as wonderful as it had been to experience the opera.

The opera and kissing all in one evening. And the night wasn't over yet.

She closed her eyes again, breathing in his scent, reaching her hand up to curl around his neck. Her fingers snuck up into his hair and she found herself tugging on a few strands, which forced his body closer to hers. Now not only were their mouths touching, but her breasts were up against his chest, her feet in between his on the pavement. His hands were at her waist, holding her still.

Silly man. As though she was going to scamper away.

She didn't want to ever stop doing this, feel the soft warmth of his lips, feel his tongue inside her mouth, her tongue responding—tentatively, then more eagerly—to his invitation.

All she could hear was their breaths, his breath a series of soft exhalations that warmed her cheek.

He drew back, and she prepared to feel disappointed that they'd stopped when he surprised her by nipping at her bottom lip, capturing it gently between his teeth. The sensation sent ripples through her whole body, and she made a noise low in her throat.

His fingers gripped her waist more tightly, and he shifted, pressing himself even closer than before. She released his hair and ran her hand down his back, her fingers splayed over his hard body.

And then he had let go of her bottom lip and

begun kissing her again, his tongue more forceful now. Making her breath come out in quick pants, making her want something that she couldn't name.

Just as suddenly as they'd begun, however, they stopped—he leapt back, his eyes wide and bright blue in the moonlight, his expression stunned.

Likely similar to hers, she thought.

"Well," she said, her voice unfamiliar to her own ears, "that was why not. Or why. I don't know which now."

He shook his head, as though bemused. Again, likely feeling the same way she did.

Unless he didn't.

What if his experience was entirely different from hers? What if this was nothing out of the ordinary and he made a habit of sticking his tongue into the mouths of random women all the time?

"I didn't—I wasn't—" he began, and she knew for certain he did not make a habit of it. This compelling, capable, and argumentative man wouldn't be at such a loss for words if it was an everyday occurrence. "Your scent, it is—what is it, some sort of flower?" he said, sounding almost awkward.

She ignored his question. "This can't happen again," she pronounced. She flailed her hands in the air. "Because if it keeps happening, then things will happen, and we will happen to end up married. And neither one of us wants *that*," she said, emphasizing the last part more forcefully than she might have.

"No," he said, shaking his head. "We most definitely do not. What's more, I cannot." He blinked a few times, then smoothed the lapels of his evening coat, holding his hand out to her when that task was finished. "Shall I escort you home?"

She paused before taking his hand, bracing herself for how much she wanted to fling herself back into his arms to try it all again. To see if it truly felt as marvelous as the opera, and catching a glimpse of the stars, and running alongside Dipper in an open park.

But she already knew the answer. She knew because every fiber of her being wanted to do it again, which meant she absolutely must not, because the inevitable eventuality of doing it again would be marriage.

Which she'd decided at an early age was not going to be for her.

And besides, he'd just said he cannot—she burned to ask why, but that might seem as though she wished to change his mind.

So it was better to tuck the memory of the kiss away and bring it out late at night when nobody would know.

"Yes," she said at last. "Please take me home."

Men I Do Not Wish to Marry: A Not at All Comprehensive List by Lady Wilhelmina Bettesford

A gentleman who is not curious. Who accepts that things are the way they are, and nothing can be changed.

Chapter Nine

$\mathcal{I}$t was customary, Bram told himself, to pay a call to a lady one had seen the evening before. It was the polite thing to do.

When have you ever been polite?

He ignored that reminder as he made the long walk from his rooms to her house in Mayfair—the neighborhoods growing gradually more affluent until he'd reached his destination, enormous town houses vying with one another for which could be the most opulent.

He had spent the morning in appointments, and had planned to spend the afternoon catching up on paperwork, but that idea had been dismissed when he'd found himself having a quite vivid daydream involving Lady Wilhelmina and strategically placed greenery. That was when he'd decided to take the polite course. For once.

The day was warm, and the sun peeked out from behind a few clouds, but it didn't look as though it would rain. A pleasant day to take a walk.

There were a few carriages parked on the street in front of her father's town house—carriages with crests, indicating the owners were Important

People who wanted others to know of their Importance.

Bram didn't even own a horse, much less a carriage. He relied on his legs or hackney cabs to take him where he was bound. If he ever truly needed his own transportation, Fenton or Benedict, the only two of them who kept stables, would lend him one, but he had never asked.

He strode up the stone steps to the house, then rapped on the door sharply. He heard the echo of the knocker within the foyer he recalled from the night before. The door swung open, the butler holding it just wide enough to peer through.

Bram extracted his card and presented it. "Mr. Townsend, here to see Lady Wilhelmina."

The butler took the card with a nod of his head. "I will see if Lady Wilhelmina is in."

Bram could hear damn well she was in—he could hear the chatter of conversation, the occasional clink of china, and tinkling laughter he knew must belong to Lady Croyde.

The butler returned within a few minutes, holding the door open wide enough for Bram to walk through. "Lady Wilhelmina is in, sir," he said.

The butler shut the door, then held his hand out toward where the commotion was coming from. A few vases of flowers were placed on a sideboard at the edge of the foyer. They hadn't been there the night before. Should he have brought flowers?

As Bram passed the table, he snatched a few stems from the arrangement, hastily shaking the water from them and trying to make them appear as if they were supposed to look like that.

"Mr. Townsend," the butler announced. His eyes

flickered to the flowers, a tiny downward curve of his mouth showing what he thought of Bram's effrontery.

Bram stood at the doorway, startled for a moment with the prospect of so much Society. He didn't normally see these types of people—or if he did, it was in a courtroom, and they were generally on the other side of the argument.

"Mr. Townsend!" Lady Croyde exclaimed, rising from her chair and coming toward him. She looked like a decorated layer cake—her head, neck, and shoulders were mostly unadorned, but then her gown was covered in increasingly complex ruffles until it reached the floor in a cacophony of fabric.

"Good day, my lady," Bram said, bowing. He held the flowers out to her, and she hesitated, her mouth pursing. "What lovely flowers, thank you." A nod over his head to the butler, who held his hand out silently. Bram handed them over, feeling like an idiot.

"Do come in," she said with a graceful wave of her hand. "What a pleasure to see you."

"Is your headache better?" he asked, remembering at the last minute that that would be the proper thing to say.

"Much, thank you. Made even better by all these visitors and flowers! My goodness, my stepdaughter is popular."

Indeed, he could now see why a few vases of flowers were outside—flowers covered every surface, and there were guests in nearly every chair in the room. A few gentlemen were present, their clothing a dark smudge among all the light, bright gowns the ladies were wearing.

Lady Wilhelmina sat at the other end of the room,

her expression set, as though she was trying her best to maintain a pleasant expression while also feeling miserable.

Bram sympathized. That awkward, uncomfortable feeling was why he eschewed polite Society, for the most part.

But his urge to see her had been stronger than his antipathy to this particular situation.

So here he was.

And now he was imitating Lord Croyde's maplike inclinations. Dear God.

"There is a seat just beyond Mina," Lady Croyde said. "Do pull that out, would you?" she said to one of the footmen standing at attention in the room.

The man obliged, and Bram made his awkward way across the room, bowing to each guest as he tried not to trip on anybody or accidentally knock someone over with his size.

And then he met her gaze, and he knew it was worth it. She looked placid enough, but her eyes were wide, showing all the emotion she was hiding otherwise: anxiety, terror, and a fierce sort of agony with which he could relate.

He sat down next to her, leaning in to speak in a low voice only she could hear.

Not that anybody was listening; Lady Croyde was relating a story involving how her beauty caused a traffic accident, because apparently a coachman was so struck by her that he didn't watch where he was going, and hit another carriage, causing broken wheels and frantic horses.

"How are you, my lady?" he asked.

She glanced over at him, her smile tight. "I am fine."

He shook his head gently. "You're not. You forget, I see you."

Her eyes widened, and she exhaled as she bit her lip. "You see me. I don't even know what that means, and yet it feels reassuring."

He resisted the urge to take her hand—to do so in a gathering like this would be tantamount to announcing his intentions.

And he had no desire to do that. Unless his intentions were to get to know her better, without any expectations. Those he could manage.

WILHELMINA GLANCED FROM under her lashes at him. Someone had given him a small plate filled with various pastries, which he'd balanced on his knee, two fingers holding it steady, while he held a fragile teacup in his other hand. Alethea must have worked swiftly; Wilhelmina hadn't even noticed food and beverage being dispensed. He looked so out of place in the drawing room—like a fearsome beast who had stumbled in for biscuits. Or no, that wasn't quite it—like a powerful god who was bemused by the goings-on of flittering fairies. While also enjoying a biscuit.

Not that Wilhelmina was a fairy. Like Mr. Townsend, she was merely a visitor. Her stepmother and all the guests fit into this world—or *flitted* into this world—in a way she never could, despite being born to it. Perhaps that was why she had started looking at the stars—searching for a place where she felt at home.

Especially pressing now that home no longer felt like home.

"What are you thinking about?" he asked.

"My lady," a voice interrupted before she could answer his question. "It was such a pleasure to see you last evening. I wonder what part of the opera you enjoyed the most?"

She squinted to see who was speaking, identifying him because his mouth still hung open from speaking and he had an eager expression on his face.

"Lord Paskins," she heard him say in a low voice.

Oh. She didn't want to tell Lord Paskins what she thought. She didn't want to share the splendor of her feelings with anyone but—but him.

Not something she should be thinking about a gentleman she had just met who was just as determined as she never to wed. Whose parentage wasn't up to what her father would expect of any potential suitor.

Because while it was apparently just fine for her father to marry his steward's daughter, it wouldn't be fine for his daughter to marry a gentleman out of her class.

But she wasn't going to get stuck inside that hypocrisy.

A gentleman who her stepmother had to *purchase* in an auction to get him to spend time with her.

But there she was. Thinking it.

Drat.

"It was nice," Wilhelmina said, raising her voice to be heard over the general hubbub.

She heard him smother a snort beside her.

And resisted the urge to elbow him in the ribs.

"I thought it was nice, too," Lord Paskins said in a cheery voice.

Another snort.

Wilhelmina felt the fatigue set in, the familiar

anxious feeling of trying to manage expectations while also remaining true to herself. Exacerbated because she knew he did indeed see her, as he'd said, could see how uncomfortable she was. If only it was just the two of them. Like last night. When they'd kissed.

Lord Paskins had risen from his chair, and was making his way toward her, a genial smile on his face.

"Oh no," she moaned under her breath, all memories of pleasant things like kissing fading away.

"I've got you," he said, and she felt something like relief course through her.

"Good afternoon," Lord Paskins said, nodding to the footman who'd pulled up a chair. He sat down elegantly, crossing one leg over the other. He was a pleasant-looking man, and if he wasn't seated near the god, she might almost call him handsome.

But everything about him paled in comparison to Mr. Townsend. His brown hair was brown, not fiercely black; his blue eyes were medium blue, not the striking pale blue of Mr. Townsend's. He was of medium height and build, nothing like the tall, powerfully built man who sat on her left, still holding that plate atop his knee, though he'd put the teacup down somewhere.

"My lord, what were your thoughts on the opera?" Mr. Townsend asked smoothly. "It was my first time seeing anything like that. I wonder what someone more experienced would say about it." He tilted his head and regarded the other man with a gently curious look.

One Wilhelmina already knew was a pretense, because if he were truly interested, Lord Paskins would have no choice but to feel it, as she had. When he'd focused his attention on her the first time they'd met, offering to assist her with finding employment or demanding to know what she was doing balancing up there, it had felt like a white light was shining on her, and there was no doubting the intensity of his scrutiny.

But he had said he would navigate this interaction, albeit not in so many words.

So this was the navigation?

Lord Paskins opened his mouth and began to speak, taking pause only to draw breath.

For over fifteen minutes.

Apparently this was the navigation. And very successful, too.

Finally, when he had apparently exhausted all of his opinions on the Italian language (too many vowels), the seating in the Royal Opera House (excellent), the quality of the people on either side of him (excellent, but one of them had a cough), and the opera in general (it wasn't a play, but it also wasn't a musical), he stopped speaking.

Wilhelmina felt as though she'd always been listening to him, she would never not be listening to him until the end of time, so it was startling when he closed his mouth.

"Well," Mr. Townsend said after a few moments of silence, "thank you. I am much more edified, thanks to you."

Now it was Wilhelmina's turn to stifle a snort, which she was much less adept at, having to pretend a cough as Lord Paskins leapt up to find a glass of water for her.

"My apologies," Mr. Townsend said, not sounding sorry at all. In fact, he sounded nearly gleeful.

"Shh, he's coming back," Wilhelmina said. Her eyes were moist from the ferocity of her snort/cough, and she slid a finger into her sleeve in search of a handkerchief.

"Allow me," he said when it became clear she hadn't thought to tuck one away. Where had the one gone from before? It wasn't like her to go out without a handkerchief.

He held out a square of crisp white fabric, free of any monogramming or anything else that would indicate its owner. She wondered if that was because he was an orphan, or just that monogramming handkerchiefs was a luxury a barrister would not be able to, or want to, afford.

She took it, dabbing at her eyes as she inhaled its scent. Most gentlemen she'd come near enough to sniff—which wasn't many, to be certain—smelled of leather, wood, and pine.

Mr. Townsend didn't smell like any of those things. Or at least his handkerchief did not.

Instead, it smelled like damp wool, old books, and the back corner of a wine cellar. It wasn't a chosen smell, she could tell. It was created because of who he was and what he did, not because he wished to present himself in a certain way.

In fact, she thought as she darted a surreptitious glance toward him, he didn't look as though he thought much about his appearance at all.

The evening before he'd worn clothing suitable for an evening out at the opera, but he hadn't worn it with any indication that he understood he looked good. Today he wore a serviceable suit of clothing, clean linen, and sturdy shoes, but nothing remarkable.

Perhaps it was because he was so forceful just in and of himself already that adding stylish clothing would make it difficult to look at him, the effect would be so blinding.

And who was she to comment on clothing anyway? She was much the same as what she'd presumed he was like—putting things on because she had to wear something, not because she wanted to wear the particular item.

Her eyes wandered to Alethea, who wore another splendidly beautiful gown. If Wilhelmina wore something so lovely, was it possible she would look nearly as good as her stepmother?

It was an idea. She could test it out, appearing at a party wearing something unusual, and see if anyone treated her differently. She already had the control of being the exact same person, so the only thing she would change was her clothing.

"And now you're thinking of something delightful," he observed.

"Do share, my lady," Lord Paskins urged.

She hadn't realized he had sat down again, as she was too preoccupied with thoughts of scientific clothing experiments, plain linen, and musty cellars.

"Oh, it is nothing," she demurred.

"It is not noth—" Lord Paskins began.

"I purchased a book the other day, and I am quite enjoying it," Mr. Townsend said smoothly. Or not so smoothly, since Lord Paskins was glowering at him.

"What book?" Wilhelmina asked, grateful she wouldn't have to reveal her sartorial scientific experiment.

"*Views of the Architecture of the Heavens* by John

Pringle Nichol." He met her gaze. "I imagine it is not advanced enough for someone like you, my lady, but for a person who is interested in the stars but knows nothing, it is quite appealing."

"I don't see the fuss about looking up at the sky in the nighttime," Lord Paskins said, apparently still peevish about being cut off. "There is so much to look at without having to squint up at some tiny point of light."

Wilhelmina had not even remotely entertained the thought of Lord Paskins as a potential husband, but that comment was enough to put paid to the notion forever. He would be the kind of husband Aunt Flora had warned her about for so many years—the kind that prioritized their thoughts and opinions over anybody else's, even when engaging in polite conversation.

Imagine if the topic was something substantial, like how a lady wished to spend her time, or if the study of astronomy was a worthwhile endeavor.

Conversations like this one confirmed her desire never to marry.

"I might have thought that before," Mr. Townsend said, "but I've found myself interested suddenly." He was still looking at her, and she felt herself start to blush.

Drat.

"I have that book as well," she said, trying to ignore the heat in her cheeks and the warmth in her belly. It seemed his words did something to her body temperature. "It is an introduction, yes, but it is so thoughtfully and wonderfully written that it is a pleasure to read no matter what your level of knowledge might be."

His lips curled into a slow smile, and now she felt as though she might actually be on fire.

This would not do. She needed to remember that someone had paid a sum, albeit for charity, that forced him to take her out. That both of them were fervent in their shared desire to remain unwed. Perhaps it was just the onset of an illness, all this heat and warmth spiraling within.

But she had the sinking suspicion she was perfectly healthy.

Drat.

Men I Do Not Wish to Marry:
A Not at All Comprehensive List by
Lady Wilhelmina Bettesford

One of the villains in a Gothic novel who entraps a heroine in his cold, drafty castle. If he had the intention of seducing the heroine in question, surely he would have tried to make his castle less cold and drafty? That he did not shows a distinct lack of thoughtfulness, even beyond the whole entrapment thing.

Chapter Ten

"Well?" Theo prompted when Bram had opened and closed his mouth a few times.

It was a few days after the opera, and Bram hadn't been able to dislodge the memory of the night from his mind. Even though he had several cases demanding his full and complete attention.

"It was nice," he replied, smothering a smile as he recalled she'd said the same thing to that talkative aristocrat.

They were in the pub closest to Bram's lodgings, which was also conveniently close to where Theo Osborne worked. Mr. Osborne, the single gentleman who had taken Theo in, was a merchant, and saw promise in Theo's charm, believing he would become an excellent salesperson. He had lived up to that early promise, and then the gentleman had died, leaving Theo with a very successful business he didn't particularly care for, but that supported at least a hundred families, so he couldn't very well just shutter it, even though he could afford to by now.

"Nice?" Theo said in a disbelieving voice. "When have you ever said anything was nice?" He narrowed his eyes. "You're not telling the truth."

"There are many things that are nice," Bram re-torted. "A warmish day with only a few clouds. Tea without sugar. Winning a few shillings at the tables."

Theo rolled his eyes. "Of course you have to argue with me about it. I didn't say things weren't nice, I said *you* never say they are." His brows drew together. "Tea without sugar?" he asked. "The other two I understand."

"Tea without sugar is flavored water," Bram explained in a lofty tone. "I require a lot of sugar. But it can still be nice."

Theo made a harrumphing noise.

"I am to escort a Lady Clara Hastings to the opera in a week," he said. "I've been to the opera, naturally—"

"Naturally," Bram echoed.

"—but I haven't been since they've renovated."

Theo picked up his ale and took a sip, then set his glass down.

"Well, since I had never been to the opera at all, I cannot tell you if the renovations make the experience more pleasant. I can just say it is nice." Bram folded his arms over his chest and gave Theo a stern look.

Which his friend ignored.

"There's something different about you," Theo continued. "It's not just the nice thing, it's—I don't know how to explain it." He leaned in and peered at Bram's face. "The mysterious lady has had a remarkable effect on you."

Bram's mouth dropped open in surprise. "How were you able to tell that?" he asked, noting he sounded aggrieved, which would make Theo go on the hunt for information even more.

Theo shrugged in mock humility as he took another sip. "When you've fallen in and out of love as often as I have, you get to know the look. It's something around the eyes," he said, pointing to his own eyes.

"I'm not in love," Bram sputtered. "The lady is most adamant about not getting married, and you know my feelings on the subject." He cleared his throat. "Besides, my plan has always been to marry someone who would never cause a stir. I cannot afford any kind of disruption to my goals. To that plan."

Theo gave an airy wave. "People always say that kind of thing, even have a ridiculous plan like you do, and then the next thing you know you're marching up the aisle with a totally unsuitable person while everyone gawks."

"More to the point," Bram continued, "the lady is a *lady*, which means her family would never accept someone like me as her husband. Not that I've considered that," he added hastily.

Theo nodded in agreement. "Now *that* is a persuasive argument. You'd have to do something remarkable, like save her from certain death, to persuade them to overlook your humble origins."

Bram winced at Theo's words, a certain event on the Blackfriars Bridge replaying itself in his mind's eye. But she'd never tell anyone about that, nor admit he'd saved her in the first place, so his lowly status was safe.

"So since you've indicated marriage is not a possibility, what do you plan to do?" Theo asked in a mild tone.

"Do?" Bram spoke in an incredulous voice. "What am I supposed to do?"

Theo lifted an eyebrow. "If you need me to instruct you—"

"Dear God, no," Bram replied hastily. Though he did have substantially less experience than either Simeon or Theo, that was obvious. He didn't know about Fenton or Benedict.

But he knew about himself. And he had kissed a few women, but he'd never bothered to do more than that. It would have complicated things, and he had his hand, which served him well.

Until now, he hadn't thought about it all that much. But now it seemed as though that was all he did think about. If this was what being in Simeon's or Theo's head was like, it was remarkable that they managed to do anything else at all.

And it wasn't as though he was having those thoughts about women in general—no, when he thought about things, he most definitely thought about *her*. About the waist he'd held when they'd kissed. About her breasts, which had pressed up against him. Of how they might feel in his hand, how he would touch and tease her.

Of her biting her lip, as she did, when in the grip of a strong emotion.

"Are you feeling ill?" Theo asked suddenly.

Bram shook his head, both in answer to his friend and also to clear it. "No, sorry. Thinking about a case," he lied.

Theo gave him a knowing look. "Of course you were," he said in a sarcastic tone. And then his expression changed. "But seriously, if you do need any advice—" he began, only to stop speaking when Bram thumped his glass on the table.

"No, thank you," he said firmly. "Can we stop speaking about that now?" he asked in exasperation.

Theo's lips twitched, and Bram resisted the urge to toss the rest of his ale in his friend's face.

Not only because it would be a waste of perfectly good ale, but also because it wouldn't stop Theo.

"But if you enjoy her company—" Theo began, only to stop when Benedict arrived, clapping Bram on the shoulder.

"Afternoon," he said, dropping into a chair at their table. He nodded to the barmaid for an ale, then glanced from one to the other of them. "Just the fellows I was hoping to see."

"How fortunate that you wandered into this pub located close to our respective offices, then," Bram remarked dryly.

"Yes, isn't it?" Benedict replied in a bland tone. "But I am here to discuss business."

"Ugh," Theo groaned. "I was just talking about this lady Bram has met recently."

"Business," Bram said hurriedly. "What kind of business?"

Benedict gathered himself, and Bram could practically see the wheels of efficiency turning in his head. Benedict was nothing if not always prepared for anything. It was what made him so good in his work. He wasn't as silver-tongued as Bram, nor as charming as either Simeon or Theo, and he definitely did not have Fenton's analytic abilities, but he had elements of all of those, making him absolutely formidable.

It was fortunate, Bram thought, that Benedict had been born an orphan and not a member of the aristocracy, because it would have been easy for a person with that much natural ability to waste it simply because a person in that position wouldn't have required it to survive.

"It would be quite helpful," Benedict began, "if the government—that is, myself and the people I work with—knew that there was a judge who was both honorable and intelligent."

This wasn't a new comment from Benedict; barristers were the only members of the law who could become judges, and Benedict had been urging Bram to aspire to that for as long as Bram had been a barrister. Bram hadn't wanted to leave his barrister work—until recently.

Benedict continued. "There are more and more people who are not well-connected socially who are embarking on business ventures, and those who have had the financial power for a long time quite resent these upstarts."

The barmaid appeared with Benedict's ale, setting it down on the table. Benedict nodded and flipped her a coin, then glanced around to make certain nobody was within earshot.

"Commerce is changing. Business is changing. But the old ways haven't yet, and that is where we need an honest judiciary system. Without you, and people like you, Bram, the people who have always held the power will be able to squelch whatever new ventures these other people start. We'll continue to have the inequities that make it impossible for people like us to succeed."

Bram's jaw clamped as he absorbed Benedict's words. The thing he hated most—the thing all five of the orphans hated most—was when a powerful person took advantage of those with less power.

It was why he had entered the law, to protect and defend the innocent and powerless, and why Theo maintained his late father's businesses instead of selling it to someone who might not care as much about the welfare of his workers. It was why Simeon ended up in the scandal sheets, because he would call out fellow artists for taking advantage of young, hungry artists, whether by charging them exorbitant fees for lessons, or by passing off the younger talents' work as their own.

And why the five of them were so bound to one another through ties of loyalty and honor.

"And so," Benedict said, "the way to secure a position as a judge is to meet the right people."

"So what you're saying," Bram replied, not without irony, "is that in order to become a judge who will preside over justice, I need to impress people in power?"

Benedict shrugged, a wry smile on his lips. "Yes. Precisely."

"What do I need to do?" Bram said, surprising himself. Five minutes ago, he would have done anything rather than put on his penguin suit and top hat—or gibus, as the case may be—again, but if it meant he could do some good in the world and spend time with Lady Wilhelmina, then—

"Shake hands. Make pleasant conversation with people." Benedict waved his hand in the air. "Do all the things that Simeon and Theo do, but without the drama."

"Hey!" Theo exclaimed. "Not that you're wrong, mind you," he said, a cheeky grin on his face.

"I can do that," Bram replied. "I will do it."

"You will?" Benedict replied, his eyebrows rising. "After so many years of my asking, why now?"

"We know why," Theo said slyly.

"Shut up," Bram replied, shooting Theo with a glare that had withered the most ferocious of opposing barristers.

Theo merely grinned wider.

"Wonderful," Benedict said, sounding relieved. "I can ensure you receive invitations for the various events—"

"And Simeon and I will sort out your wardrobe," Theo added.

Bram opened his mouth to ask what was wrong with his wardrobe, then realized he could likely use help in that area. Not that he would admit that to his friends. Besides which, they already knew.

"I'll begin as soon as the first invitation arrives," Bram promised.

And he would be able to see Lady Wilhelmina again. Not that that was why he had said yes to Benedict's request. Or at least, not that that was the main reason he had said yes.

If he could right wrongs and spend time with the only person besides his four closest friends who had ever intrigued and challenged him?

How could he possibly say no?

"No."

Wilhelmina emphasized her word with a strong shake of her head, even though neither her father nor Alethea acknowledged her vehemence. Instead, Alethea continued explaining her idea as if Wilhelmina hadn't spoken.

They were in the room where her father had first introduced Alethea—the room had changed, due to Alethea's efforts, but Wilhelmina was reminded of that day every time she walked in.

It was ten days since the visit to the opera. At first, many gentlemen had paid calls on Wilhelmina, bringing flowers and compliments in equal measure. But after a week or so, the calls had dwindled, so that only Lord Paskins and Mr. Breson, an older merchant with bad breath and a tendency to dribble tea down his shirtfront, were regular visitors.

Which was why Alethea had had her brilliant idea.

"Mr. Townsend is here, my lord," the butler said, making Wilhelmina emit a squeak as her eyes widened.

"Send him in, please," Alethea said in a serene tone of voice, completely ignoring that her stepdaughter was currently imitating some sort of rodent.

"No, I will not—"

"Mr. Townsend." The butler withdrew as that gentleman entered the room.

Alethea rose, extending her hand. "Good afternoon, Mr. Townsend. I am so glad you were able to respond to my note."

A note? Alethea had sent him a note? Regarding this request?

Wilhelmina wanted to dissolve into the cushions.

"Please do sit down," Alethea said, indicating the seat next to Wilhelmina.

He nodded toward her and her father, then sat beside her on the sofa. She caught his scent, the combination of old books and wine, a scent that shouldn't have been appealing, and yet absolutely was. He was freshly shaved, and the clean lines of his face made her catch her breath all over again, as though this was the first time she had noticed his handsomeness.

It was not the first time. It likely would not be the last.

"You mentioned a service I could do for you," Mr. Townsend said. "Are you in need of legal work?"

Alethea emitted a tinkling laugh, one that Wilhelmina suspected she must have practiced, since it was so delightful. "Oh no, nothing like that." She gestured toward Wilhelmina. "Mina's father and I were discussing the opera, which led us to discussing Wilhelmina's future—"

Wilhelmina heard Mr. Townsend—Bram—swallow. Was he thinking this was a conversation about marriage? Dear Lord, please don't let him be thinking that. That would be even more mortifying than what Alethea was actually going to say.

"My future, which has nothing to do with you, Mr. Townsend," Wilhelmina said quickly as Alethea took a breath. "Thank you so much for paying a call, but I believe that my stepmother is mistaken. We do not require anything from you."

"But we do," her father interrupted, sounding aggrieved. "Why else would we ask him here?" He followed that up with a grumbling noise indicating his displeasure. A noise Wilhelmina had been hearing a lot more of lately. Basically, any time she was in the room with him. It generally ceased when Alethea arrived, which told her everything she needed to know.

But the solution Alethea and her father wanted to enact was an extreme measure.

"Yes, as I was saying, we are thinking of Mina's

future. And the day after the opera there were so many gentlemen who came to call, and we think that was because they saw her with you, Mr. Townsend."

Mr. Townsend, wisely, did not speak.

"Mina's future happiness depends on her finding someone to marry," Alethea stated. As though it was the truth. "And you are, by all accounts, a very persuasive gentleman."

Mr. Townsend's expression was wary. He hadn't leapt up and run out of the room yet, but Wilhelmina could tell he was weighing the option. She wished he would, so he wouldn't have to hear what Alethea was about to say.

"It's nothing like that," Alethea assured him, likely gauging his fear he was going to be forced to marry Wilhelmina. She gave a trill of laughter. "The earl has been very clear that he wants Wilhelmina to marry someone of her own class." She tapped her husband's arm. "One shocking marriage in a family is enough, wouldn't you say?"

Wilhelmina closed her eyes in mortification.

"No, it is that your escorting her to the opera caused several gentlemen to see Mina in a light they hadn't before. As a potential spouse. So I thought that if you were to *pretend* to be interested in Mina that we could get that same increased interest from other gentlemen, gentlemen who might actually wish to marry her."

"And who would be a good choice for a husband," her father added, his meaning clear. Because of course he did.

It wasn't enough to ask a gentleman to pretend to be interested in your daughter because she was too unappealing on her own merits, but then you had to insult the gentleman's antecedents on top of that. Well done all around.

"You would be helping us out a great deal," Alethea added. "Especially Wilhelmina." Even though when Alethea had told her the idea, not half an hour before, Wilhelmina had been unable to speak for five minutes, but had spent the following twenty-three and a half detailing why it was such a horrible idea, and that she would not agree to it.

Alethea merely listened, a slight smile on her mouth.

"This is an odd thing to ask," her father said, at which Wilhelmina snorted. "And you would have no reason to do this, except that I have heard that you might wish to become a judge." He cast a speculative eye on Mr. Townsend. "I can speak to a few people, once Wilhelmina is safely married."

"I don't expect you to say yes," Wilhelmina said, turning to face him. "In fact, I would prefer that you not." Despite the enticement her father was offering. She met his gaze, trying to convey how strongly she did not want this; it was embarrassing, it was disrespectful, and it might have the intended side effect of getting her married off to somebody who was only interested in her because of another gentleman's interest. How was that a basis for a lifelong commitment?

"Mina, you have to get married sometime." Alethea's tone was impatient. "Where would I be if I hadn't married your father?"

Back on my father's estate with your parents? Leading a happy life being beautiful and entertaining several offers of marriage? But Wilhelmina didn't think Alethea would appreciate her answer.

"It is what ladies do," her father pronounced.

She opened her mouth to argue, but snapped it shut again. There was no point to it. It was clear what her father and Alethea wanted, and it didn't matter what Wilhelmina herself thought. At best, they would listen and refuse to change their minds; at worst, they would further limit her activities until she was forbidden to do any of the things she loved.

Wilhelmina felt as if she was being closed in from all sides. He still hadn't answered. Why hadn't he answered? There was no possibility he would agree to this charade, was there?

Oh God.

He looked past her to Alethea, opening his mouth to speak.

Please say no, please say no, please say no.

"It would be my pleasure," he said at last, still not meeting Wilhelmina's gaze. What had happened to the gentleman who was aggravating, stubborn, and argumentative? He was agreeing without even one objection? One stipulation?

What was he doing? Was he that desperate to become a judge?

"Excellent," Alethea said, sounding smug. Of course she did; she was going to get her stepdaughter out of her house forever, merely by asking a gentleman to pretend to like her.

And Wilhelmina could refuse, of course, and walk away from him when they were in public. But that would be incredibly rude in the first place, and would likely result in even more oversight of her behavior in the second, which would have the opposite effect of what she wanted. No more visits to the Stars Above Society, no more long walks with Dipper, nothing except sitting in this house being watched over.

She was entirely dependent on her father for another six months. Could she stand to be closed up in this house for six months?

If this was even a fraction of what marriage felt like—to be unable to make your own decisions—then Wilhelmina definitely wanted no part of it. Agreeing to this farce now meant that the next six months might not be completely miserable. Only partly miserable.

"We'll be attending the Langleys' party in two nights," Alethea said.

"As will I," Mr. Townsend replied. And then, finally, he looked at her. She couldn't read what was in his expression. Her mind still whirled with what had just happened—the worst part was that her father agreed with his wife that she would need subterfuge to convince a man to marry her. And that he didn't and wouldn't understand that she did not wish to be married.

But if she were to be permitted more than one worse part, it would be that Mr. Townsend would agree to something that she was so clearly against. Where was the person with whom she thought she had so much in common? Did he also agree that she would need some sort of deceitful maneuver to attract a potential spouse?

Was it possible to punch someone in the nose and burst into tears at the same time?

"And now, if you will pardon me, I must get to an appointment." He rose as he spoke, giving her a brief nod, then taking Alethea's extended hand and, after an awkward pause, lowering his head to drop a kiss on it.

"Good day, my lord. My lady." He turned back to her. "My lady."

And then he was out the door before Wilhelmina could say a word.

**Men I Do Not Wish to Marry:
A Not at All Comprehensive List by
Lady Wilhelmina Bettesford**

A gentleman whose only impetus for marriage is that another gentleman is pursuing the lady in question. Marriage is not a competition sport.

Chapter Eleven

He couldn't leave without trying to explain. But he also couldn't just linger in the foyer, hoping that she would magically appear before her father and stepmother realized he was still there. Instead, he'd rushed out as if he had somewhere to be, when actually he just wanted to keep himself from sharing his opinion on what her father and stepmother had asked him to do.

He hoped Lady Wilhelmina would be angry enough to follow him when he left, so he kept his pace slow, listening for any movement behind him.

And if she didn't? He'd send her a note, perhaps asking her to meet him on Blackfriars Bridge.

"Mr. Townsend!"

Thank God. He didn't want to have to wait any longer than was necessary to speak to her.

Bram's steps slowed, and he braced himself before turning around.

She stood facing him like a wrathful angel, her expression fierce and unhappy and proud. It hurt him to see her like that. Even in the short time he'd known her, he'd realized there was so much more to her than people usually saw.

But he saw her. And he saw the raw emotion in her eyes, the pain of what her father and stepmother had asked wounding her to the core.

"I can explain," he said, holding his hand out to her as he walked back down the street.

"What is there to explain?" she said in a clear, loud tone. A few people walking by gave them curious glances, which she ignored. "You agreed to this ridiculous . . . *stunt*, and now you say you can explain?" She gave him a derisive look. "Are you so desperate to change professions?"

"Come with me," he said, taking her arm. "And I will."

"I can't wait to hear it," she bit out, yanking away from him. She kept pace beside him, however, so it seemed he was going to get the opportunity to share.

Since they were near her father's house, however, there wasn't a convenient pub they could just pop into and have a pint while he told her why he'd agreed. Besides which it would be even odder for a lady to enter a pub anyway, so there went that idea before it even was a possibility. Instead, there was only a long stretch of road with massive houses on either side, and not even one with a large garden they could pretend to be admiring.

Finally, when he was about to pull her into somebody's shrubbery, he saw a small park, enclosed with iron fencing. It was probably private, only for the residents of the street's use, but he didn't think anyone would throw them out. At least not before he had a chance to explain.

This would be a true test of his argumentative skills.

They walked through the gates, seeing only a few people in the space: some children and their nurses, a few maids in groups of two and three, likely stealing fifteen minutes away from their employers' houses.

Benches ringed a small garden, and he nodded toward the closest one. "We can sit there," he said, jerking his chin toward it.

She made a grumpy noise, but walked toward the bench, settling herself at one end and glaring up at him.

He sat as well, keeping to the other end of the bench.

"The thing is—" he began.

"That you said yes to this proposal that I have no wish to be part of!" she interrupted.

"Not a proposal," he pointed out, unable to resist. "The proposal is supposed to be later, and will definitely not come from me."

"This is no time for jokes," she replied, her eyes narrowing.

She was truly angry.

He couldn't blame her. But he could try to tell her why he'd said yes.

"Fine. No jokes," he said, holding his hand up in a gesture of surrender.

"Why?" she said after a moment. "Is it the opportunity my father dangled in front of you?"

Her voice was quiet, though he heard a note of strength indicating she wasn't defeated. Good. He wanted her to push back against him, against the plans her father and stepmother had for her.

He took a deep breath as he met her gaze. "It is my job to reason things out, to weigh the costs of any action. To forecast things to the end. I saw that your father and stepmother were determined—*are* determined—to marry you off."

He rose, since he was accustomed to making his arguments while standing, and this was an argument he needed to win. "I didn't want them to turn to someone else, someone who is not me."

"Just because I kissed you—" she said, color flooding her cheeks.

"Someone who might talk about what he had been asked to do," he continued, as though she hadn't spoken, "or would take their job so seriously you would be in actual danger of marrying, when I know that is the last thing you want."

"It is," she said, her tone vehement. "Which is why your assisting in this project is not at all helpful."

"The last thing you want," he repeated. "I know that. I know *you*. Even though we only met a month or so ago it is patently obvious—to anyone who would pay attention—that you would chafe in a traditional marriage. I doubt a husband would tolerate his wife hopping up onto parapets, for example—"

"It was to see the stars," she exclaimed, sounding as though that was a reasonable explanation.

"And I cannot imagine that you would be satisfied by a daily round of visits, shopping, and taking tea."

"No," she replied simply. "I cannot and will not marry. I could not tolerate it," she said, her expression pained.

"So this tactic—agreeing to what your stepmother suggests—gives you freedom and time to decide for yourself what you want to do next. No, you cannot just run off to the country—can you?"

he said, struck that perhaps she did have other op-
portunities.

"No," she said. "Not for another six months. Six
months from now I will receive my inheritance."

From the tone of her voice, she might have just
said six thousand years.

"But if we operate under the pretense that I am
courting you, you can strategize on how to do what
you want. At least until you get your money."

"Why would you do this?"

It wasn't the same question as before; this time her
voice held genuine surprise, as though nobody had
ever put themselves out for her before.

"Because it's the right thing to do," he said.

"Because it's the right thing to do?" she repeated.
Of all the things for him to say, she wasn't expecting that. Not because it wasn't the right thing to
do, although actually she wasn't certain what the
right thing was in this situation. At least, there
wasn't anything she could think of. Or rather, all
the things she did think of would not work.

But because he thought it was his responsibility.

"You swear this isn't because I kissed you, is it?"
she blurted out, her eyes widening as she realized
what she'd said. "I mean, you don't owe me anything. It's not as though I go around kissing every
gentleman I meet, if that is your concern." In fact, he
was only the second gentleman she'd ever kissed—
the first was when she was nine years old, and the
gentleman in question was the son of her mother's
friend.

He'd run out of the room crying.

"No, of course not," he replied, his expression
one of disbelief. "It was a lovely kiss, surely you

know that?" And then he gave her a confused
look. "How are we actually discussing the quality
of a kiss?"

"Well," she said, sounding frosty to herself, "it
did seem as though it was important." And if she
could go back in time and ask that boy just why
he'd cried perhaps she would be better at it all by
the time she tried for a second time.

And now she must sound pompous to him.
Though how one could be pompous about a kiss,
she didn't know. But just because she didn't know
how to do it didn't mean she wasn't doing it.

Just like her kisses.

"I promise you, it was," he replied, taking his seat
on the bench again, his arm stretched over the back.
It appeared as though he was trying not to smile,
and she didn't know if that was because he found
her fretting amusing, or because he was concerned
he would offend her. Likely both.

"So how is this going to work?" she asked. She
didn't want to keep talking about the kiss, though
of course she couldn't stop thinking about it.

He shrugged. "We'll spend time together in public." He frowned in confusion. "Isn't that how courtship works? Even a pretend one?"

She flung her hands up in the air in a gesture of
frustration. "I have no idea. Aren't you supposed to
know these things, what with being you and all?"

Now he looked even more confused. "What do
you mean, me being me? I assure you, my lady, I
do not have a history of pretend courting. I only
participated in that auction because it benefited the
home where my friends and I grew up. And because
Benedict insisted."

"Not because of that," she said, waving her hand in dismissal. "But because of your appearance."

"Because you think I am handsome?" he said, sounding puzzled.

"Of course because you are handsome! Goodness, have you never looked in a mirror?"

How could he not know? It was as clear as the nose on his face. And as clear as his remarkable blue eyes, or the sharp planes of his face, or the breadth of his shoulders.

"My appearance is neither here nor there," he said. "I am not sure you understand how this all works," he said.

"No, I do not," she replied, allowing her aggravation at his determined slowness to seep into her tone. "Which is what I have just said."

"Oh," he said, sounding taken aback. "So you did. My apologies, my lady." He raised an eyebrow. "It isn't often I lose the thread of what I'm saying. It's a rather important element of my profession, after all. And yet here you are doing it. Well done."

"And you'll ensure no other gentleman tries to press his suit with me?" she prodded.

"I can't promise that," he began. "Because the whole point of this, according to your stepmother, is to get other gentlemen to notice you. But I can promise that it will take an enormous effort for a gentleman to actually propose to you. We'll do our best to make it seem as though there will be an imminent announcement of our engagement, so as to dissuade potential suitors."

"But won't Alethea and my father try to make it so that doesn't seem likely?" She frowned as she worked out what might happen.

"And risk having their scheme found out?" he retorted. "No, because if they do anything to make it seem as though this is not real, then either people will think something is wrong with you if they had to resort to this subterfuge, or they will be horribly embarrassed, or both." He gave her a pointed look. "I cannot imagine your father would tolerate being embarrassed. Besides which, it's only for six months. We can manage this for at least six months."

"You don't just know me, you seem to know my father very well also," she commented wryly.

"It is my job to know people," he said. Sounding smug.

"I thought it was your job to stay focused on a discussion?" she shot back.

"Both are true, my lady. Just as it can be possible for me to say I very much enjoyed our kiss, but that I do not want to marry you."

She felt the heat come to her cheeks. "And I feel likewise, Mr. Townsend."

"'Mr. Helpful,' you mean to say," he replied, his beautiful mouth curling into a smile.

Men I Do Not Wish to Marry:
A Not at All Comprehensive List by
Lady Wilhelmina Bettesford

Whichever gentleman first suggested that a lady should not be given the same education as he is entitled to receive. Just ask yourself why any gentleman would not want a lady to be as well educated as he—because he knows he is not as intelligent? Because he wants to keep the lady from doing what she might be able to, given the proper opportunity? Whatever the reason, it's deplorable.

Chapter Twelve

I need your help," Bram said bluntly.

He'd been the first to arrive at the Peckham Club, having sent notes to his friends to meet him there that evening. It wasn't their usual book club evening, which would be in another two weeks.

Benedict had arrived next, followed by Theo and Simeon, who were bickering about an essay they'd read, and then Fenton had appeared, looking as though he'd just woken up.

Perhaps he had. One never quite knew with Fenton.

"Bram needs help," Theo said, glancing around the room. "Has Bram ever asked for help before?"

"There was when he needed to be garbed for the opera," Simeon said. "Only recently, though."

"And as I recall, Bram didn't ask, but was required to accept our help," Theo replied.

"What help do you need?" Benedict asked.

Fenton didn't speak, but kept his gaze focused on Bram's face. A sure sign he was actually paying attention, for once.

"There is a lady—"

"Oh, the mysterious lady!" Theo crowed.

"Shut up, Theo," Benedict commanded. "And she isn't mysterious any longer," he added.

"This lady, Lady Wilhelmina Bettesford, is in the unenviable position of being an unmarried woman in her father's house, and her father has just arrived with a new bride, one who is five years younger than the lady."

"Are you going to rescue her, Bram?" Fenton said, somewhat unexpectedly.

"Rescue? No. Her father made it very clear I would be an unwelcome husband."

The four other men all bristled to varying degrees. But they understood, all being orphans themselves, that their cloudy origins would affect every aspect of their adult lives.

"Perhaps you're the founder's child," Simeon said, nodding toward Bram. "And he can reveal himself at the last minute, wielding a marriage certificate and a title."

"When I ran the calculations, Bram and I were the least likely to be the son of the founder," Fenton said, running a hand through his hair. "As I recall, the three of you were more likely than the two of us. But there was no certainty that the founder's child was even one of us. It might be someone else entirely."

"And besides which," Bram added quickly, "I don't have time for marriage. My work keeps me too busy." *And she would be entirely unsuitable, no matter how appealing I find her.*

"I'm busier than you," Theo said, "and I still find time for socializing."

"Yes, and you still have time when your socializing goes awry to come complain to us," Simeon said.

"Can we get back to what Bram is talking about?" Benedict said, sounding irritated. Of the five of them, Benedict was the one most likely to get annoyed when their conversations veered off into odd pathways. Bram was a close second, when he wasn't the one doing the veering.

Bram inclined his head in thanks. "What the lady's stepmother proposed was that I pay attention to Lady Wilhelmina in an effort to get other gentlemen to also pay attention, which might lead to an actual marriage proposal."

"Seems rather complicated to me. Is the lady that unattractive?" Simeon asked.

"No," Bram said, suppressing the urge to punch his friend for even asking the question. "No, she is—she is unexceptionable."

"She's the one you attended the opera with?" Theo asked.

"Yes. And after that, apparently, the lady received more attention than she normally gets. Which she doesn't like—she has no wish to be married."

"So why is she doing this?" Fenton asked.

"Her father and stepmother are behind the scheme. If Lady Wilhelmina refuses to go along with their plans, they could limit her activities or cut off her allowance. If she makes her antipathy to the entire marital institution known, she will be seen as unpleasant, and she will be limited in what she does."

"Rather hamstrung no matter what she does," Fenton observed.

"Yes, which is why I agreed. I know she doesn't wish to marry, and I hope to help her."

"Why?" Simeon asked. The same question she had asked.

"Because it's the right thing to do." The same answer he had given her.

They nodded, as though that was what they'd expected him to say.

"So what I'd ask is that you, if you happen to meet the lady yourselves, pay attention to her, at least enough so that others notice. I don't expect you to rush into Society—"

"God forbid," Fenton said fervently.

"But if you are there, and you see me and the lady, try to make a stir."

"Does this mean you'll be needing more evening clothes?" Simeon asked.

Bram sighed. "Yes. Yes, it does."

Simeon and Theo both grinned at Bram's clear dismay.

WILHELMINA LIFTED HER chin as she waited with Alethea and her father to be announced.

It was two days after Mr. Townsend had agreed to Alethea's preposterous suggestion. And while she understood why he had said yes, she did not at all support the premise: that she was so forgettable or mediocre that she would require a gentleman's attention to garner other gentlemen's attention. Or that she needed a gentleman's attention in the first place.

But she knew not to argue the point. Alethea was clearly just as stubborn as her father, and both were apparently determined to get her married off and out of their house.

If only her father had met Alethea after Wilhelmina had received her inheritance. Then she could have gracefully left and set up her own residence, and she would just be viewed as an eccentric, and wealthy, spinster.

But because she wasn't quite old enough to be a spinster, but too old to qualify as a reasonable marital prospect, she was in a hellish limbo that forced this charade.

That was why she was wearing the gown she was, for example; it was much fancier, and much more expensive, than her usual evening wear.

Made of silk and satin, the gown was pale blue, with tiny puffed sleeves just barely clinging onto her shoulders; its bodice molded to her figure, and then it billowed out into layers and layers of fabric, each layer progressively more flimsy, until the top layer, which was a delicate tulle.

Alethea had hunted through her jewelry collection to find a blue topaz necklace whose pendant was nestled right between her breasts. Wilhelmina wore white elbow gloves and satin slippers that were so delicate as to make her feel that she was barefoot.

She had to admit she looked lovely. It was irksome, that Alethea had such an unerring eye for fashion.

"Now remember," that lady said in a hushed tone, "Mr. Townsend will be here, and will be paying particular attention to you. You should smile, but not too much; speak with him, but not excessively so; and whatever you do, don't have more than two dances with him."

"Lord and Lady Croyde. Lady Wilhelmina Bettesford," the butler said.

Here we go, Wilhelmina thought to herself.

She waited as her father and Alethea descended the few steps into the ballroom, her father already preening with pride at having his young, lovely wife on his arm. Wilhelmina followed after, her eyes darting around the room in search of—

There. There he was. Standing near the wall, his arms folded over his chest, glancing around the room with that penetrating gaze. She would relish the opportunity to see him at work, arguing a point of law with someone who wasn't nearly as clever or well-spoken as he.

Not that she knew for certain that his opponents wouldn't be as clever and well-spoken as he, but she strongly suspected it.

Their eyes met, and he began to walk toward her, his gaze now focused entirely on her. An inappropriate shiver ran through her—she was supposed to still be angry with him that he was going to carry out Alethea's mad plan, even though he had given several excellent reasons why he should.

"Good evening, my lady," he said in a low voice. "Ready?"

"Mmm," she murmured.

"Good evening, my lord, my lady," he continued in a louder tone. Her father and Alethea greeted him amicably, striking the perfect balance between friendliness and a natural superiority of class.

"Could I have the first dance, my lady?" he said, returning his attention to her.

"Yes, thank you," Wilhelmina replied. This was all pretend—he was just as strong in his desire never to be married as she—and yet she felt that tug, that pull of attraction, between them.

Of course attraction could occur between two people who had no intention of making their relationship official. And of course the opposite could be true, and frequently was—a married couple had little to no caring for one another because they had been paired up for financial, Societal, or other reasons. Anything but love.

That was why she wanted none of it, even without having heard Aunt Flora's admonishments on the subject for years. Or seen her own mother's vivacity dim.

"You are looking awfully fierce," he murmured as he took her in his arms. The music hadn't yet begun, so it felt odd to be encircled in his hold without a purpose.

"I suppose I am feeling awfully fierce," she replied. At least she could speak the truth to him—she wouldn't have to prevaricate on her feelings, or her reluctance to be in this situation, or anything of that sort. At least they'd established that.

"Because of this?" he said, lifting his fingers off her waist to gesture to the crowd.

She exhaled, but didn't answer.

The music began, and several other couples joined them on the dance floor. Wilhelmina didn't have a lot of practice dancing; her father had hired an instructor, but Wilhelmina had figured out fairly quickly that Mr. Cavendish much preferred gossiping with the footmen than teaching her, so she finagled it that there was always a reason for Mr. Cavendish to make an inquiry of a footman or two, giving her time to herself.

Time she usually spent reading.

Perhaps explaining why she'd stepped on so many feet during her first and only Season.

So it took all her concentration to focus on the movements. He was frowning as though concentrating as well, and she felt relieved that he wasn't remarkably good at dancing. The last thing she wanted was to look like a clumsy buffoon sailing around the dance floor with an elegant gentleman.

Well, no. The last thing she wanted was to be in this situation in the first place.

But the whole "poor dancer with an excellent partner" thing came a close second.

He moved as though conscious of his strength, holding it in so he wouldn't hurt her. Keeping himself locked down rather than exhibit what his musculature could do.

Which just made her wonder what his musculature could do.

Not the kind of thoughts she should be having at the moment.

"Can we—?" she asked, gesturing toward the doors leading out onto, she presumed, some sort of terrace.

"If you wish," he said.

They picked their way through the dancers, him with his hand still on her waist as she led the way.

It felt nice to have him at her back—literally. And figuratively, she supposed, though she wasn't certain he would be able to accomplish what he'd promised.

The air was cool outside, and she lifted her head and took a deep breath, feeling the air fill her lungs. The night sky was mostly cloudy, but she gazed up at it nonetheless, hoping to glimpse a constellation or two. Perhaps a planet, if she was lucky.

"Is this so people will notice?" he asked, his voice all rumbly.

"Is what so—oh God, no," she said, horrified that he might think she was so manipulative.

"Oh," he replied. "Then why?"

She exhaled, still gazing up at the sky. "I don't like crowds," she said simply. "That is, I feel both too seen and entirely unseen," she continued, turning to meet his gaze. "Not that that makes sense."

His eyes caught the light, the dramatic blue making her breath catch. Again.

Really, it was ridiculous that he was so good-looking.

"It makes sense," he said, making the flutter in her stomach settle. She hadn't realized her stomach was fluttering until it stopped.

He reached out to take her hand, his warm skin on her fingers like comfort.

"I promise you," he said, sounding as fierce as she must have looked earlier, "that you won't have to be with anyone who doesn't see you. That you will make it through without having to compromise who you are or what you want."

She almost believed him. "You must be very effective in the courtroom," she said at last, her voice soft. "You are very persuasive."

His mouth curled up in a delicious smile. "When there is something I want, yes."

Men I Do Not Wish to Marry: A Not at All Comprehensive List by Lady Wilhelmina Bettesford

Someone who criticizes how you manage the household, but has no constructive advice for how it should be done—just that you are doing it wrong.

Chapter Thirteen

The point, Bram reminded himself, was not to flirt with her. Though actually the point *was* to flirt with her. But not in private, in the darkness, with only a few stars and a cloud-covered moon to see them.

And yet he hadn't been able to resist. She looked vibrant, and lovely, and delicious. It would be disingenuous to say he would find her just as enchanting if she didn't look as she did, because of how appealing her brain was. But it would also be wrong to say that he wouldn't be nearly as enticed by her if she didn't have that brain resting inside that beautiful head.

"And what do you mean by that?" she said, a note of challenge in her voice. "You are not supposed to be telling me you find me attractive. Unless that isn't what you meant?" she added.

"It is what I meant," Bram said. He still held her hand, though he wished it was her bare hand, not covered by a glove. "When I say something to you, Wilhelmina, it is because I mean it. I won't lie to you."

"Oh," she said on a sigh. Her gaze met his in the moonlight, and she drew the plushness of her lower lip into her mouth, biting it with her strong, sharp teeth.

The movement inspired something in him, something he recognized as desire, though he had never felt it this strongly before. He wanted to plunge his hands into her hair, freeing it from the pins so it would flow around his fingers, then draw her close and place his mouth on hers. Knowing her lips would be warm, and soft. That he would pull her close against his body, feel her curves pressed against him.

No wonder Simeon and Theo were both so ludicrous in love, if this was how they felt most of the time.

"I wish you could kiss me here," she said in a low voice. "Or rather, I wish I could kiss you." A hint of humor inflected her tone.

"You'd like to take command, then?" he asked.

She kept her eyes locked with his as she removed her fingers from his to roll down the glove of her left hand, peeling it off and sliding it over her arm. Then she took his fingers in hers, the contact of skin to skin like a lightning bolt through his body.

"I would. I just did," she said, arching a brow.

His cock stiffened, and he swallowed a few times, his eyes never leaving hers.

This was dangerous. They weren't supposed to actually *do* anything—just give the pretense that they were.

And yet here they were on some random aristocrat's terrace, undressing one another with their eyes. Her literally undressing herself, though it was only a glove.

"I promise I won't like you either. *Bram*." She said his name like a vow, an oath she'd sworn.

"Christ, Wilhelmina," he said, raking his hand through his hair, his other hand still clutching hers. "What in God's name are we going to do?"

That brow again. "Do?" She shrugged. "Whatever we want, I suppose." The corner of her mouth curled up. "I suppose if we do something sufficiently scandalous, that will take care of my problem as well as you pretending interest in me."

"I'm not pretending," he said sharply. He knew she knew that, but he needed to tell her anyway. It all felt so important, that she know some of this wasn't true, but that the crucial things were. "I can be interested in you without wanting to be married to you, after all. And I presume you feel the same way about me."

"I do," she said firmly. "Though if I did have to marry, it might as well be you. Not that I want to, however," she added quickly.

"Thank you," he said in a dry tone of voice.

She swatted him on the arm with the hand he wasn't holding. "We said we would be honest with one another. The truth is, I would like to kiss you nearly as much as I don't wish to marry you."

He choked on a laugh.

"And it all works out," she continued, "because if we are truly interested in one another, then it will be less difficult to play at this whole courtship thing."

"What about the kissing?" he couldn't resist asking.

"Oh, that," she said, glancing around the terrace. She grabbed hold of his arm and pulled him toward a small set of stairs that presumably led to the gardens. They walked down, him following in her wake, and she scuttled to the other side of the terrace wall.

Nobody would see them unless they peered over the edge.

"And here we are," she said, putting her back against the wall and grasping his lapels. "Now you are to kiss me."

WILHELMINA WAS SURPRISED at her own boldness. But since their goals were firmly aligned—no marriage for them, nothing beyond this pretense—then the fact that they were mutually interested in one another would not lead to anything permanent.

She could kiss him and keep her independence. Very few women in her social circle could say the same thing.

She tilted her head up as she pulled him down, using the lapels of his evening coat as leverage.

And then his mouth was on hers. Warm, insistent, intoxicating.

She released his coat, instead putting her hands at his waist, sliding her fingers along the fabric of his waistcoat, pressing into the hard strength of his body underneath.

He made a growling noise deep in his throat, and then his tongue was in her mouth, exploring and questing. She chuckled against his lips, then tangled her tongue with his, the distant noise of the party receding as she heard only the hitching of their breaths, the rustling of fabric as they shifted against one another, his hand at her waist, gripping her tightly so that it was hard to move. Not that she had any intention of going anywhere.

Which she would tell him if his tongue wasn't in her mouth, and vice versa.

Her palm flattened against his chest, her fingers splayed as she drew her hand across its breadth. Feeling the hard strength of him. If he wasn't wearing clothing, she would be able to hear his heart beat.

Was it beating faster because of this?

Or did he do this type of thing all the time?

He was remarkably good-looking, after all. Likely women flung themselves at him every day.

Which would be lowering if not for the fact that if he *did* do this frequently, it would mean that much less to him. So she could plan on doing it more.

His hand, meanwhile, had slid onto her hip, the warmth of his skin seeping through the layers of her gown. She wanted to curl up into him, to press herself against him, let her body mold against his.

And yes, she knew exactly what she wanted. She'd read enough books on her own to know what happened between married couples at night. She'd never felt the urge so strongly, however, to do those things as now.

It felt as though his warmth was flooding her skin, making her pulse with a kind of sensual energy.

She put her hand into his hair, tugging gently as they continued to kiss. He groaned again, and she tugged a little harder, making the hand on her hip tighten. It seemed he liked that.

His other hand was still at her waist, but his long fingers were splayed out, and with just a bit of upward motion he'd be touching her breast. Which, she realized, ached to be touched.

She squirmed so as to encourage his hand to where she wanted it—not in the place she wanted it most, since that would be lower than her breast. But the place that would be the next expected move.

He understood her cue, his palm covering her breast. His fingertips resting on the skin above her breast.

"Mmm," she moaned, and pushed off the wall, eager to get her body closer to his.

At which he stumbled backward, breaking the kiss, his hands grabbing onto her arms as he tried to steady himself.

He didn't fall, thankfully, but the moment was over.

She was mournful about its end, of course, but it was also hilarious to her that her attempt to do more resulted in doing less.

She met his gaze, her mouth swollen from their kissing, her body tingling where he had touched her.

And she smiled, then began to laugh, until he joined in on the laughter, both of them realizing that they should be as quiet as possible, what with being unchaperoned and unseen.

They both covered their mouths with their hands, trying to smother their snorts and guffaws, which just made them laugh harder.

She shook her head, unable to speak, and jerked her head upward, then walked away from him, still laughing. "Give me five minutes," she was able to say, then walked sedately to the terrace, trying to make it appear as though she'd been there the whole time.

IT WAS GOOD she had said five minutes, because he needed that time to settle himself down. By which he meant his erection to subside. He'd never had this happen before, him having an inconvenient erection. His courtroom appearances were thankfully free of any such occurrences, mostly because he was far too often doing last-minute preparations for the case to get sidetracked by an attractive person. Or interest thereof.

Not to mention that he had never felt this strong attraction to anybody before. Of course he had natural sexual urges, but a few minutes with his hand had sorted those out.

He didn't like not being in control of his body, of his reactions, which was likely why he hadn't had this kind of experience before. But with her—he wondered what it would look like, what it would feel like, if she took command, as she'd done just a few minutes before.

But taking command of more, letting himself forget to think and just feel.

Only all this thinking about feeling, ironically, was not helping the whole erection situation. Because he was thinking of how she felt pressed against him, and what she'd sounded like when she'd uttered her soft moans. How he'd wished he could ruck up her skirts and press his way inside, pushing her back against the wall, perhaps hoisting her up so she could wrap her legs around him.

For a person who had never actually done the thing itself, he certainly had a lot of thoughts and ideas about the experience. Though that was true in general; that was how he was successful at his work. Being able to imagine any kind of situation, regardless of whether he himself had experienced it, made him a compelling debater.

"A surprise to see you here, Mr. Townsend."

Bram started, relieved to be shaken out of his thoughts, but not necessarily pleased to see Lord Paskins.

The other man wore his usually benign expression, but Bram thought he saw a hint of—malice? Disdain?—in his eyes. Of course it could just be Bram's imagination and guilty conscience.

After all, he knew Lord Paskins had been pursuing Wilhelmina, and Bram had just been kissing the lady in question below the terrace. Even though he had no intention himself of pursuing her.

But he also knew Wilhelmina would never willingly accept Lord Paskins's suit, so he couldn't feel too guilty about it.

"I am here with Lord and Lady Croyde, and Lady Wilhelmina," Bram said, straightening himself up to his full height.

And now he was being ridiculous—puffing himself up like a rooster displaying his coxcomb.

"Of course you are," Lord Paskins said with a smug expression.

What was he up to?

"I would have thought you would be too involved with your work to do something so frivolous as attend a party. But I would imagine the allure of Lady Wilhelmina's dowry might overcome your antipathy to social events." Lord Paskins accompanied his comment with a kind of conspiratorial look that made Bram bristle.

Shouldn't he be off sharing his mundane thoughts on things he'd done recently? Before, Bram had only thought of the other man as a boring nuisance. But now he was realizing that the banality of the other man's demeanor hid his more unpleasant character-istics.

"I have no—" Bram began, then shut his mouth. He couldn't admit to this gentleman, as much as he wished to, that he had no interest in Lady Wil-helmina's dowry. Then the whole charade would be exposed before they'd barely begun, and who knew what gentleman Lady Croyde would choose next? Perhaps even one like this Lord Paskins here—seemingly mild on the outside, but almost conniving on the inside.

Or he was reading too much into the man's char-acter, but he'd also gotten very good at that, thanks to his profession.

Also it didn't take a particular insight to surmise that young, unmarried gentlemen would be inter-ested in young, unmarried ladies with large inheri-tances.

"It's an inheritance," he said suddenly.

"What?" Lord Paskins replied.

"Lady Wilhelmina has an inheritance, not a dowry. Which I am given to understand will be hers in six months."

Lord Paskins looked suspicious. "But her father is very fond of her." He raised an eyebrow. "I presume her father will settle money on her when she is mar-ried, especially since it appears the lady might need a little bit of help for that to happen." He raised a brow. "A dowry on top of an inheritance could make any lady seem appealing."

Bram gritted his teeth, trying to remind himself that punching the condescending lord would garner attention he did not want, and that Wilhelmina almost certainly did not want. "Yes, and her father has also recently married himself."

Bram hoped the other man would be clever enough to put those things together and figure out what he meant. He certainly didn't want to say aloud that the new Lady Croyde was likely keenly interested in her husband's fortune. That the new Lady Croyde was likely keenly interested in having her own children, a boy, who might supersede Wilhelmina's standing in her father's eyes.

And now it had to have been at least five minutes.

"If you will excuse—" Bram began, only to be interrupted.

"Good evening," Theo said, glancing from one to the other of them.

"Good evening, Mr. Osborne," Lord Paskins said, his easy smile reappearing.

"Evening, Theo," Bram said.

Theo gave a pointed look toward Bram's clothing. "You look quite presentable," he said, unable to keep a note of astonishment from his tone.

"Thank you," Bram replied, resisting the urge to roll his eyes. He could dress himself properly, it just wasn't something he'd ever placed much importance on before. Never mind that Simeon had assisted earlier that day. But he would never admit that to Theo.

"I came with Benedict—he's off in one of the other rooms discussing politics." Theo's disdainful tone revealed what he thought about that. "But I wanted to meet your Lady Wilhelmina," he continued, giving a sly look toward Lord Paskins.

"Yes, she is in the ballroom, I believe," Bram said.

He nodded to Lord Paskins in a clear gesture of dismissal, but that gentleman walked with them as they returned, Bram spotting Wilhelmina at the edge of the dance floor.

She was not precisely surrounded by a multitude of gentlemen, but there were at least three of them clustered around her.

The plan was working.

He had to make certain it wasn't working too well, however. He'd promised her, after all.

So he swept through the crowd, Theo and Lord Paskins trailing behind, walking up to her with, he hoped, the attitude that he had the most claim on her.

"Lady Wilhelmina," he began, indicating Theo, "may I present my friend Mr. Theodore Osborne?"

Her eyes went from him to Theo, and then her mouth curled into a smile as she extended her hand to Theo. "A pleasure to meet you, sir," she said.

Bram found he didn't like that she was smiling at Theo. And then found that he didn't like his own reaction on top of that dislike. He couldn't be jealous of her, not when they'd both stated their intentions. It was just, he told himself, that he knew Theo was as likely to fall in love with her as Bram was likely to start an argument.

Which was to say very likely.

But he also knew that she had no desire to pair herself with anybody—even somebody as charming as Theo was. She had a plan, he'd figured out; it was just that she hadn't seen fit to share it with him yet.

"Good evening, Lord Paskins," she added, her smile dimming a little.

Which Bram tried not to be incredibly cheerful about.

"You attended the opera with this fellow?" Theo said, jerking his thumb toward Bram. "I've been trying to get him to more cultural events, but he always has the excuse of work. But now that he has gone to the opera, my lady, what else would you suggest he see?"

Wilhelmina blinked. "Uh . . . I don't know that I am the person to ask, Mr. Osborne. That was my first time at the opera as well."

"Did you enjoy it?" Theo asked.

Her expression grew dreamy. "It was splendid. People telling an incredible story through singing, and I would have never imagined it would be so good, and yet it was."

"You'll go again, of course," Theo said, glancing toward Bram.

"I would be glad to accompany you to the opera, my lady, should Mr. Townsend find himself too busy with work to do so," Lord Paskins said.

Bram suppressed a huff of annoyance. Though he did have to give credit to the other man; not only had he offered to take Lady Wilhelmina to something she would greatly enjoy, he also subtly reminded her that Bram might not value her as much as he did his work, and also that he did work for a living and wasn't just an aristocrat who'd been born into an indolent lifestyle.

Though that was a bit judgmental. But then again, so was Bram.

"I would very much like to attend the opera again, my lady." He turned to address Lord Paskins. "Thank you for the offer, but Lady Wilhelmina's enjoyment is more gratifying to me than a few additional hours of work."

"Bravo," Theo murmured.

She met his gaze and blushed, and then he realized how she might take what he'd said—about her enjoyment, when they'd just been kissing one another in the garden.

And then he colored, too.

Men I Do Not Wish to Marry:
A Not at All Comprehensive List by
Lady Wilhelmina Bettesford

Any gentleman at all. No matter how blue their eyes are, or how intelligent they seem.

Chapter Fourteen

Wilhelmina nearly pinched herself to make certain this was reality. There were no fewer than five gentlemen standing around her, and at least two of them—Mr. Townsend and his friend Mr. Osborne—were exceedingly handsome.

She could see why Alethea enjoyed the attention she received because of her beauty, though Wilhelmina imagined it would be exhausting to have this attention all the time. One would want to run home and hide under the covers for a bit, just to recover.

Or she would. She didn't think Alethea would have that wish.

She'd never experienced this before. When she'd first made her debut, she'd taken pains to keep herself to herself in the corners, and not so subtly discouraged anyone who might possibly take an interest in her. Then there was her stepping on feet, which discouraged anyone who hadn't gotten the hint already.

And she was going to go to the opera again! She should have thought of that before, that she could go again if she wanted to. There was no need for her father and his wife to purchase someone to take her either, since she had two gentlemen offering.

Plus she had somehow made Mr. Townsend blush. She wasn't certain quite what she'd done, just that she'd met his gaze after they'd spoken, and then pink had flooded his cheeks. She would not tell him, of course, but his blushing made his appearance move from devastatingly handsome to adorable.

While still being devastatingly handsome.

"Mr. Townsend, I would very much enjoy going to the opera." But she wouldn't be rude to Lord Paskins, even if he thought staring up at the stars was idiotic. He couldn't be blamed for his ignorance. "And my lord," she said to Lord Paskins in a gentle tone, "if there is something else you would enjoy doing—" she began, only to pause as Mr. Townsend began to cough.

"Apologies," he said when the coughing fit was done. "Just something catching in my throat."

"I imagine so," his friend Mr. Osborne said, his intonation making it sound as though there was something more he was referencing.

"I've purchased a carriage recently," Lord Paskins replied. "Perhaps I could take you for a drive? Say on Friday?"

Wilhelmina nodded before she had time to think about it.

Perhaps there was something to Alethea's plan, after all—she would not be doing these things if Mr. Townsend hadn't agreed to the fake courtship. Though did she really wish to go driving with Lord Paskins? Likely not. But she would like being outside, since the only times lately she could go outside were when she was being whisked to the dressmaker's or taken to a party such as this one.

If she just went out for the occasional drive with eligible gentlemen, perhaps the careful watch her father and Alethea had on her would relax, and she would be able to do more of what she wanted. It was something she should test out. Rather like a scientific theorem of increasing disregard for what she did, as long as it was in the pursuit of marriage.

Ridiculous, but there it was.

"My lady," Mr. Osborne said, "would you do me the honor of granting me a dance?" He held his hand out to the dance floor, and she took it, allowing him to escort her out onto the floor.

The music was just starting up, and they stood still for a moment, his expression amused. At something she had done? She didn't think she was being funny. Perhaps it was inadvertent humor?

"Do you have a question for me, my lady?" he asked as they began to dance.

A waltz. She had very little experience with waltzing; all she knew about it was that it helped if she counted "one, two, three" in her head while moving her feet, but that made answering his question—or talking in general—quite difficult.

He was a remarkably good dancer, unfortunately. Because she knew she must look awfully incompetent compared to him. But perhaps that was for the best, because then prospective suitors might write her off as a potential bride because of her inept footwork.

Which seemed as preposterous as choosing a life partner because you visited them a few afternoons at their house, but she wasn't the one in charge, so that was how it was done. Though not for her, because she would not be squelched like that. And she knew full well that marriage for her would be a squelching: of her joy, of her research, of her relative autonomy.

If her husband didn't want a dog in the house, he could get rid of Dipper without even speaking to her about it.

She didn't think, if she were to marry Mr. Townsend, that he would do any of those things. But he was just as adamant as she that he did not want to marry, so the point was moot.

Even though the thought kept dancing around in her mind, particularly annoying since that dance was far more adept than her own physical attempts.

"My lady?" Mr. Osborne prompted.

Oh right. She owed him an answer to his question, not an internal railing against the system she was currently taking part in, albeit under pressure.

"I was wondering"—*two, three*—"how you know Mr. Townsend. It seems as though you are good friends."

It wasn't what she was wondering, because she knew the answer already, but she couldn't ask him why he looked so amused. First because he'd have to come up with a lie if he was laughing at her, and second that if he could tell her what he was smiling about, he would have done so.

Likely she was saying the same thing in two different ways. She was proud she'd been able to come up with a response, even if he did have to ask her twice.

"We are," Mr. Osborne said, looking past her shoulder to where they'd left Mr. Townsend. "He

and I met at the Devenaugh Home for Destitute
Boys." He returned his gaze to her. "We are both
orphans."

"Oh," Wilhelmina replied, envious of their closeness. Though also aware that their closeness was
formed through their respective tragedies. "I imagine that would forge a strong bond." She tilted her
head in thought. "Rather like the three stars in Orion's Belt."

"Pardon?" Mr. Osborne said, looking confused.

"Alnitak, Alnilam, and Mintaka," she continued.
"Together, they form a constellation. We cannot
speak of one without speaking of the others, and in
fact, we tend to speak of them as one unit."

"We?" Mr. Osborne said, his eyebrows raised.

"Astronomers. I am an astronomer," she said, not
without a hint of pride in her voice.

But unfortunately, that moment of boasting meant
she lost her count, and so she stepped squarely on
Mr. Osborne's foot, making him wince.

"Oh, goodness, I am sorry," she said. They had
stopped dancing, and now the other dancers were
whirling around them, glares on their faces.

"Would you—?" she said, gesturing toward the
doors that led out onto the terrace.

"Theo, I can escort Lady Wilhelmina. You should
go take care of your foot," she heard Mr. Townsend
say. More glares directed toward them now that
there were three people standing in the middle of
the dance floor.

"I'll do that," Mr. Osborne replied. He didn't look
at all bothered, beyond his initial reaction, that she
had stomped on his foot. In fact, he met her gaze
and winked, before walking off the floor. Though

his stride did have a bit of a hitch to it, as though he was favoring the foot.

"I am no good at this," she muttered. No, she did not want to find a life partner this way, but neither did she want to cause pain—literal pain—by her very existence. Or more specifically, her foot's very existence.

"On the contrary, my lady," Mr. Townsend replied. "You are excellent at it." He gestured to the dancers, most of whom were now just avoiding the middle of the room where they stood. Not glaring any longer, thank goodness. "Everyone here is aware of who you are and that you are open to trying new things, even if you are not immediately good at them."

By now, he had walked her back to the terrace, and they stepped outside. She breathed in the fresh air, now conscious of how oppressive the heat and odors were inside.

"You're not actually talking about my kissing, are you?" she said, narrowing her gaze at him.

Instead of answering, he had another coughing fit, which she was beginning to suspect was caused by his being surprised.

"No, my lady, I have no complaints there," he said when he'd cleared his throat a few times. "It is unusual to speak about kissing nearly as much as doing it, however."

She shrugged. "I like to analyze things," she said. "Don't you?" She gestured between them. "Isn't that part of your profession also? You have to prepare your arguments, don't you?"

"I do," he confirmed. "We have much in common."

"We do," she confirmed. She tilted her head and

gave him an appraising glance. "If I had any desire to marry, you might make an adequate husband."

"Adequate?" he said, his brows raised.

"Though your friend Mr. Osborne is quite pleasant as well," she mused. "He is such a good dancer, and very gracious about my stepping on him."

"You think Theo would be adequate as well?" Mr. Townsend asked. His voice held a hint of a snarl, and she wondered if he and his friend had argued recently.

She shrugged. "If I had any desire to marry, I suppose so. But since I don't," she continued in a bright tone, "I'll just be pleased that there are two gentlemen, at least, who would not make me miserable." She would not tell him that he was the only one she had any desire to kiss. A desire that had, unfortunately, only increased after their terrace-adjacent incident. She hoped it wasn't like her stargazing—that the more she did it, the more she wished to. Because that would be an untenable situation to be in.

Men I Do Not Wish to Marry:
A Not at All Comprehensive List by
Lady Wilhelmina Bettesford

Someone who does not have a hobby. It could be the most ludicrous hobby—collecting rocks, for example, or wanting to try every variety of food there is—but a hobby-less man is a very dull man.

Chapter Fifteen

*A*dequate.

She thought he would make an adequate husband.

Bram's fingers itched with the urge to grab her to him and show her just how *adequate* he could be—kissing her until she was breathless, for example, or using his considerable talents of persuasion to change her mind about his adequacy. Or lack thereof.

But what would be the point? Nothing, except for soothing his bruised ego. He was already committed to not marrying her, not only in her eyes, but in her father's and stepmother's. Two very different reasons, but it didn't matter—they would not and could not marry.

"I suppose," he said slowly, "that if I had any desire to marry, you would be my first choice as well."

She blinked in surprise, then frowned when she'd processed what he'd said. "You have a first choice, which implies you have a second choice also. Possibly even a third." She folded her arms over her chest. "I would like to know who those other choices are."

She sounded outraged, and he tried to keep from smiling in satisfaction.

"It doesn't matter, does it? Since neither one of us wishes to marry. In fact," he said, gesturing back toward the party, "the whole point of this is to keep you from having to succumb to that state. If you can just hold out for—six months, I believe?"

"Six months, yes," she said tightly.

"And while we are conducting this fake courtship, we can discuss what it is you truly wish to do instead."

She gave him a suspicious look. "*We* can discuss? When we spoke about it, you said this subterfuge would give me time to decide what I want. How did this," she said, twirling her fingers in the space between them, "become a two-person endeavor?" She gave an emphatic nod, then folded her arms over her chest again. "Besides," she continued, "who's to say I don't already have a plan in mind?"

God, he loved sparring with her like this.

"I believe, my lady, that it became a two-person endeavor when you kissed me."

"I did not cede my rights just because I pressed my mouth to yours!" The color in her cheeks was bright pink, and her eyes flashed fire.

"Did I say that?" He imitated her position, folding his arms over his chest. "Remind me when I stated—or even implied—that a kiss bestowed rights of decision-making."

She glared at him. A long moment of silence stretched between them until finally she exploded, flinging her hands up in the air in exasperation.

"You didn't! But neither did I ask for your help."

"I am offering to help, as a friend would." He leaned in to speak softly in her ear. "As a friend who has kissed you. And would like to again."

She exhaled sharply, blowing the air up so wisps of hair fluttered around her face.

"I will not withdraw from my pretend courtship of you," he continued, noting her set expression with an internal lick of pleasure, "so we might as well make the best of the situation." He nodded toward her. "Tell me. What is it you want?"

He thought for a minute she was going to say she wanted to beat him with her shoe, but she stayed silent for a long few minutes until she finally exhaled.

"I have many plans," she said at last. "Most of which you cannot help me with," she continued, making him want to argue. But she kept speaking before he could demand to know just what it was he couldn't help with. "I do want to go to the next Stars Above Society meeting," she said at last. "And—" she went on, then stopped.

He waited, but she didn't say anything else.

It was a start. Eventually, she would tell him what she truly desired. And, perhaps, he would figure out why knowing was so important to him.

"It is the least I can do," Bram said, adjusting his cravat in the mirror.

"Who are you talking to?" Fenton asked, lifting his gaze from the book he had been reading.

Bram met his friend's gaze in the mirror. Fenton was seated on his bed, his long limbs tangled over one another, his spectacles catching the light of the candle that stood on Bram's bedside table.

"You, of course," Bram said, giving Fenton a confused look. There wasn't anybody else in the room. Fenton had agreed to accompany Bram and Wilhelmina to the Stars Above Society for additional respectability, as though anyone with an interesting theorem and a pad of paper couldn't make Fenton wander off, never to be seen again.

Bram was relieved Fenton had so much money from his investments, since he was unlikely to be able to hold a position like he, Benedict, and Theo had, positions where people were required to be at certain places at certain times with certain information.

But he never forgot a book club meeting or when he'd promised one of the rest of them he'd do something. Fenton had his priorities clear, to be sure. Bram admired that.

"Why is it the least you can do?" Fenton asked. "The least you could do is do nothing. Isn't that the case?"

Of course Fenton would choose to argue semantics. Their Wollstonecraft disagreement had occurred when Fenton had posited that advocating for the rights of women was a biased position, since it denied the rights of men. When Bram had pointed out that men had all the rights because they had made the laws, Fenton had agreed, but said the ideal situation would be one where all rights were equal.

A fine theory in theory, but it would never be implemented, not without first recognizing the rights of women, Bram had argued.

And then the punching had begun.

"Yes," Bram replied through a clenched jaw, "that is true. The second to least thing I can do is escort Lady Wilhelmina to the event she most wishes to attend."

He'd paid clear and obvious attention to her at a few subsequent parties, where he'd noticed—to his chagrin and, he presumed, to hers—that more and more gentlemen were beginning to notice her.

As much as he knew Wilhelmina would not want to admit it, nor be pleased by the results, her stepmother's plan was working. A few gentlemen had gone so far as to ask Bram what his intentions were toward her, and then had reminded him of his humble origins.

As if he wasn't acutely aware of them at all times.

"She seems intelligent," Fenton observed. "She would be pleasant to keep company with."

Bram whirled around to face his friend. "What are you saying?"

Fenton shrugged. "Just that one could do worse than her, I suppose." His face lit up with a devilish look, a very non-Fenton type of expression. "She isn't the least one could do, is what I am saying."

Bram's hands curled into fists, and Fenton collapsed into a heap on Bram's bed, holding his sides as he laughed.

"It is so easy to rile you up, Bram," Fenton said when he could speak again. "We know you say you don't wish to marry her, but it seems you also don't wish her to marry anyone."

"Because that is what *she* wishes," Bram replied shortly. He gave himself one last glance in the mirror, then jerked his head toward the hallway that led to the stairs. "We should go. We don't want to be late."

"*You* don't want to be late, you mean," Fenton replied, but was quick to get off the bed and walk behind Bram as he made his way to the front door.

"THE MEETING OF the Stars Above Society is now in session," its president, Mr. Muller, proclaimed.

The Stars Above Society did not have as many

members as the Royal Astronomical Group, nor did it have as much prestige. Which was why Wilhelmina was allowed to attend as a guest, though she was denied membership.

That she knew more about astronomy than half of the society's actual members never failed to irk her, which was another reason to want to publish her paper, if she was ever given enough time from all this Societal traipsing-about nonsense. And she would submit the paper under her own name—not that she hadn't considered submitting under a male pseudonym. But if her work was to be recognized, she wanted to be recognized as well. Free and clear of all pretenses that she was a usual kind of person, content with doing the usual kinds of things.

But to be able to do that, she needed to convince her father and stepmother that she had done everything possible to get herself married off, but had been ultimately unsuccessful.

Alethea had wanted to argue that Wilhelmina should not attend the meeting this evening, but Wilhelmina had been well prepared, presenting her stepmother with a list of the society's members, including their marital status and rank in Society. It was quite a detailed and thorough list, making Wilhelmina glad she had such a scientific mind.

Mr. Fenton Ash, Mr. Townsend's friend, sat on her left, while Mr. Townsend himself sat on her right. They had taken seats toward the back of the room, since the front was reserved for members.

Mr. Townsend's eyes had narrowed when she'd told him of the restriction, and she had been unsuccessful in suppressing her pleasure when it had looked as though he was going to argue the point.

It was only when his friend Mr. Ash had pointed out that the only person who truly cared where they were seated was her, and she did not want to stir up trouble, not after finally getting some grudging respect for her knowledge.

"The first order of business," Mr. Muller continued, "is the submission of articles for the next Stars Above Society journal, *The Stroke of Venus*."

Mr. Townsend began to cough again, while Mr. Ash's head snapped back before he turned to look at his friend, his eyes wide.

When Wilhelmina gave him an inquisitive look, he shook his head and withdrew a handkerchief, putting it to his mouth before averting his gaze to the floor.

"The submission deadline is in four weeks," Mr. Muller said. "We have already accepted a few papers from our members"—at which point he nodded toward the row of gentlemen who sat in the front rows—"and we have limited space."

Wilhelmina wanted to leap up out of her seat and go home to work on her paper at this very minute, only it wasn't as though she would be allowed any peace if she arrived home earlier than was planned.

"You're planning to submit," Mr. Townsend said in a low tone.

She gave a startled jerk in her chair, grateful—for the first time—that she was seated so far back that nobody would notice. "How—what do you mean?" she asked.

He gave her a conspiratorial look. "Because of how your body tightened when that oaf," he said, nodding his head toward Mr. Muller, "announced the deadline."

"You think Mr. Muller is an—no, that's not important right now," she said, her words bursting from her. "I—did you see my notes? How did you know?"

He kept his gaze on her, making her feel as though he could see into her soul. It was uncomfortable, because she had never felt that kind of deep knowing he inspired in her. But it also felt comforting in a way she'd never felt either.

Aunt Flora and Dipper were her family, but neither one of them understood her.

Until now, it had seemed as if nobody understood her.

And yet here he was.

"I know because I know you, Wilhelmina," he said in a low tone. "Because I see you."

"Oh," she said, the exhalation emerging from her lips before she could think. The one person—the only person—whom she could say might possibly understand her, and he was the only person she'd explicitly said she would never have a future with.

Well done, Wilhelmina.

But you don't want a future with him, she reminded herself. With him, with anyone.

Until now, living in a quiet cottage with Aunt Flora and Dipper had seemed like paradise. A refuge from men who wished to tell her how to live her life, simply because she was a woman. Men who refused to admit she could know as much, if not more, than they did about something. Men who assumed she would be happiest if she was married and bore children, and that would be the extent of her life.

"What is your paper on?" he asked, seemingly unaware of how much torment he'd just stirred up.

Damn him. As if his handsome looks hadn't already made her into a flibbertigibbet, his complete and total understanding made her recognize her future self would always be lacking something.

She wished she had fallen on anybody else on that bridge.

Though she truly did not. She was glad she had fallen on him, because now she might have a chance for the life she truly wanted.

And she did want it, she assured herself. It was just that this new idea was taking flight in her head—probably after some time contemplating it, she'd realize that he didn't really understand her, it was just that she was starved for any kind of camaraderie.

"I can explain it later," she said in a whisper, nodding to the front. "It's too complicated for now."

"Of course it is," he replied, but he didn't sound dismissive, or sarcastic, or anything but earnest. It sounded as though he respected her, and wanted to hear what she had to say.

"The next order of business," Mr. Muller said, having apparently gone over the details of the submission process, "is a plan to increase our membership."

Wilhelmina couldn't help but make a noise of disgust.

"Because they won't allow you in?" Mr. Townsend said, accurately analyzing her meaning. Again.

"Mmm-hmm," she muttered.

"We propose a debate on the nebular hypothesis, with one person taking the side of Sir Herschel, and the other side Lord Rosse's ideas. As all of us are aware, the topic is quite controversial, and should stir some interest."

Wilhelmina inhaled sharply.

"What is it?" he asked.

"The Earl of Rosse has just built a new telescope," she explained. "It is my wish to journey to Ireland to see it."

"Ah, so you will admit to what you want," he said smugly.

"That is not the—wait, what are you doing?" she said as he held his hand up and rose from his seat.

"Mr. Muller," he began as all the people in the rows ahead of them turned to look at who was causing the interruption. "If I may?"

Mr. Muller looked peeved, but made a motion to proceed. "You are?"

"Mr. Bram Townsend," Mr. Townsend replied, inclining his head. "I am accompanying Lady Wilhelmina Bettesford to your meeting. She has introduced me to the delights of astronomy."

Wilhelmina furrowed her brow at his words. They hadn't discussed astronomy beyond his retrieving her from a bridge he deemed as being too dangerous to stand on. Though he had bought a book on astronomy, she recalled. And she had pointed Sirius out before—never mind that, she thought hastily.

"And?" Mr. Muller said, sounding impatient.

"Lady Wilhelmina is not a member of your organization," Mr. Townsend continued.

Wilhelmina froze in her seat. He wasn't going to—

"And if I might, I would suggest that instead of debating your nuclear hypothesis—"

"Nebular," most of the attendees corrected.

"Whatever," Mr. Townsend said, waving a dismissive hand, "you should perhaps debate whether people such as Lady Wilhelmina—a fervent fan of the stars—should be admitted to your society. I would imagine such a debate would garner a great deal of interest and would attract many new members, regardless of the debate's outcome."

The proposition caused a collective gasp in the crowd, while Mr. Muller's expression darkened.

"I cannot consider your proposal, sir, since—"

"Hold on a minute," one of the gentlemen seated in the front row said. He rose and turned to address Mr. Townsend.

Wilhelmina recognized him as one of the oldest members of the society, both in terms of his membership and his age. She had never spoken with him, though she had listened appreciatively when he had talked about how far the study of astronomy had come in his lifetime.

"What this gentleman is proposing has merit, Mr. Muller, members of the society. Lady Wilhelmina." He nodded toward Wilhelmina in acknowledgment. "Even if we do not choose to admit members of the fairer sex to our society, we do have to admit that a debate on the topic is certain to raise awareness, and not just because we compare unfairly to our larger counterpart."

The Stars Above Society and the Royal Astronomical Group had long been competitors, with the latter receiving the bulk of financial and prestigious support from Great Britain's wealthy astronomical dilettantes.

Mr. Muller's expression tightened, and Wilhelmina waited as he considered it. "Fine," he said at last, sounding reluctant. "We will put it to a vote. Of the members," he added, shooting a pointed glare toward Wilhelmina's group; whether it was directed at her or Mr. Townsend, she supposed it didn't matter.

"If the vote carries," Mr. Townsend said, "I would like to participate in the debate, as it is my profession."

Wilhelmina found herself leaping to her feet before she knew what she was doing. "As would I," she said, her eyes widening as she realized what she'd just done.

"I'll calculate the odds of each side winning," Mr. Ash added, but he spoke in a tone only Wilhelmina and Mr. Townsend could hear.

"Not helping," Mr. Townsend shot back.

"If you will excuse us," Mr. Muller said pointedly. "All nonmembers should leave the room for voting. To be clear, we are voting on which debate to select—the nebular hypothesis or the right of women to join our group."

Wilhelmina rose, followed by her two companions, and the three left the room, the only people there who were required to leave, since everyone else—all the other men—were members in good standing.

Men I Do Not Wish to Marry:
A Not at All Comprehensive List by
Lady Wilhelmina Bettesford

Mr. Muller, the President (and Oaf) of the Stars
Above Society.

Chapter Sixteen

"What were you thinking?" she said when they had made their way downstairs to the entrance hall.

"I'm fairly certain I know what *I* was thinking, but what were *you* thinking?" Bram retorted.

"Not a lot of thinking going on at the moment," Fenton said in a mild tone.

"Not helping," Bram and Wilhelmina said in unison. Fenton shrugged, then withdrew a notebook and pencil from his pocket and began to scribble furiously.

"You realize that this kind of notoriety will reflect badly on—oh!" she exclaimed, her eyes widening. "Was this a plan to ensure nobody would actually want to offer for me because I'm too scandalous?"

Well, no, he hadn't thought that. But it was a clever idea, so he wouldn't admit he hadn't thought of it.

What he had thought of, to be honest, was that it wasn't fair that she was so enamored of this subject, but the people who shared her enthusiasm wouldn't allow her to participate fully, as she should be able to. That it would render her possibly unfit for marriage in some gentleman's eyes was an unexpected bonus.

So he assumed a smug attitude and nodded in confirmation.

"But if I become too scandalous, Alethea and my father will restrict my activities. So I am not certain your plan is a good one."

Bram felt himself start to bristle at the implication that a plan he hadn't thought of until she'd mentioned it was not a good plan. Yes, he knew he was being ridiculous, but even plans he hadn't thought of deserved a champion.

"None of that matters," Bram said decisively. She looked unconvinced. "What does matter is that you are allowed to join your society. Isn't that what you truly want?"

Her lips tightened, and then she gave a slow nod.

"And this ensures you the opportunity to have it where you didn't before. The whole point of this," he continued, waving his hand in the air between them, "is to figure out what you truly want."

"I want to have my work published," she said in a low tone.

"Pardon?"

"My work. My theories. I've been working on a paper to submit to *The Stroke of Venus*. But all of this," she said, making the same gesture he'd just done, "is impeding my ability to do so. Not just because of having to attend parties and be too tired from speaking with people to settle down to work, but because Alethea has ensured almost every minute of my day is filled with something. Loads of meaningless, banal somethings that are apparently what I should care about more than anything actually useful."

He could hear the pain and disappointment in her voice.

"So if we succeed, and you are able to join the society, will that give you a better chance to have your work published in the journal?" He couldn't bring himself to say *"The Stroke of Venus,"* it was just too likely he'd burst out into giggles, like when he'd first discovered his interest in the opposite sex.

"I don't know," she admitted. "I suppose it might. Though again, that notoriety might mean that Alethea and my father decide I am too rebellious in my attitudes, and try to constrict me more than they already do."

"Or the notoriety will establish you as an intelligent woman who is determined to get what she seeks." He raised a brow. "There is always more than one way to approach a problem."

"Spoken like a true barrister," Fenton interjected, startling them both. Bram hadn't realized his friend had even been paying attention; his focus had appeared to be entirely on his notebook.

"Gentlemen and lady," Mr. Muller said, speaking from the top of the stairwell, "we have taken a vote, and if you would like to return, we can announce the results."

Wilhelmina took Bram's arm, marching them both up the stairs with a brisk determination, as Fenton followed behind.

"WELL," WILHELMINA SAID as they exited the building, "that was not what I'd expected."

The society had voted to allow the debate. Mr. Muller had been clearly unhappy about the results, but he had to abide by the membership's majority. Not only that, but they were willing to allow Wilhelmina to argue her position, while Mr. Townsend argued the other side, despite neither of them being members of the society.

Wilhelmina surmised that that way they could avoid any possible negative outcome because they weren't actually arguing the points themselves, they were just hosting the discussion.

"What side will you be taking, my lady?" Mr. Ash asked.

Wilhelmina jerked her head up, the idea not having even occurred to her. "You mean—am I arguing for the equal inclusion of anybody who wishes to join versus a restrictive policy that excludes people who might have a fervent interest in the subject?"

"Precisely," Mr. Ash replied, his expression puzzled, as though not understanding why Wilhelmina was clarifying.

"I am, of course, equally capable of either opinion," Mr. Townsend interjected.

Wilhelmina considered it, then startled herself by saying, "I will take the side that is opposed to allowing women as full members."

"I rather thought you might," Mr. Ash said in a mild tone.

If she weren't so concerned with her own thoughts, she might spare one for Mr. Ash, who seemed to continually offer the most unexpected words at the most unexpected times.

She wondered if he and Mr. Townsend were friends because reacting to whatever Mr. Ash might say would keep Mr. Townsend's arguing skills rapier sharp.

"You're driving out with Lord Paskins?" Mr. Townsend said, perhaps trying to one-up Mr. Ash on the unexpected conversational swerve department.

Though Wilhelmina doubted even the verbally adroit Mr. Townsend could do that.

"Yes, tomorrow."

"Do you have a plan for how to deal with him?" Mr. Townsend continued. "Because he has indicated he wishes to pursue you, and I know you do not wish him as a husband."

Wilhelmina snorted. "No, he is probably ahead of Edward Oxford, but behind Henry Prince."

"Do you have a comprehensive list, then?" Mr. Ash inquired.

Wilhelmina shook her head as she chuckled. "No, because I don't wish to marry anybody. As Mr. Townsend knows."

"But who would be on that list besides myself, if you were to make one?" Mr. Townsend asked.

Wilhelmina gave him an amused, if also annoyed, glance. "I think the list would be Men I Do Not Wish to Marry rather than Men I Would Marry—the latter would have precisely one name on it."

Mr. Townsend looked startled, but Mr. Ash merely asked, "And who would that be?"

"My dog, Dipper," Wilhelmina replied, laughing aloud at Mr. Townsend's expression.

Men I Do Not Wish to Marry:
A Not at All Comprehensive List by
Lady Wilhelmina Bettesford

John Hatfield.

   Mr. Hatfield was a confidence man, one who leveraged his own absolute confidence into tricking everyone he came in contact with. Not only was Mr. Hatfield a forger, but he presented himself as belonging to certain famous families, securing credit for his immoderate lifestyle. What's more, he presented himself as not being married when he absolutely was, committing bigamy on top of his other crimes. No, thank you.

Chapter Seventeen

"My lady," Bram said, inclining his head toward Wilhelmina's stepmother.

Lady Croyde was dressed in yet another gown that made her look like a pastry—an entirely impractical pastry, one ornamented with icing and cream and weird little brightly colored bits.

The kind of pastry Bram longed for when he'd been in the Home, but had realized wasn't worth all the longing when he'd finally gotten a chance to try one.

Lady Croyde was not nearly as insubstantial as a pastry, however; standing in the salon, her sharp gaze took in her surroundings, noting how closely Lord Paskins sat next to Wilhelmina, which Bram had also noticed.

And then promptly wanted to correct. Preferably by tossing him out the window, since Bram doubted he could succeed in persuading Lord Paskins to depart peacefully. Not when there was money involved, and not when Lady Wilhelmina herself was so appealing.

Not that Bram thought Lord Paskins shared the latter opinion.

When Lord Paskins looked at Lady Wilhelmina, Bram surmised, he saw pounds and pence, not her warm, intelligent gaze or wide mouth.

"You're looking rather ferocious," Benedict remarked, making Bram start.

"Why are you—?" he began, but Benedict cut him off.

"You asked that we create some sort of gentlemanly barrier around the lady," Benedict said, nodding toward Lady Wilhelmina, "and I know Theo and Fenton have already done so, but neither I nor Simeon have. So I'm here."

"Thank you," Bram said stiffly, wishing Benedict didn't look quite so much like he could be the mysterious aristocrat's son—handsome, commanding, and completely comfortable, no matter what setting he was placed in.

"May I introduce you to Lady Croyde?" Bram said, noticing that Wilhelmina's stepmother was regarding them with a questioning look. "Mr. Benedict Quintrell, this is Lady Croyde. She is our hostess. Lady Wilhelmina is her stepdaughter," Bram added.

"Yes, she couldn't be my actual daughter," Lady Croyde said in a trill, "because she is five years my senior!"

Bram didn't have to look over at Wilhelmina to confirm her reaction. He had heard her sharp intake of breath, even though likely nobody else in the room had. It wasn't the first time, he imagined, that Lady Croyde had made the same remark.

What was he doing, being so intently focused on her? He was ignoring his work, which he usually did too much of, he had forgotten Benedict's request, and he was fantasizing about tossing men out of windows.

And, on top of it all, he hadn't even started to read the next book for their monthly meeting. He didn't even recall what it was.

"It's *Love in Excess; Or, The Fatal Enquiry*," Benedict said.

Had Bram spoken aloud? He must have. He was so distracted he couldn't even keep track of his words. Or Benedict was just that intuitive.

He needed to remember his goals, one of which was not to get married to anyone. Another of which was to at least start the next book club book.

Even though the first goal made him want to argue with himself, never a good sign. It was just one step from there to deciding he'd been wrong, and Bram was never wrong. At least, not that he would admit.

And *Love in Excess* just seemed like far too pointed a choice.

"Are you going to introduce me to Lady Wilhelmina?" Benedict asked, sounding impatient.

Bram took another exasperated look at Benedict's generally handsome elegance and nodded. The two made their way to the other side of the room, where Lady Wilhelmina was seated with Lord Paskins, a pained expression on her face.

"Good afternoon, my lady," Bram said.

Lord Paskins's expression tightened, and Bram darted a quick glance toward the nearby window. "Good afternoon, my lord," he continued. "My lady, allow me to introduce my friend Mr. Benedict Quintrell."

Benedict executed a flawless bow as Lady Wilhelmina murmured something polite.

"Would you like to join us?" she asked brightly, gesturing toward two seats a few feet away.

Bram moved the chairs closer before one of the attending footmen could do it, dragging his opposite Lady Wilhelmina, Lord Paskins on his left. Benedict sat on his right, facing Lord Paskins, a pleasant smile on his lips, his expression smoothed into what the rest of them called his Benedict Face—diplomatic, calm, without revealing anything that might be going on inside his mind.

Bram thought, belatedly, he should have mentioned Lord Paskins was one of the gentlemen Lady Wilhelmina did not wish to marry, but it seemed Benedict had figured that out already.

"Lady Wilhelmina went driving with me yesterday," Lord Paskins said, sounding smug. "She commented that my new horses were—what did you say?"

"Attractive?" Lady Wilhelmina replied, sounding hesitant. "At least they were a lovely dark brown, both of them, and they had all the requisite limbs."

Lord Paskins's expression grew even tighter, while Bram suppressed a laugh.

"I am not much of an expert on horses," Lady Wilhelmina added, unnecessarily.

"My lord," Benedict said, "do you have a large stable?"

Lord Paskins launched into a lively discussion of how shrewd he was when it came to buying horseflesh, how he always managed to pay the least amount for the best quality, and then, finally, a list of all the horses he owned. Bram stopped paying attention when Lord Paskins went into a thorough description of Blaster's markings.

He rose under the guise of getting some tea, then moved his chair so it was angled behind Lady Wilhelmina's. He sat as Lady Wilhelmina twisted her body so she could see him.

"This is dreadful," she said in a whisper. "I didn't know it was possible for there to be so much conversation about horses."

"It's more like a monologue, but I understand your point," Bram replied. He scooted his chair closer, so close he could see the fine bones of her collarbone.

He'd never realized the collarbone would be something that would fascinate him, and yet here he was. His fingers tingled with wanting to touch her there, feel her skin and the flutter of her pulse.

Put his mouth there softly, gently, as he licked his way up her neck. Perhaps ask her to explain the difference between stars and planets as he undid her gloves. Pulled the pins from her hair. Slid her gown off her shoul—

"Bram."

Benedict's voice intruded on his fantasy, and he suppressed a groan of frustration.

"Pardon?" he said instead, trying to make his expression as smooth as possible, and not as if he was calculating how many buttons ran down the back of her gown.

"I've just been telling Lady Wilhelmina about our monthly gathering."

"Fiction," she sniffed.

"I don't like fiction myself much either," Lord

Paskins interjected. "All that making things up. It's not proper."

"Because otherwise it would be nonfiction," Bram said through gritted teeth.

"What have you read, my lord?" Benedict asked smoothly, no doubt aware that Bram now wanted to thwack Lord Paskins over the head with a copy of the biggest work of fiction he could find—*The Pickwick Papers*, perhaps, or *Les Misérables*, both of which were quite hefty tomes—and *then* fling him from a window.

"Nothing," Lord Paskins replied, sounding proud. "I peruse the papers, of course, and sometimes what they publish is fiction"—at which point he looked arch, as though he'd said something clever—"but nothing more than that."

"And you, my lady?" Benedict continued. "What works of fiction have you tried?"

Lady Wilhelmina frowned in thought. She looked ferociously adorable, even though she was likely about to say something irksome.

"You know," she began slowly, "I realize I might have dismissed the genre because of a few bad experiences." She looked at Bram. "When we first met—that is, when we met at the auction," she said, coloring. Likely because the first time they met was on that bridge, only neither one of them was supposed to mention it, at least not in public. "When we met at the auction, you said you read a lot of books, and I might have been rude."

"Inadvertently, of course," Lord Paskins exclaimed, glaring at Bram as though it was his fault.

"No, quite vertently, I believe," Lady Wilhelmina replied earnestly. "The books I was given to read were books I did not choose for myself. The books I chose for myself were entirely different, and I think I resented the formers' existence for keeping me from the latter."

"Bram is the most well-read of us," Benedict said, gesturing toward him. "He can recommend something, if you want to try again."

Her eyes lit up, and he felt an answering lift in his heart.

Only he wasn't supposed to be responding to her like this. To be thinking anything about her beyond helping her out of her situation.

What had become of the man who'd insisted he was too busy for romance? Too busy to bother finding a wife, that his life was fine as it was?

The man who knew that if he ever did marry, he'd have to marry someone unremarkable. Someone who wouldn't disturb his peace in the slightest, nor cause anyone else to question his character, despite his birth.

That had all seemed fine enough, before.

He hadn't known until he'd met her what his life was lacking.

And now that he'd seen her, he couldn't unsee any of it.

Men I Do Not Wish to Marry:
A Not at All Comprehensive List by
Lady Wilhelmina Bettesford

Victor Hugo.

Any gentleman author who thinks I have time to read his thousand-page book greatly undervalues my time. I don't care how extraordinary it is, or how extraordinary he thinks it is. If he can't say it in fewer than one thousand pages, I don't want to read it.

Chapter Eighteen

"Drat," Wilhelmina said, frowning down at the page.

Not that the book wasn't good; it was. And that was the problem.

Mr. Townsend had written down a list of fiction recommendations, and she'd headed to her favorite bookshop to purchase a few. The proprietor had been startled to see her head away from where the scientific tomes were kept, and she had to explain—defensively, if she was being honest—why she was interested in buying novels when she had never been interested before.

And now here she was with Mary Shelley's *Frankenstein*, devouring its pages as if she didn't also have her own paper to write and a debate to prepare for.

She nearly jumped out of her seat when a knock came at the door.

"Come in," she called.

Mrs. Windham appeared, followed closely by Jones, her maid.

"That Mr. Townsend is here," Jones said.

"If I could just have a word—?" Mrs. Windham asked, glancing between Wilhelmina and Jones.

Wilhelmina hastily put the book down, shoving a hair ribbon into the pages to mark her place. "Of course," she replied. "Do you mind if Jones makes certain I look—?" she said, her words trailing off when she realized what she was saying.

I want to look as good as I can for the man I will not be marrying.

I say I am not a flibbertigibbet, and yet here I am.

"Yes, of course," Mrs. Windham replied.

Wilhelmina accepted, for the moment, her flibbertigibbet status and went to sit at her dressing table. Mrs. Windham perched on the end of Wilhelmina's bed, Wilhelmina meeting the other woman's gaze in the mirror.

"It is Mr. Townsend I wanted to ask about," Mrs. Windham said, her voice higher than usual. "I—who are his people?"

Wilhelmina frowned. It wasn't as though it was a secret, but it felt odd to be gossiping about the gentleman waiting downstairs. But Mrs. Windham wouldn't ask if she didn't have a reason to.

"He is an orphan," she replied, noting Mrs. Windham's pinched expression as she spoke. Was the housekeeper as much of a snob as Wilhelmina's father? She wouldn't have thought so, but then Mrs. Windham had been spending a fair amount of time with Alethea—perhaps the latter had confided the earl's concerns about Mr. Townsend.

"His people are his four fellow orphans, and the five of them are closer than actual siblings," Wilhelmina continued. "Is that what you wanted to know?"

Mrs. Windham nodded and rose. "I'll just go see what Lady Croyde might want for the dinner menu," she said, bustling out of the room.

That was odd, Wilhelmina thought. But if she toted up all the odd people and odd questions that she encountered on any given day she would have no time for anything else.

Jones, meanwhile, was fussing with her hair and not improving the situation, Wilhelmina thought ruefully. "That's enough, Jones," Wilhelmina said.

"I could just—" her maid said, gesturing to a piece that was dangling down instead of being neatly pinned back.

"No, it's fine," Wilhelmina said, shaking her head, the errant hair tickling her face. "I'm coming down."

He wasn't in the foyer, which must mean that their butler had put him in the salon. She ran down the stairs, turning the knob and entering the room, leaving the door ajar as was proper.

Dipper followed exultantly behind, apparently delighted that she was no longer sitting in her room with her nose in a book.

Mr. Townsend whirled around at her entrance, his handsome face lighting up with a smile, which grew even wider when he spotted Dipper.

Wilhelmina tried not to be jealous of her own dog.

"You're the famous Dipper," he said, reaching down to scratch Dipper's ears. Dipper immediately leapt up onto Mr. Townsend's trousers, though he was too small to do more than touch his shins.

"Down, Dipper," Wilhelmina ordered.

Her dog did not listen to her.

"Down, Dipper," Mr. Townsend said, and her dog—*her* dog—immediately complied.

"Hmph," Wilhelmina said with a sniff, but she was smiling.

"I came to ask if you would care to go for a walk

with me. I would take you for a carriage ride but I do not own a carriage," he said, a wry look on his face.

She let out a surprised laugh. "Well, thank goodness, because if you were going to lecture me on how you chose your horses or what kind of style your carriage is—"

"You mean if I were to Paskins you?" he interrupted, his voice sounding amused.

She had to laugh again. "I imagine that trait is not limited to Lord Paskins, Mr. Townsend."

He advanced toward her, his eyes focused on her face. "Call me Bram. Please."

She swallowed, startled by the intensity of his request. "Why? I mean, yes, it seems that we should be on a first name basis, given that—" And then she felt herself color, and his smile grew deeper.

He took her hands in his, and both of them stared down at their interlaced fingers. It felt both comfortable and terribly uncomfortable to hold hands with him. But not uncomfortable in an unpleasant way—more like her entire body was made up of excited prickles.

All of which she knew was due entirely to him.

Somehow, he'd stirred her imagination—and other parts of her—so that all she wanted to do was go turn the key in the lock and fling him down on the sofa so she could experience what she thought she never would.

How was it fair that people—ladies, specifically—were only supposed to feel the heady rush of passion with someone you'd pledged to be with for the rest of your life? Shouldn't ladies be allowed to sample, as men were? What would happen if it turned out you and your life partner were incompatible? Or he changed over the course of your time together?

"It's not fair," she muttered, still looking down at their hands.

"What isn't?" he asked, sounding genuinely curious. "Because if there is one thing I excel at, it is bringing justice." He stroked her skin. She wasn't wearing gloves, and the contact sent a sizzle down her spine.

Between the prickle and the sizzle, she was in danger of becoming her own star nebula.

She raised her face to his, staring into his blue, blue eyes. It was so unfair for him to be so handsome and so kind. It made her think of things she knew she didn't want.

But she did want right now.

"If only there was a nearby terrace," she said softly.

"What isn't fair, Wilhelmina?" he demanded. "You're trying to distract me with your terrace talk, but I won't be dissuaded. Barristers are very good at sticking to the subject, I assure you."

She exhaled. She hadn't realized she was trying to deflect—but he'd seen it. Not only that, but he'd called her out on it, which made her even more keenly aware of how intelligent and thoughtful he was.

"I can't just be who I am," she said at last, her voice just above a whisper. "I have to pretend to be someone who enjoys going out in Society when I do not. I have to pretend to be someone who likes needlework, when I do not. I cannot admit that all I truly want to do is—is live somewhere where I can see the stars."

His eyes searched hers, and she felt a lump come to her throat. This was not what she was supposed to do—she was supposed to flirt with him in public, look suitably appealing without looking too appealing, and deflect all marriage proposals.

She wasn't supposed to be admitting things she'd barely admitted to herself.

"Isn't that why we're doing this charade?" he asked, sounding entirely reasonable. "So that you can do what you want, which I gather is stare up at the sky for the rest of your life?"

She gave a snort of laughter, then her humor subsided.

"What do you want to do right now, Wilhelmina?" he asked. He still held her hands. She didn't want him to let her go.

She took a deep breath. "I want to go on a walk with you, Bram."

HE NOW KNEW what she wanted, or at least he thought he did—if only he could say the same about himself. Before meeting her on that bridge, he would have said he was, if not happy, at least content. He had his work, he had his friends, and he had ambition.

He'd be a judge eventually, if things went as he wished. He'd have a wife eventually, one who supported his work, not worried about her own. One who would behave properly.

But now he realized what he *didn't* have. Her. Or someone like her—a partner to share kisses and conversation with in equal measure. A person who would mock him as well as his friends did, but also soothe him when he was hurting.

And though he'd said "someone like her," he had

the unfortunate feeling that he would be happy with *only* her. And now that he knew what she wanted, which was a life entirely unencumbered by marriage, or gentlemen, or any kind of the usual course for a well-bred female, he knew he could never have her.

They were walking along the same path they'd taken when he'd agreed to her stepmother and father's scheme, but now her hand was looped through his arm, and she was looking around interestedly, her expression warm and enthusiastic.

Her maid trailed behind them, holding Dipper's leash. Wilhelmina hadn't wanted to bother with requiring her maid's presence, but then Alethea had appeared and announced that now that Mina was actually popular—something that seemed to startle both of the ladies in equal measure—more people would be paying attention to what she did, so she couldn't do anything to possibly cause a scandal.

Bram hadn't missed the mischief sparkling in Wilhelmina's eyes at that comment.

The day was temperate but not too sunny. The sky was mostly gray, not holding a promise of rain but definitely not promising sunshine either.

And then Bram realized, as he glanced up at the sky, that that was what his life would be like: no rain, but no sunshine either.

"What are you thinking about?" she asked. "You just gave the heaviest sigh, and if you don't wish to walk with me, you could just say so."

He snorted as he shook his head. "No, it's quite the opposite. Not only do I want to talk with you, Wilhelmina, but I wish we were alone so I could"—

tell you how I feel about you—"practice our respective kissing skills."

"Oh," she said softly. "I didn't think you needed practice."

Well, that warmed his soul. And other places, he had to admit.

"I haven't had much," he said. "Practice, that is."

She stopped short, jerking her head around to stare at him. "What? You mean someone like you"—she gestured, her hand indicating the entirety of him—"doesn't have experience? What does that say about us mere mortals?"

"I don't know what you mean," he replied. "It hasn't come up before now. At least not much."

"How is that even possible?" she asked. "Unless you are so particular—oh my gosh, are you so particular? And then I forced myself on you and perhaps you didn't—"

"I think we've established I wanted to kiss you as much as you wanted to kiss me, Wilhelmina," he said, a note of laughter in his voice. "There was no forcing, I promise you."

"Oh. Well, thank you," she said in a quiet voice.

"But speaking of practice," he said quickly, "we should practice our debating skills."

"Won't that be cheating? I mean, we are going to debate one another, so we're going to practice debating one another?"

"It's not cheating, but I can see your point. We'll need to keep the argument fresh for the actual debate, but we can practice debating other topics." He turned to grin at her. "Topics like which pets are better, dogs or cats?"

"Dogs, of course," she shot back.

"What is the best kind of nut?"

"The best kind of—it has to be almonds," she replied, with nearly as much authority as she'd answered on the pets question.

"Fenton swears it's the Brazil nut," Bram said, shaking his head in dismay.

"I think we can and should all agree the Brazil nut is the least good nut." She shared a smile with him. "I think practicing my debate skills with you would be excellent. And Alethea and my father cannot object, since the debate will bring me to more notice, particularly since I am espousing the other side. That women should not be allowed into the SAS, for example."

"SA—oh, right," he said. "I'd forgotten."

"We can practice at my house," she continued. "It will be entirely respectable, and it will only add to the fiction that you are courting me."

He felt his chest get tight. It *was* a fiction, there was no possible way he would be allowed to court her for real, even if he wanted it. Even if she wanted it. But the most important point of all of it was that she did not want it; she had been absolutely clear on that point.

"And," she said in a sly tone, "perhaps we can practice some other things. If I am going to achieve what I want, I will not be doing any of that. I mean, I suppose I could—"

At which point Bram's chest tightened more, since he already wanted to defenestrate the imaginary people she'd be kissing in the future.

"But I don't think I will, since I'll be too busy and it would be altogether too complicated."

He exhaled, not realizing he'd been holding his breath while she was speaking.

"Do you know," she said brightly, "how much I am looking forward to the next few weeks? I never imagined, when I went to look at the stars, that I'd be discovering all these new adventures."

"Though I do not recommend hopping up onto bridges in search of more of them," he said dryly.

"Not without a Mr. Helpful to assist, that is," she replied, taking his arm again.

Men I Do Not Wish to Marry:
A Not at All Comprehensive List by
Lady Wilhelmina Bettesford

William Mathias.

Mr. Mathias, a Devonshire resident, constructed a wall to prevent people from riding or walking across a footpath leading from his house to the local village. When the wall was torn down—repeatedly—he constructed an iron gate. Mr. Mathias's gate was likewise demolished, and he was jailed and fined, again repeatedly, for his refusal to allow progress to, well, *progress*. Can you imagine what being paired to such a stubborn fool would be like?

Chapter Nineteen

You will need to take the dog out at least once a day."

"A dog gets better treatment than a wife," Wilhelmina muttered.

"Pardon?" Mr. Townsend—Bram—said. She heard Jones smothering a giggle behind her.

"A cat does not care if it has a name, it will not come when called," Wilhelmina replied. *Also a better situation than a wife's, who can be summoned at any time.* This time, she kept her thoughts to herself.

"A dog's bark can disturb your peace."

"A dog's bark can warn you when something is wrong," she retorted.

He frowned, then held his hand out in explanation. "What we're doing now is not debating. We're arguing."

"What's the difference?" Wilhelmina asked, genuinely confused.

They were in the newly redecorated and decluttered salon, which meant there was room for Mr. Townsend to pace, which apparently he needed to do when debating. Or arguing. She didn't know which.

She sat on the sofa, watching him walk up and down in front of her. There were worse views.

He planted himself in front of her, a stern look on his face. "An argument is one where we trade opinions back and forth. A debate follows a formal order of logic."

She tilted her head to look up at him. "So if I were to list the reasons a dog is better than a cat, leading up to my ultimate conclusion, that would be a debate?"

He smiled down at her in satisfaction. "Yes. Exactly. Do you want to try again?"

They'd been at it for a half hour, far longer than Wilhelmina would have ever imagined discussing pets.

"Jones," she said, "would you mind fetching us some water?" She turned to her maid, who was already getting up. "Just leave the door open. We'll be fine."

"Yes, my lady," Jones said, darting a quick, admiring glance toward Bram.

"Take your time," Wilhelmina called after her. "Go ahead and have some tea, if you want." The maid scurried down the hallway.

Bram's eyebrows lifted. "Take your time?" he said, knowing Jones was out of earshot. "Did you have some other activity in mind while your maid is away?"

Wilhelmina waved her hand. "I just don't see the point of boring Jones to tears because it is too scandalous for us to be left alone. I know she likes to talk to Cook, and I know she'd much prefer having a cup of tea in the kitchen to sitting here listening to us. Plus I am too self-conscious with having someone else around."

"What will you do when we're in front of all the members of the SAS and whomever else comes to watch the debate?"

She shrugged. "I don't care about any of them. I don't know them. Jones works for me, but she also has her own preferences and opinions, some of which I know. So I am more likely to be aware of those when I am here than when I am in front of a group of strangers."

"It does make an odd sort of sense," he said.

Well. *That* was irresistible—having a gentleman admit she was right. As though she didn't already find him irresistible.

"Speaking of the debate, what will you do if you cannot march up and down while you make your points?" she said, gesturing to the path he'd taken.

He immediately sat down next to her, stretching his arm over the top of the sofa. "I can debate sitting down as well."

She looked over at him, raising an amused eyebrow. "And what about other distractions?" Because once he'd asked what she had in mind she couldn't keep herself from thinking of that . . . and that . . . and some more of that.

"What do you have in mind, my lady?" he said, his eyebrows waggling. She burst into laughter at his knowing look.

"How about this?" she said, getting up to her feet only to sit back down facing him, her legs on either side of his body.

He glanced toward the door instinctively.

"That's part of the distraction," she said, putting her hands on his shoulders. His strong, strong shoulders. "It takes a few minutes to boil water for tea, for Cook to persuade Jones to try a scone or two, and then a few more minutes where they gossip before cleaning up. You've got approximately ten minutes to state your opinion."

"My defense," he corrected.

She rolled her eyes. "Fine. Your defense. Go ahead and present your ideas while I attempt to distract you."

His hands slid around her waist, and then he drew her closer. She could see the dark stubble and sharp planes on his face. Up close, his eyes were dazzling—so blue she thought she could swim in them.

"Or you might distract me," she murmured.

"I like your plan. Go ahead." He looked at the clock that stood in the corner. "Ten minutes."

"Go!" she said, then lowered her mouth to his neck.

"What I will prove today, ladies and gentlemen," he began, "is that the SAS should not be restricted in its membership for any reason other than that the person is not interested in the sky."

"Excellent start," she said against his skin.

"Thank you. I like how you are starting as well," he said.

"I haven't even started," she said, then licked his skin right below his jaw. He inhaled sharply, and his hands tightened on her.

She bestowed soft kisses along his jawline, relishing the feel of his stubble on her mouth.

"If we are to impose arbitrary rules on membership," he continued in a strained voice, "why not decide that people with brown hair cannot join? Or that you must own a cat. Since we know cats are the superior pet."

By now she was up to his ear, and she took his lobe in her mouth and bit gently, at which he squirmed under her. His hands were moving up so that his palm was now on her breast, and she shifted forward so she could feel the warmth and pressure of his hand.

"Cats are not the superior pet," she said, sliding her hands down his arms and then putting them on his chest. She ran her palm under his jacket on his shirt, wishing she had more time to explore underneath everything.

But she only had—"Five minutes, right?" she said.

"Mmm-hmm. And I've only just begun."

"As have I," she said, the same feeling of discovery and excitement she'd only before had when looking up at the sky.

"Limiting membership means that the SAS will not have the benefit of the intelligence, expertise, and money that potential members would bring. Why restrict a group to only one type of person when all types of people love astronomy?"

She couldn't kiss him on the mouth—that wouldn't be fair, since he wouldn't be able to speak at all—but she could feel the strength of his chest under her fingers as she kissed him very close to his lips, but not so close he couldn't still talk.

"You are dangerous, Wilhelmina," he said in a low voice. "But you cannot distract me. Not when I have a point to make."

It was on the tip of her tongue to tell him she could feel his point just under her bottom when they heard the sound of footsteps and she leapt off him, sprinting to the chair to the side of the sofa.

She met his gaze and grinned just as Jones returned, followed by Mrs. Windham, who held a tray.

The latter froze when she saw the two of them, and Wilhelmina did a quick furtive analysis of their respective clothing. All was fine, though his jacket was still pulled to the side, but that wasn't anything more than usual.

"Where should I put this, my lady?" Mrs. Windham said, her voice strained.

Wilhelmina gestured to the table in front of the sofa. "Just there, thank you." She exchanged a questioning glance at Jones, who shrugged as if to say she didn't know.

"I had Cook send up some of her biscuits, my lady," Jones said. "And tea, as well as water."

"Thank you, Jones, that was very thoughtful."

Wilhelmina poured tea for both of them, secretly delighted he took his tea the same way she did: with a dash of milk and a lot of sugar. Jones settled herself back in the corner, discreetly picking up a book—likely a work of fiction, Wilhelmina presumed, though that thought wasn't tinged by her usual disdain.

She was changing, she had to admit. Changing because of him, and also because of herself. Figuring out what she wanted and what she did not want.

What she wanted was to do more discovery of the Bram Star. How his skin would feel, what it would be like to have him touch her in certain places without fabric between them. What would please him, and what would please her.

An entirely scientific, albeit salacious, study.

BRAM SHIFTED IN his seat, hoping he could disguise his erection until his cock realized it was time to calm down.

He had not expected this Wilhelmina, although perhaps he should have, given that she had initiated their previous encounters. But this Wilhelmina—this bold, confident woman who knew precisely what she wanted to do—was entirely alluring. Even more so than he'd thought before, and he'd been fairly smitten before.

He was in so much trouble. And in for so much heartache. Because while he could imagine that she would want to do more of this type of activity again, he knew she didn't want to do it forever.

It would end, and he would know just how Simeon and Theo frequently felt. At least he would be able to ask them for advice on how to mend his broken heart?

Because, hell and damnation, he'd gone and fallen in love with the woman who'd fallen on him.

The irony was not lost on him.

He loved her. This ridiculous, impulsive, intelligent woman who didn't want anything—or anyone—to interfere with her plans for her life.

Who would accept a kiss but would refuse to accept a commitment.

"Mr. Townsend?" He heard her voice as if from a distance, and realized he was wasting the precious time he had left with her—by thinking about her.

Again, the irony was not lost on him.

"Pardon, my lady?"

"*Frankenstein* by Mary Shelley. One of the books you recommended. I have been reading it, and I have to say I find it absolutely compelling."

She sounded astonished, as she had following the opera. Her tone held a note of wonder as well, and a feeling of agony swept over him—agony because if she fell in love with fiction, as he did, then she would be even more of an ideal partner.

It was ridiculous. He was the dispenser of justice, the person whose tremendous skills of argument were going to ensure this woman—this strong, brave, and yet circumstantially limited woman— was not going to have to do something she did not want to.

And he didn't know when her enthusiastic spirit might emerge. If he was a judge, if he was supposed to have a wife who epitomized respectability, he couldn't very well marry a woman who had her own thoughts about . . . about *everything*.

"*Frankenstein*," he said abruptly, willing himself to focus on her now rather than how they would be in the future. "It is fascinating, and I find myself examining the layers of the story every time I read it."

"You've read it more than once?" she said. "I can't imagine—"

"You've read your books on astronomy more than once." It was a fact, one he didn't need confirmation of.

She nodded slowly, but her expression was confused. Adorably confused, if he had to put an adverb on it.

"But fiction—you read the story, and then you know the story?"

His mouth curved into a slow smile. "My lady, a well-written book is about far more than just the story itself. It is about life, and common experiences, and underlying human concerns. Reading a book more than once reveals more of its beauty—rather like looking at a bouquet of flowers from all sides. It's not possible to comprehend the depth of a book, an excellent book, from just one reading."

"Oh," she said softly. It was clear she was absorbing his words, and once again, he felt awed that this intelligent woman, who was obviously as stubborn as he, was willing to listen to him.

As he was willing to listen to her.

"So what have you discovered in reading *Frankenstein*?" she asked, sounding genuinely curious.

"My experience will be different from yours. I don't want to color your opinion of the work before you've finished it."

"I've nearly finished it," she admitted. "I stayed up far too late reading, in fact." Her expression was rueful. "Perhaps it's not for the best that I have found other things to occupy my brain—there is no possibility of my learning how to do needlework or exchange idle talk with random people in my social sphere."

He gave her a wry look. "It is not as though you were planning on doing that anyway."

He heard her maid smother a snort of laughter.

She drew herself up in an exaggeratedly proud attitude. "No, you are correct. But I did not anticipate being so concerned about a literal monster when I agreed to read your recommendations."

He held his hands out in a gesture of surrender. "That is what great literature does, my lady. It makes you care about the monsters."

She considered that also, tilting her head in

thought. "I suppose it does. Though I still will never have sympathy for Lord Paskins."

"That is because there is no possibility of an author choosing to write about someone like Lord Paskins."

She grinned in response.

Men I Do Not Wish to Marry:
A Not at All Comprehensive List by
Lady Wilhelmina Bettesford

Someone who will not try something because they've already decided they don't like it. Yes, I am looking at myself.

Chapter Twenty

*L*urid is far too mild a word for this book," Benedict remarked, sounding almost stuffy.

It was the evening of their monthly meeting, and Bram had barely finished reading *Love in Excess*, which was not usual for him. Usually, he devoured the book within a few days of their deciding which one it was to be, and he'd be the first to be discussing it.

Not now, however. When he wasn't paying close, but not too close, attention to Lady Wilhelmina, he'd been thinking about her, and strategizing a way for her to live her happiest life without having to resort to subterfuge.

Thus far he had not been successful.

"Is that what your life is like, Simeon?" Theo asked in a deceptively mild tone of voice.

All of them knew better—Theo was the most sharp-tongued among them, and his rapier wit had gotten him in plenty of trouble through the years. It was only because the man who'd taken him in was so wealthy and so indulgent of his son's fierce intellect that he hadn't been punched in the nose more often.

As it was, he had gotten punched enough that his

father had gotten a private boxing tutor for him, which meant that Theo was as lethal with his fists as he was with his hands.

"No," Simeon replied smoothly, refusing to take Theo's bait. "My life is far more orderly. And I would not make the mistake of thinking one lady in my bed was another one entirely. If you're too much of a lout to be able to discern the essential differences between people—" He shook his head.

"I imagine that kind of life would be far too complicated," Fenton said, making everyone turn their heads toward him.

"How so?" Bram asked.

From Fenton's expression, the answer was obvious, and they were all idiots for not understanding. He sighed. "Because you're always having to remember who you think you're in love with and putting off all those people who think they're in love with you."

"Just like you," Simeon and Theo said in unison, each looking at the other.

Benedict raised his hands between them. "Stop. We're not talking about the two of you, for once. We are discussing the book."

"We should talk about Bram," Fenton said.

"About me?" Bram said, surprised.

Fenton nodded. Again, his expression revealed he thought it was all perfectly obvious.

Most people in the world were slower to comprehension than Fenton—except when it came to things like common niceties and idle conversation. He was abysmal at any of that.

"Bram has fallen in love with Lady Wilhelmina," he stated.

There was a stunned silence, and then Theo tilted his head back in laughter, Simeon following soon after. Benedict met Bram's gaze with a look of concern on his face, and Bram himself felt simultaneously relieved and appalled.

"You're not denying it," Benedict observed.

Bram inhaled deeply, then shook his head. "No, I'm not."

When the laughter had subsided, Theo directed a piercing look toward Bram. "What are you going to do about it?"

"You're not going to instruct me on anything," Bram said sternly.

Theo's expression got puzzled for a moment, then he uttered another bark of laughter. "Not that. Though if you do need assistance, there's no one better than either me or Simeon."

"Assistance in what?" Simeon asked, glancing between Theo and Bram.

"Nothing," Bram said shortly. "And the answer is the same for what I am going to do about it— nothing. The lady has made it very clear she does not wish to get married." His throat got tight. "I will not ask her to do something that she is so clearly against."

"What about your famous powers of persuasion?" Simeon prodded. "Surely you could give her a dazzling display of your rhetoric and she would swoon into your arms. Or something like that," he finished with a shrug of his shoulders.

"You are quite persuasive when you want to be," Benedict said in his solemn tone. Bram felt momentarily proud—it was difficult to get a compliment from Benedict—then gave an emphatic shake of his head.

"No. I might have grown . . . fond of Lady Wilhelmina—"

"In love with," Fenton corrected.

"But that gives me even more incentive not to make her miserable."

"It might be miserable being married to you," Theo mused. Fenton flung a piece of cheese at him, which bounced off Theo's chest and onto the floor. "But we would be terrible best friends if we just allowed you to foreclose on your future."

"No," Bram said, even more firmly than before. "You cannot."

Images of what it would be like if they were to have a future together danced tantalizingly in his head—the two of them working in their respective offices, joining one another for tea and then dinner, discussing what they'd been doing and how much they'd learned that day. Then retiring to the bedroom, where the two of them could learn even more, exploring one another's bodies, and what made each of them gasp in pleasure or bite their lips in delicious agony.

"You're overruled," Benedict said, startling Bram out of his reverie. "That look on your face—"

"We owe it to you to try," Fenton said, surprising everyone. Fenton wasn't the type of person who tried; he just *did*, regardless of what anyone else thought.

Bram folded his arms over his chest and looked at each one of his friends in turn. "Fine," he said at last. "But I won't help you. I can't do that to her. It has to be something she wants, not that I persuade her into. And it's over if she says it's over."

"Are you going to tell her, then?" Simeon asked interestedly.

"Tell her what? That I've fallen in love with her and my four idiotic friends are going to try to convince her to marry me when that's the last thing she wants? I don't think so."

"Oh good," Simeon replied. "It would be harder if she knew." He paused as he thought. "Not impossible, but harder."

"And what will happen—if you four are successful, which I highly doubt—when she has a burst of inspiration about some astronomical theorem in the middle of a dinner party or something? What then?"

Fenton gave him an incredulous look. "You adjust, Bram. It's what people in love do."

And how did he know? Had Fenton ever been in love himself? If he had, none of the others had known about it.

"We have to persuade her first," Benedict reminded them. As though already mentally preparing a checklist of what to do and when to do it.

"You four are ridiculous." Though a part of him wondered if they would be able to do anything to make any of this better.

And it reminded him that even if he ended up miserable and loveless, he wouldn't be alone—he had his chosen brothers, and they would always support him.

That, at least, was a bit of comfort.

"MINA!"

Wilhelmina froze, a few feet from the front door. She'd thought she could get away, just for a few hours, to do some research at the library, but Alethea was far too aware of everything that went on in the house.

She turned, trying to look as innocent as possible. "Yes?" She pointed to the door. "I was just going to—"

"I know what you were going to do," her stepmother cut off. "And it was not going walking in the park in your best outfit, or taking some time to rest so you look as good as you can this evening. Which means that you cannot do it, whatever it was."

"I might have been going for a walk," Wilhelmina objected.

"Not without your maid, and not in that outfit," Alethea sniffed. "Come into my sitting room, we need to have a talk."

Wilhelmina glanced down at what she was wearing. It wasn't her best gown, but it also wasn't her worst.

Her stepmother's standards were clearly a lot higher than her own. Unfortunate that didn't also apply to more important things such as who you might have to spend the rest of your life with.

She trailed Alethea upstairs, walking into her sitting room, which was adjacent to her bedroom. Alethea had redone this room as well, and now it was a fairy-tale paradise—all soft shades of pinks, beiges, and gently hued whites.

Wilhelmina sat gingerly on a remarkably silly-looking piece of furniture, a tufted sofa that would barely fit two people.

Imagine if Mr. Townsend and his length tried to sit on it . . . but that just brought up ideas of other things that could be done on the sofa, and she should not be thinking about any of that.

Not when Alethea was looking so stern.

"What is it?" Wilhelmina asked.

"You and Mr. Townsend appear to be spending far too much time together."

Wilhelmina blinked, then shook her head as if to clear it. "I'm sorry—what? Wasn't it your scheme that he pretend to court me?"

"There is a difference between pretending to court and monopolizing," her stepmother replied.

"Shouldn't you be having this conversation with Mr. Townsend, then?" Wilhelmina asked, annoyed.

Alethea waved a hand in dismissal. Even her gestures were elegant, Wilhelmina noted sourly.

"He is supposed to pay court to you, but you do not have to always receive his attentions. It would look odd if he were to stop or ease his pursuit, but if you were to spend time with other gentlemen, that would be preferable." Alethea gave her a hard look. "You are supposed to be engaged by now."

Wilhelmina pondered whether what she'd wondered might happen was already true—that Alethea was with child, and was even more eager for her stepdaughter to be out of the Croyde household. Alethea could have her room for her children, and wouldn't have to deal at all with Wilhelmina except during prearranged visits.

If that was the case, no wonder Alethea wanted her gone so much. Did her father feel the same way? And how terrible was it that she didn't know?

She and her father had never been that close, but since his marriage they'd gotten further apart.

She cared for Alethea, in a way—her father was so much happier than before. She hadn't seen how lonely he was. But how awkward and potentially awful would it be if she managed not to get married, only to feel even more of an outsider in her own home until she could finally leave? While she watched her father, Alethea, and their children love one another? And belong?

"Well," Wilhelmina said at last, "I will see if I can find other gentlemen who would like to pay as much attention to me as you've persuaded Mr. Townsend to." It still stung that her father and Alethea thought that she needed a pretend suitor, but she had to admit the plan was working—she had many more dance invitations than before, and flowers were routinely delivered when they never had before.

Granted, she couldn't remember most of the gentlemen, but they were out there somewhere. They just paled in comparison to Mr. Townsend.

Just thinking about him—of what they'd done when Jones had gone to fetch tea—made her all warm and tingly inside.

"Excellent," Alethea said, sounding pleased. "Your father and I will be expecting at least one of them to make an offer by the time we remove to the country."

Wilhelmina felt her throat constrict. Now she had an actual deadline by which they expected her to have committed to spending the rest of her life with someone.

How could she possibly do that?

Aunt Flora had told her so many times not to let it happen. No matter how charming the gentleman might appear, it didn't change the fact that if the two of them got married, one of them—him—would have all the rights, and the female in the equation had none.

It would be stifling. She wished, perhaps for the

first time, that she had friends other than Flora and Dipper. That there were other women of her age and in her situation she could ask about it all.

For the first time, she didn't think she had all the answers.

"MY LADY," SHE heard a voice say at her side.

She, her father, and Alethea had gone to yet another party that evening, with Wilhelmina determined to—well, she wasn't sure what she was determined to do. Just what she was determined not to do, which was to engage anyone's interests enough for them to think they had a chance at marrying her.

She turned, surprised to see Mr. Ash. As far as she knew, Mr. Ash was the least sociable of Mr. Townsend's friends, and that even included Mr. Townsend, who looked uncomfortable at these types of parties.

Unless he had snuck away to kiss someone—or more accurately be kissed—in a dark garden or something.

She should not be thinking about that.

"Yes, Mr. Ash?"

Mr. Ash frowned, looking confused. But he had spoken to her first, had he not?

"Call me Fenton. Mr. Ash is not—well, I don't know who that might be."

Now it was Wilhelmina's turn to look confused, but she dismissed it, shrugging as she replied, "Fine. Mr. Fenton, then."

"Just Fenton," Fenton said.

"Fenton. Was there—?" Short of being incredibly rude and demanding to know what he wanted—

besides correcting her on the use of his name—she didn't know what to say.

Well, it wasn't as though she worried about making certain this gentleman liked her. Even though she would like it if he did—he seemed very kind.

"Was there something you wanted?" she asked, hoping nobody was in close enough proximity to hear her.

"Yes!" he exclaimed, as though surprised by his own answer. "Yes, there is. I was thinking—that is, we were thinking—that you might wish to practice your debating skills."

Thoughts of what had happened last time she tried to debate made her cheeks turn bright red.

"Yes?" she said hurriedly, hoping he wouldn't notice the change in her complexion.

"And we thought we could all assist," he said. "Myself, Bram, of course, Benedict, Theo, and Simeon." He gave her a piercing look, one very much at odds with what she'd previously thought of him—that he was adrift in his own thoughts. She wondered how many people underestimated him on any given day. "You can see for yourself how good Bram is at his profession, and perhaps you can learn from him."

"Was this Mr. Townsend's idea?" she asked.

Fenton shook his head. "No, he doesn't know about it."

"But—?" she began, but then stopped. Clearly Fenton and the others had some sort of plan and also clearly they wished to help her prepare for the debate, so she wouldn't question the former too much for fear of losing out on the possible instruction.

Though she hadn't quite decided if she wanted to win or lose the debate. If she won, she'd have argued against allowing people such as herself to join the SAS; if she lost, she might have as little chance to join by virtue of the fact that she'd lost.

No matter what happened, however, she would be showing that a woman could engage in the same pursuits as a man did—arguments, looking at stars, and the like. That had to mean something, didn't it?

And, she realized, spending time with these gentlemen would fulfill Alethea's demand that she spend time with people other than Mr. Townsend. Alethea didn't have to know that Mr. Townsend was also there; just that Wilhelmina was with gentlemen not named Mr. Townsend.

"Excellent," she said at last. "When do we start?"

Fenton's expression was gleeful. "Why not tomorrow? Benedict said he would be free to come collect you."

"Collect me? Where will this take place?"

Fenton waved a nonchalant hand. "At the Orphans' Club. That is, the Peckham Club." He frowned. "Though you'll have to wear gentleman's clothing to enter," he said. "That won't be a problem, will it?"

The myriad complications of locating, donning, and then leaving the house in gentleman's clothing immediately leapt to her mind, but she only shook her head. "No."

She'd figure it out. It felt like an adventure, and it would be something she'd learn from on top of that—the very best kind of adventure.

"Wonderful. Benedict will come pick you up at three o'clock." Fenton peered over her head. "Oh, and there's Bram! I'll be off. Don't mention this plan to him, will you?"

Wilhelmina shook her head again, and Fenton darted away, leaving Wilhelmina feeling as though she'd been blown about by a very strong wind.

"Good evening," Bram said, bowing.

"Good evening, Mr. Townsend," she said, sounding a little breathless.

Men I Do Not Wish to Marry:
A Not at All Comprehensive List by
Lady Wilhelmina Bettesford

Jack Sheppard.

Mr. Sheppard was a criminal who began committing small thefts, and then escalated to grander ones. Not only did he not repent for his crimes, he was able to escape prison several times after being arrested. While this kind of clever ability might seem appealing at first, imagine what he would do if he was to be trapped in a marriage to a woman he no longer loved?

Chapter Twenty-One

"*Y*ou did what?" Bram said, blinking at Fenton, who stood opposite, a pleased expression on his face. Bram had danced with Lady Wilhelmina only once, having to cede the field to a seemingly unending supply of young gentlemen her stepmother introduced her to.

And Fenton was at the party also, which was very odd.

"We're going to sneak Lady Wilhelmina into the club so we can assist with her training for the debate. Honestly, Bram, you should be happy. Not only will you get to spend time with, may I remind you, the woman you love, but you will also be helping her with something important to her."

"But sneaking her in—if she's discovered—"

Fenton shrugged. "Then her reputation will be ruined and nobody will want to marry her, which is her purpose, isn't it?"

Bram closed his eyes and rubbed his temples. The musicians playing in the corner of the ballroom now sounded incredibly loud. "That limits her options, Fenton. If she's ruined, she'd have no choice but to remain unmarried."

"You'd marry her, wouldn't you?" Fenton asked in a reasonable tone of voice.

"Yes, but I don't want to *have* to marry her." *Also, if she marries me, she assumes the burden of my birth. I can't do that to her, not unless it is her free choice.*

It didn't pass his notice that he wasn't as adamant himself about not wanting to marry her because she would disrupt his life.

He might welcome the disruption. But she wouldn't.

"Have to marry who?" Simeon said. He stood to Fenton's right, looking dashing and elegant and casually artistic.

"What are you doing here?" Bram said.

Simeon waggled his eyebrows. "Helping," he replied, no doubt trying to sound enigmatic. And, Bram thought sourly, succeeding.

"Did you know about this plan?" Bram said, gesturing toward Fenton.

"Is it a plan where someone has to marry someone else?" Simeon asked. "If so, no, I don't. If it's the one where Lady Wilhelmina comes to the club, that one I know about."

"You two are unbelievable," Bram said, turning his eyes upward in exasperation.

"I am, aren't I?" Simeon said in a smug tone of voice. "And if you'll excuse me, I have a lady to dance with."

He strode away, heading directly toward Lady Wilhelmina, while Bram forced himself not to run after.

Simeon was just too damn charming.

"This is my dance, I believe," Mr. Jones said, bowing low over Wilhelmina's hand.

She had met Mr. Jones for the first time earlier that evening, and she was surprised that he'd asked her to dance. But then she'd seen him with Mr. Ash and Mr. Townsend—though she should start calling him Bram, shouldn't she, given how many times their lips had been pressed against the other's—so he must have been another one of the orphans.

He was audaciously and vibrantly handsome, dressed in a not quite British gentleman way. More as though he was visiting from a foreign locale and deigning to appear in his finery to dazzle Society. His coat wasn't black, it was dark blue, as were his trousers. His waistcoat was a multitude of colors, colors she would never have imagined putting together, but somehow worked.

It was his appearance that made everything come together, however. His hair was a rich brown, and wavy, falling just so over his brow. His smile was sly and knowing, and his eyes—more deep rich brown—held a wicked glint.

He held his arm out for her, and she took it, meeting Bram's gaze as Mr. Jones escorted her to the dance floor.

She couldn't help but feel a thrill at Bram's narrowed eyes, as though he was perturbed his very attractive friend was escorting her onto the dance floor.

Though that kind of response was precisely the kind of response Aunt Flora had warned her about—Flora's husband had been an incredibly jealous sort, so much so that Flora had to tell him precisely what she was doing at any given hour so he knew she was not seeing any other gentleman.

Would Bram be a jealous husband?

She would never know, she told herself.

"Bram has spoken of you," Mr. Jones said.

Wilhelmina was trying to count the steps—one two three, one two three—so didn't absorb his words at first. "Spoken of me?" she asked, stumbling, but thankfully not stepping on his toes. Did he talk about how often she seemed to run her lips onto his? Dear Lord, please don't let him be talking about that.

"He mentioned the astrological society, and the debate," Mr. Jones replied, easily negotiating graceful dancing with complex conversation.

She envied that.

"Ah," she said, relieved. Things she could discuss in casual conversation without fear of setting her cheeks on fire.

"And that you were hoping to join," Mr. Jones continued.

"Yes, which is why he proposed the debate. I'm still not certain that it is the best idea—" she said, before missing her count and landing on the side of her foot, making her falter.

Mr. Jones caught her, a wry smile on his mouth, and she had to admit she felt a little breathless—not just because of the misstep, but also because he was so undeniably good-looking. She'd gone through twenty-four years of her life without having any gentleman pay attention to her, so having it now in such abundance was a bit overwhelming.

Though as she reflected on it, there was only one handsome gentleman she wished she could do more than dance with—and he was currently glowering at her and her partner from the edge of the ballroom.

Mr. Jones caught the direction of her gaze, and his smile widened. "It seems that Bram would like to debate *me*—perhaps posing an argument between his fist and my face." He sounded positively gleeful, and Wilhelmina had to wonder if that was how they normally dealt with one another.

"Have you read *Frankenstein*?" she asked hurriedly, hoping to change the topic from the one where Bram was jealous of her.

Though it did feel pleasant.

"Yes, though the idea of cobbling together an entity out of scraps wasn't appealing." He raised an eyebrow. "It would have been far preferable to make a creature that was aesthetically pleasing."

"*That* is your criticism? That the monster wasn't attractive enough?" She spoke without thinking, then realized her tone was sharp.

Mr. Jones didn't seem to mind at all; in fact, he met her gaze and grinned, his white teeth nearly sparkling. "I can see why you and Bram get along so well."

"Why?" she blurted, then rolled her eyes at herself. She didn't need to know what this incredibly charming, if wrong-opinioned, gentleman had to say.

"Because you are both so argumenta—oh, Bram, there you are."

Bram stood in the middle of the dance floor, an unmovable rock in the sea of swirling people.

"Did you want something?" Mr. Jones asked, a wicked tone in his voice.

Wilhelmina shook her head, then stepped out of Mr. Jones's embrace and took Bram's arm, leading him away from the dancers. She spotted doors to the outside, and quickened her pace, still holding on to him.

Bram's chest was tight. He'd strode up to them as if
he had a right to, an urgent clarion sounding in his
head: "Mine."

But she wasn't his. She wasn't going to be his, not
even if all of his friends somehow managed to persuade her she might actually like him.

For God's sake, he already knew she liked him.
She'd kissed him, multiple times, and clearly enjoyed
his company.

But he couldn't have her and also give her what
she wanted most: her freedom. Never mind that he
refused to give her what he'd vowed never to
give anybody: the stigma of his birth.

Damn it, he was going to have to be one of those
self-sacrificing heroines in the Gothic romances he
liked to read late at night. Denying themselves for
the good of the other person. A premise he'd always
scoffed at.

Until now. Damn it.

"Did you have something to say, or did you just
want to march onto the dance floor and glare?" She
gestured back toward the room. "If it's the latter, we
can return so you can resume your glaring."

"I was not gla—" he said, then stopped, clamping
his lips shut.

She gave him a knowing look. "You know you
were. It's fine, didn't we agree we would be honest
with one another?"

Suddenly Bram's cravat felt as if it was constrict-
ing his neck. He wasn't being honest with her. If he
was, he would tell her that he had true feelings for
her, feelings he wished she might reciprocate.

Enough of that. If he kept up this line of thinking

he'd have to go find a menacing castle and hole up in it as he waited for interfering ghosts to appear.

"I suppose I was glaring," he said slowly. "I thought perhaps it would help the charade if other people thought I was jealous of the attention being paid to you."

A total lie.

Though the jealousy part wasn't; he wasn't comfortable with someone as suave and assured as Simeon spending time with her. What if Simeon went and fell in love with her, too? He could see it happening, Simeon fell in love constantly, even more than Theo.

"Ah," she said, sounding surprised. "I appreciate the effort, but I doubt anyone is paying that close attention to me."

I am, he wanted to growl.

Instead, he shrugged, saying, "You would be surprised."

"Your friend Mr. Ash asked me to come to your club to practice for the debate." She stepped closer to him, putting her hand on his arm and looking up into his face.

God, she was lovely.

"Is that all right with you? I get the feeling Mr. Ash tends to just"—and she made a vague gesture in the air—"do what he wants without checking with anyone first."

He barked out a laugh. "He does do that. Very clever of you to gauge that after only a few meetings with him."

She raised her eyebrows. "So you are saying I am intelligent and observant, Mr. Townsend?"

She fluttered her hand in front of her face. "You flatter me."

"As only you would wish to be flattered," he replied with a bow. "Most ladies want to be told they are beautiful and dance wonderfully."

"You know I don't dance wonderfully," she said pointedly. Her cheeks turned pink. "And you needn't answer the other," she said.

"I think you're beautiful, Wilhelmina," he said in a low tone.

"I think we had better go out onto the terrace," she said, her color heightening even more. "I feel as though I need some air."

"Air?" he murmured, tucking her hand through his arm as he began to walk with determination toward the doors leading outside. "Is that what they're calling it these days?"

She laughed, a forthright, proud, and confident laugh that made all the people in their immediate vicinity turn to look at her. She met their gazes directly, but she clutched tighter to him, and he felt an urge to wrap his arm around her shoulders and draw her closer.

To protect her, even though it was clear she didn't need protecting.

"ALETHEA—MY STEPMOTHER—told me I should stop spending so much time with you," she said as they walked onto the cool terrace.

There were several other people out there, and Wilhelmina nodded vaguely in their respective directions. She didn't know who they were, and she knew herself enough to know she didn't care. The people she cared about she cared fiercely about, but that was very few: her father, Aunt Flora, Dipper, Alethea, she supposed, and now Bram and his brotherhood of orphans.

"Wasn't the whole point that we should spend time together?" he asked, sounding confused.

"That's what I thought!" she replied. "Apparently it's more complicated than that. So I imagine she will be very happy I danced with your Mr. Jones."

"Just don't fall in love with him."

That surprised her.

"I won't," she said firmly. How could she fall in love with anyone else when he was right here? "If I fell in love with anyone, it would be you. And that hasn't happened, so I think I am safe." She spoke with a certainty she most certainly did not feel, though she didn't dare even think that it wasn't a certainty.

"Yes, thank goodness," he said shortly.

"But that doesn't mean I don't wish to do more of those things we do together," she said. "If you feel the same."

She made a vague gesture in the air, feeling her face get hot all over again.

Was there a way to tell a person one wished to kiss them without turning into a furnace?

She didn't think so.

"You mean—?" And he made an equally vague gesture, a knowing smile on his mouth.

"Precisely," she replied.

HE TOOK HER arm and led her into the corner. Unlike the other terrace, this one didn't have convenient steps leading to a secluded area. But it did have a tree overhanging the corner where they stood, and if they positioned themselves well enough, they wouldn't be seen.

If they were seen, then her reputation would be irrevocably ruined and they would have to marry. He couldn't hope for that, even though a part of him did.

He was not being logical, at least not where she was concerned. Not anymore.

Not, in fact, since he'd rescued her from that bridge.

He guided her to the shadowy depths offered by the tree's thick leaves.

"It's still not safe enough here," he muttered. He couldn't risk it. Couldn't risk her. She had no idea what it was to be tarred with such a disreputable reputation, even though it was only the circumstance of one's birth. Which, he wished he could point out to the many disapproving people, happened when he was far too young to have any say in the matter.

"If I don't care about my reputation, why should you?" she asked.

Because I love you.

"Because if you are ruined instead of married, you will never be able to make your own choice about your life."

"What if I choose to be ruined?" she said, speaking in a light tone. She couldn't know what it was like—the talk, the stares, the outright disdain.

"You have no idea, Wilhelmina," he said slowly. "You cannot even speak like that. It's—" Images of the numerous times he'd been mocked or over-looked because of who he was ran through his mind.

"Fine," she said, sounding grumpy. "We'll have to figure out another way."

Chapter Twenty-Two

"Well, this is an adventure," Aunt Flora said, her tone excited.

She, Wilhelmina, Mrs. Windham, and Dipper were in the attic where all the detritus from the house was stored—there was much more than there had been before Alethea. Now there were boxes and storage chests filled to bursting with knickknacks, small tables, a variety of chairs, and bins of drapery and other assorted fabrics.

There were also a few storage chests filled with Lord Croyde's clothing, which was why they were in the attic in the first place.

Mrs. Windham had caught them on the way to the attic and insisted on helping, concerned—she said—that Aunt Flora would fall or Wilhelmina would catch ill.

She kept shooting odd glances toward Wilhelmina, but Wilhelmina presumed it was because Mrs. Windham was worried in general about her. As it happened, Wilhelmina hadn't seen much of the housekeeper since Alethea had arrived—Mrs. Windham was working harder than ever.

"How elegant do you wish to be?" Aunt Flora

asked, withdrawing an evening coat from one of the chests. Dipper poked his nose into the chest, then immediately withdrew it and released a powerful sneeze.

"I'm not going to the opera or anything," Wilhelmina replied. If only she was. Though sneaking into the Peckham Club was far more of a unique experience, and she had to admit to feeling a thrill at the whole enterprise.

"That is unfortunate," Aunt Flora replied, folding the coat and putting it back into the chest. "Why did your father keep all these anyway?" she asked. "Not that they aren't helpful, but he might've given them to his valet or donated them to charity."

Wilhelmina's mouth twisted. "I wonder if he and my mother thought they might have another child. A boy." Because right now the earl's title was to go to a distant cousin, unless he bore a male heir.

A much more likely possibility, now that he and Alethea were wed. And presumably doing the things married people did—which she would not think about again, thank you very much.

Mrs. Windham made a strangled noise, and both Wilhelmina and Aunt Flora made concerned noises, which Mrs. Windham waved away.

"How about this one?" Aunt Flora said, withdrawing another garment from the chest.

She handed it to Wilhelmina, who shook it out, releasing a cloud of dust that floated in the air. Wilhelmina stepped back, holding the coat at arm's length and assessing it.

It was made of excellent material, a little dated, but not so much that it would be noticeable. The good thing about gentlemen's clothing was that it was less easy to identify a particular era, at least for the clothing from this century. Any earlier and she might have had to confront the possibility of wearing some sort of frock coat made in a bright fabric with embroidery all over it.

This coat was dark, though it was hard to see if it was black or blue. She slid it on, shaking her arms through the sleeves and adjusting its fit. The coat was too big, of course, but again, it wasn't so much that it would be obvious to a casual viewer.

"Are there trousers in there, too?" Wilhelmina asked, peering at the chest.

"Indeed," Aunt Flora said, sounding triumphant.

"I can pin everything up so it fits better," Mrs. Windham said.

The trousers matched the coat, it seemed, and Wilhelmina shrugged out of her day dress to try it on. She pulled her chemise up to her waist and drew the trousers up—they were loose in the waist, and too long, but those elements could be easily fixed.

"I'll wear my own shirt-blouse, and find a hat somewhere. Father won't miss one of his work hats if I take it for just one night."

Aunt Flora turned to her, a curious expression on her face. "You said you will be donning a disguise, but you haven't said what for." She gave Wilhelmina an expectant look.

"I'm infiltrating a gentleman's club," Wilhelmina said.

Mrs. Windham coughed again.

Aunt Flora's eyes widened. "Well! Doesn't that sound exciting!" And then her expression narrowed. "Just make certain you don't end up in a

compromising situation. You know how gentlemen are."

Wilhelmina gave her a half smile. *No, I don't,* she
wanted to say. *I don't know how they are, but I plan to.*

"Let me take these to my workroom," Mrs. Windham said when Wilhelmina had removed everything
again. She left the two of them alone, with Wilhelmina
hoping her aunt wouldn't pursue her line of thought.
Unlikely, given her aunt's usual line of thought, which
was scattered, if one was being generous.

But if Aunt Flora knew what Wilhelmina was
planning on doing, she'd be terrified. Aunt Flora
thought all things male were to be feared, and Wilhelmina was beginning to suspect that not every
gentleman was as awful as Aunt Flora's husband
had been.

But she still couldn't feel comfortable with the
thought of aligning oneself with the same person
for the rest of one's life—fine, so it was very possible
a prospective husband for Wilhelmina wouldn't be
abusive like Aunt Flora's husband had been, but it
was still very likely that his very presence would
constrict her. He would expect her to have children,
and keep a home, and not want to stare through
telescopes or go to random earls' country estates to
stare through even bigger telescopes.

But before she settled into her confirmed spinster
life, she was going to partake of the advantages normally only accorded married women.

After she infiltrated a gentleman's club.

BRAM LEAPT OUT of his chair every time he heard a
noise outside their regular meeting room.

"You should just stay standing," Fenton observed.

Bram growled at him, but he followed his advice.

"How will she get in?" Bram said suddenly. "She's not a member, obvio—"

"Benedict will tell them she is his young cousin. Everyone knows Benedict would never lie."

"Ah," Bram said.

Eventually, the door opened, and she stepped in, glancing wide-eyed at everyone in the room with her gaze landing, finally, on him.

Benedict accompanied her, and Bram felt a wash of jealousy come over him; not that Benedict had interest in her, but anybody who got to spend time with her that wasn't him made him envious. They'd arranged to have Benedict fetch her since her step-mother wanted her to keep company with other men—Benedict was still not acceptable as a suitor, given his birth was as suspect as Bram's, but he was a different specimen of unacceptable, which had to count for something.

She wore nondescript gentleman's clothing, a battered hat on her head. Her hair was presumably tucked into the hat, since none of it hung around her shoulders. She'd tilted the hat forward, no doubt to disguise her face even more, but now she swept the hat up and off her head, her hair tumbling down from its prison.

Her expression was delighted, and he was pleased he and his friends had been able to make her so happy, even if for a short period of time.

"Well," she said, rubbing her hands together, "so this is a gentleman's club."

"Welcome, my lady," Simeon said, making a sweeping gesture as he bowed.

She grinned.

"We've got a seat for you just here," Theo said, indicating a chair set in front of the fireplace. There was a small fire burning in the hearth; it was a warm summer night outside, but Fenton argued every time that they have a fire because it was far friendlier than staring at ashes.

Sometimes Bram wasn't certain what kind of logic Fenton used, just that it was unfamiliar to his own reasoning.

She went to the chair, giving a last look toward Bram, and sat herself down, taking special care to adjust her coat. "I don't know how you men do this," she muttered, and Bram laughed aloud.

"We don't know how you manage all those skirts and underthings," Simeon said, a hint of mischief in his tone. "Perhaps after we work on your debating skills you could teach us about them."

"We won't be doing anything of the kind," Bram burst out, making his four friends howl in laughter as Lady Wilhelmina gave him a wry look.

"You know he just said that to annoy you," Fenton observed.

"And it succeeded!" Simeon crowed.

"Can we get to the point of us being here?" Bram said, his tone impatient.

"We won't be debating pets or nuts, will we?" Lady Wilhelmina asked, glancing from Bram to the rest of them. "Is this what you do here usually?"

"Pets or—? No," Theo said, giving his head a decisive shake.

"We usually discuss books," Bram explained. "This evening we are not."

"Oh!" she exclaimed, her face brightening. "Did

you discuss *Frankenstein* during one of your evenings?"

"We did," Bram replied. "Did you—are you still liking it?" he asked.

"Very much so," she said. "I do not think the point of the book is that the monster is made of stitched-together parts," she said pointedly, shooting a quick glance at Simeon, who smirked in reply.

"The two of you are debating what?" Benedict asked, his calming tone clearly trying to stem the conversation back toward their purported topics.

"Whether or not ladies should be allowed to join the SAS—the Stars Above Society," Lady Wilhelmina said.

"Only we cannot practice that specific topic since it would be cheating," Bram added hastily.

"Goodness knows we cannot possibly aid you in *cheating*," Simeon said dryly.

"It wouldn't be fair!" Wilhelmina protested.

Bram felt his chest warm at how they shared those behavioral norms as well.

"Fine, fine," Simeon replied, waving his hand at them. "We will have you debate another topic in preparation for your grand one."

"I know," Fenton said, popping up from his seat. "What if we were to debate marriage?"

"Debate . . . marriage?" Bram echoed, wishing his friends weren't quite so determined to assist him while also not being very good at hiding it.

Subterfuge was foreign to Fenton, whereas it was second nature to Simeon and Theo.

"Excellent idea," Benedict said.

Benedict was also not good at subterfuge, Bram realized.

"Marriage?" Lady Wilhelmina said in a faint tone.

"Nothing any of us wish for, mind you," Benedict said in a far too hearty tone. "Now, my lady, which side will you take?"

Bram held his breath as she considered it.

"I would like to take the side against marriage," she said at last.

Making his heart hurt.

"And I will be in favor, then," Bram replied, trying to sound as though he agreed.

"Excellent. Let us stage the scene," Simeon said, dragging one of the small end tables to the middle of the room. "This will be your podium. Theo, move that chair over here?"

Theo obliged, dragging one of the wooden chairs, not the grand upholstered one, to sit beside the table.

"And the other?" Simeon said, jerking his chin toward Fenton. Fenton looked perplexed for a moment, then spotted the first chair's match and brought it to the other side of the table.

"We will be the judges," Simeon announced, going to sit on the sofa that was in front of the long table where their food was usually placed.

Benedict nodded, sitting beside Simeon, while Fenton and Theo found their own seats.

"Uh—" Bram said.

"Hardly an auspicious start," Simeon commented.

"Shut up," Theo commanded.

"Well." Bram straightened. "Marriage is a long-standing institution that benefits both partners."

He heard Wilhelmina utter a derisive snort.

"No rebuttal from the other side until it is your turn," Simeon said sternly. Lady Wilhelmina did not look chastened, but at least she didn't say anything else.

"As I was saying, marriage is a long-standing institution that benefits both partners."

If only he could persuade her, even if he didn't win the debate tonight. If only he could persuade himself.

Men I Do Not Wish to Marry: A Not at All Comprehensive List by Lady Wilhelmina Bettesford

The type of man who responds to your polite query "How are you?" with a twenty-minute talk on just how he is.

And then doesn't ask how you are.

Chapter Twenty-Three

Marriage is a long-standing institution that benefits both partners.

Wilhelmina sat in her chair, her mind spinning from all the new experiences: wearing trousers, being in a gentleman's club, being alone in a room with no fewer than five men, each of them interesting in their own distinctive way.

It was hard, in fact, to concentrate on what Bram was saying, and focusing on what he was saying—being able to respond to what he was saying—was the whole point of the evening.

So she tried to forget about the atmosphere, the company, and her clothing, and focus on the debate.

A topic she had very strong opinions about.

What had Bram said? *An argument is one where we trade opinions back and forth. A debate follows a formal order of logic.*

"A marriage consists of an agreement between parties to join their lives together."

"It's not a merger, Bram," Mr. Osborne said.

"The same applies to you," Mr. Jones admonished. "No talking."

"And if the marriage is an equal one, both parties get as much as they give." He glanced toward her, his expression inscrutable. "A marriage can enhance the wealth of both wife and husband, even if the two are not themselves wealthy. For example, an intelligent wife will be able to see what the husband could do to increase his business where he might not have realized an opportunity. The shared love and other benefits"—at which he turned bright red, and all of his friends began to laugh—"will make both partners happy."

"Both, Bram?" Mr. Osborne said with a quick, knowing glance toward Wilhelmina, who now found her own cheeks starting to heat.

"Yes, both," Bram said firmly before Mr. Jones could remind Mr. Osborne about the no-talking thing.

Well. At least she knew if they managed to accomplish what she wished to, she would have as much pleasure as he would. Not that she didn't already know that; she knew Bram was considerate, and kind, and found inequality in anything distasteful.

"A marriage that is between two people who respect and like and love one another can only make each partner happier than if they had stayed alone."

He took a deep breath, then looked at her. "You have the floor, Lady Wilhelmina."

Wilhelmina rose, smoothing the lapels of her jacket and drawing her hair back away from her face. Bram sat down in his chair, clasping his hands loosely between his legs. He regarded her with an intense curiosity, a look that said he was paying the utmost attention to what she was about to say.

It wasn't what she was used to.

At least, not until she'd met him. And his friends, she realized.

How had she existed for so long without having anyone want to hear what she was saying? Who believed her thoughts and opinions were worth something?

Aunt Flora listened, sometimes, but she was more likely to seize on something that related to her own life than to empathize with anything Wilhelmina felt.

Dipper always listened, of course, but he seldom had anything to offer in return.

What would it be like if she had friends as he did? People to listen, to converse with, to debate against?

It did feel lonely being her, she had to admit. Which she hadn't realized until recently. To feel as though no one truly listened.

But from the first time she'd met him, on the Blackfriars Bridge, he'd paid attention to her. To her words, to her opinions, to her thoughts. Even if he disagreed and wanted to argue with her—he listened.

It was intoxicating.

She took a deep breath and began to speak. All five of the men were quiet, their eyes on her as she presented her argument.

BRAM WITHDREW A handkerchief from his pocket and wiped his hands. He was normally implacable, even in the face of the most difficult cases, but this evening was different.

Because she was here.

His palms were sweaty, and his clothing felt itchy and uncomfortable, even though he knew it fit perfectly, thanks to Simeon and Mr. Finneas.

He hadn't made the best presentation for his side—he knew that—but he hoped she'd gleaned some of what he felt during the course of his speech. He couldn't tell her how he felt, he wouldn't put her under that obligation, especially since it came with an illegitimate gentleman.

But if she knew—if they could just partner up, as he'd described in his argument, and figure out how to make it work.

He thought they could come up with something. Maybe.

"Marriage is an antiquated notion that benefits the gentleman in the partnership far more than the lady."

Well, so much for convincing her as to anything.

She cleared her throat, looking as though she was trying to avoid his gaze.

"I cannot speak for the benefits the gentleman might receive," she continued. "But I can speak to what a marriage purports to offer a lady." She held her hand up as she began to tick off her points. "One, a marriage provides protection. Because other gentlemen are not to be trusted." Her eyebrow rose. "But how is a lady to know that the gentleman she chooses is to be trusted?"

Another tick of her finger. "Two, a marriage can only be instigated at the gentleman's request. What of the lady? If she feels that the gentleman would be a good pairing for her, why can't she say so? Instead, she's got to make it as clear as she possibly can without seeming forward." An eye roll accompanied that statement, added to with a chorus of mumbled agreements from everyone but Bram.

"And three, how is either party to know that the person you select at the time is going to be the person you wish to be with forevermore? You are not allowed to change your mind, even if the situation makes you miserable." A memory of something crossed her face, and he regretted not asking her more about her mother. Presumably there was something there that made her aware of what time could do to a relationship.

"There are many more items I could cite, but I am running out of fingers and out of time. Thank you for your attention."

She executed a bow, as though she truly was the gentleman she was garbed as, and sat back down in her seat, looking expectantly at the judges.

There was a moment of silence, and then Fenton began clapping his hands enthusiastically. Simeon and Theo joined in, both of them shooting sly glances at Bram, whereas Benedict dipped his head in a slow nod.

She flushed, and lowered her head, and Bram thought he saw her eyes get bright, as though they were teary.

"Thank you, gentlemen," she said in a soft voice when the applause had died down.

Benedict rose out of his chair, holding his hand out to Wilhelmina. "I think you will do splendidly at the debate, my lady. He will comport himself well, of course," Benedict continued, nodding to Bram, "but you will be a worthy opponent."

"Thank you," she said again.

Bram went to the table and poured out a measure of wine, handing her the glass. She took it, their fingers touching as their gazes met, and Bram felt an almost overwhelming rush of emotion. Goddamn it.

He had found the person he wished to spend the rest of his life with—only because he loved her so much, he couldn't tell her.

Even he couldn't argue his way out of that predicament.

Men I Do Not Wish to Marry:
A Not at All Comprehensive List by
Lady Wilhelmina Bettesford

Henry VIII.

Chapter Twenty-Four

"Say it again," Simeon said, holding Bram's cravat just out of reach.

Bram gritted his teeth. "Simeon Jones is the handsomest, most charming man in the world." He folded his arms over his chest. "Now will you help me?"

It was the morning of the debate, and Bram had been beset—entirely unexpectedly—by a bout of nerves.

He'd argued impossible cases, and won. He'd battled his way through the Inns of Court to become a barrister, despite his ignominious birth. He'd faced standing on a stage being bid on by a group of eager ladies, and yet all of that paled in the face of what he was feeling now.

Because he was going to square off against the woman he loved. Because if he won, she might be able to achieve her greatest dream of joining the Stars Above Society, and would vault toward it, leaving him behind without a second glance. If he lost, she might still achieve her greatest dream because of the notoriety attached to her surprising win.

No matter what happened, he knew this might be the last time he would see her. He couldn't imagine her father and stepmother would allow him to continue the farce of his courting her. The talk would be too great, the potential for scandal too risky.

"There," Simeon said, doing something Bram didn't understand to his jacket. "You look good."

"At least as good as he's going to look," Theo said, a wry grin on his face.

"Shut up," Simeon and Bram said in unison.

"You'll be fine," Benedict said in a reassuring tone. Fenton, who Bram would have sworn was not paying attention at all thanks to the enormous book he was engrossed in, raised his head and nodded in agreement.

The five of them were crowded into Bram's small rooms, all of them having appeared within minutes of one another, even though none of them had spoken to the other about showing up.

It was just the sort of thing found brothers did, Bram reasoned, feeling unaccountably maudlin. Or maybe accountably so; after today, or maybe even after a week, his found brothers would be the only people in his life. Again.

"You all have to promise to stay quiet," Bram warned, glancing at each of them in turn. "No piping up to say that Mary Wollstonecraft must've met a few bad gentlemen to have such an opinion"—at which point Fenton tossed his book aside and leapt out of his chair—"or that if ladies joined the society they wouldn't have time to fall in and out of love with certain gentlemen." Which made both Simeon and Theo flush.

"We will," Benedict promised, then glared at the others. "Won't we." It wasn't a question.

"Let's go, then," Bram said, consulting his watch. "I've got an argument to win. Or to lose."

"You'll always be a winner to us," Theo said, patting Bram's shoulder with a wicked smile on his face.

Bram shook his head, grateful, at least, that he had these four to weather the rest of his life with.

"AND WHERE ARE you going?"

Wilhelmina sighed as she heard Alethea's voice.

"Out with me," Aunt Flora said in the firmest voice Wilhelmina had ever heard her use. "She has promised to visit with a friend of mine, a lady who is also a widow. We plan to discuss how to transform our old clothing into drapes, tablecloth linens, throw rugs, and the like. Would you like to join us?" she added brightly.

Wilhelmina didn't have to look at Alethea to know her stepmother shuddered. "No, no, thank you. We will see you later, then."

Wilhelmina smothered a laugh, then she and Aunt Flora hastened out the door.

"Thank goodness you agreed to come with me," Wilhelmina said as they were safely outside.

Her father's carriage waited for them, the coachman doffing his hat when he saw them. He came forward and held his arm out to Aunt Flora, who took it with a coquettish smile.

Interesting, Wilhelmina thought.

"Mr. Williams has promised not to share the details of our outing with my brother," Aunt Flora said, giving a nod to the coachman.

He was an older gentleman, still fit and with most of his hair. She glanced from Aunt Flora to him and back again, her suspicions aroused.

"That is very kind of you, Mr. Williams," Wilhelmina said as he assisted Aunt Flora into the carriage.

"No kindness, my lady. It's a privilege to be able to help Lady Flora out."

He helped Wilhelmina in, then leapt onto the seat, urging the horses forward right after.

"Thank you for coming," Wilhelmina said.

Aunt Flora gave a short nod, her tight expression revealing her anxiety. She didn't like going out very much, but she had recognized the need to keep the debate from reaching her brother's or Alethea's ears, and had readily agreed to accompany Wilhelmina to the SAS.

It was a short trip, and soon Aunt Flora was seated among Bram's friends, being flirted with by Mr. Osborne and Mr. Jones, watched out for by Mr. Quintrell, and given all sorts of arcane information by Mr. Ash.

Wilhelmina and Bram stood waiting to go onto the stage for the debate, Mr. Muller alternating his glares between the two of them.

Bram held his hand out to her. "I wish you the best of luck, my lady," he said in a normal tone, then lowered his voice to add, "My dear."

She shivered as she took his hand, nearly gasping as his fingers made contact with hers. She'd removed her gloves to wash her hands, damp because of her nervousness, and she hadn't bothered putting them back on. They were just going to irk her, and she didn't need any more irkedness at the moment.

"Thank you," she said, inclining her head. "Bram," she added, more softly.

His eyes flared with heat, and she shivered again, wishing they were near a terrace or at least alone so she could kiss him.

Because, she knew quite suddenly, she wanted to kiss him. Not just now, but frequently, and for several days in succession.

She wanted—she wanted *him*. She didn't dare say, not even to herself, in precisely what category she wanted him beyond today. She couldn't. She owed it to her plans, to her aunt, to her strongly held and oft-stated belief that marriage was nothing more than a contract that benefited only the male.

But she *did* know with absolute certainty, as she stood there still holding his hand, that she wanted him and she would have him.

Once, perhaps, or for a few hours, or however such things were measured—she had no idea, not having considered the idea before meeting him.

She'd think about all the other things later on.

Though uncertainty about her future was leaking in, likely through the same aperture she'd opened to allow for the chance of further relations with him.

Would it be so bad, to be contracted to a male if it was this male?

Though she knew he didn't want that as much as she didn't.

Would she get bored with him?

She strongly suspected she would not. And that thought terrified her.

"Are you all right?" he asked, his tone concerned.

"Fine," she said brightly, pasting a smile on her face. "Just running over the debate points. My apologies if my expression—"

"I see you," he interrupted. "Remember? I know you have a lot depending on the outcome of this performance. I promise to do my best. Or do my worst."

"No!" she flung out, then clapped a hand over her mouth, surprised at her own outburst. "No," she repeated, more softly this time. "Do your best. Whatever happens will happen."

"It's time," Mr. Muller said, sounding peeved.

Likely he would remain peeved no matter what occurred. Someone, namely Bram, had dared to challenge Mr. Muller's views on the world.

"Oh no," she breathed.

"You're not all right," he said, taking her arm.

"Mr. Muller, can we postp—"

"I am fine," she said, straightening and shaking his hand off her arm.

But the traitorous thought that perhaps she wasn't absolutely correct in her assessment of the world made her head spin. What if she was being like Mr. Muller, implacable when there was a clear need for change?

Not that she was Mr. Muller; for one thing, she was taller. And she knew more about astronomy than he did.

But still.

"I will state the rules of the debate and then present you," Mr. Muller was saying as they walked onto the stage.

There was a smattering of applause, which Mr. Muller hushed by holding his hand out for silence.

"Here we go," Wilhelmina breathed. "Time to change some minds."

He gave her a crooked smile as Mr. Muller began to speak.

BRAM WISHED HIS chest didn't feel so tight, and that it was more comfortable to breathe.

Being in love with the person you were about to debate was not the easiest task. It was a good thing he had never had such feelings for his opponents in court, since he might have given up the idea of being a barrister long ago.

"Each side will have five minutes to present his or her viewpoint."

Mr. Muller stood in the center of the stage, in front of both Wilhelmina and Bram, as he explained.

Bram saw his friends toward the back of the room, the same place they had sat when he had proposed the idea. An older lady was seated in the middle of the group, Theo and Benedict on one side, Fenton and Simeon on the other.

As he looked at them, Benedict gave him a reassuring nod, the rest of them too engaged in conversation with the older lady to notice his gaze.

"If the audience has questions, each side will have a minute to respond, then will be given a final two minutes to wrap up their argument. Then," Mr.

Muller said, turning to look at both Bram and Wilhelmina, "the membership of the SAS will vote on the winner."

"Lady Wilhelmina will go first," Mr. Muller said. "I will indicate when your time is up." He walked to the side and stepped down to the main floor, taking a seat in front of them and giving a nod to Wilhelmina.

She clasped her hands and took a deep breath.

"Ladies and gentlemen," she began, her voice strong and clear, "we are here today to ask if women should be allowed to join the Stars Above Society. My position, which I will prove today, is that they should not. And here is why."

She stepped from behind her podium to stand where Mr. Muller had just been. She wore an elegantly ruffled gown in a pale pink color, looking exactly like what a young unmarried lady should.

But he knew better. He knew the lady who wore that clothing was fiercely independent, proud, intelligent, and passionate.

"Astronomy is the purview of the wealthy," she continued. "The most recent example is the Earl of Rosse, who has built the largest telescope to date. The earl has funds at his disposal, funds he chooses to spend on astronomy. His wife, presumably, does not have a say in how he spends his money. If she shares his passion for the stars, she would not be able to do anything about that because everything she owns belongs to her husband. I hope, for her sake, that she does share his passion, since astronomers can talk at length about their favorite subject."

This drew chuckles from the audience, and Bram saw a few of the stuffier-looking gentlemen visibly relax.

"Astronomy needs to have this influx of money in order to further its exploration. It needs as many people as possible to champion the study of it so it can develop and grow as we all wish it to. The stars can teach us so much, and if astronomy is considered to be anything less than a worthy investment, it will stagnate. I know from personal experience how some gentlemen see ladies' interest in their favorite pursuit." Which drew more, albeit more subdued, chuckles. "There is nothing I want more than for every person who can do so to spend time, thought, and yes, money, on astronomy. Societies such as the Stars Above Society are not for dilettantes, nor for people who cannot assist in a meaningful way. Therefore, it is my position that women should not be allowed to join."

She turned and nodded her head to him before stepping back to her side of the stage.

And now it was his turn to speak.

He had been startled by her argument, a remarkably cynical one: that the society should not allow women because it would impede the potential strides in astronomical exploration. He'd assumed she would fall back on stereotypes about the respective genders, making the argument that ladies couldn't possibly comprehend the enormity of the stars. That they were needed at home, rather than outdoors on bridges looking up.

But her argument didn't even consider the possibility that women might not have the intelligence to be astronomers; perhaps they could, perhaps they couldn't, but the fact was they couldn't afford to invest, and investing in astronomy was the only way to make it grow.

Fascinating.

He took a deep breath, then began to speak.

**Men I Do Not Wish to Marry:
A Not at All Comprehensive List by
Lady Wilhelmina Bettesford**

Ivan the Terrible. No explanation needed.

Chapter Twenty-Five

Wilhelmina barely heard what Bram was saying. She was flooded with emotions, emotions she didn't know what to do with.

She was pleased she had presented her argument well, even though she disagreed with its premise. She, Aunt Flora, and Dipper had spent a few hours as Wilhelmina crafted her points, Aunt Flora giving encouragement whenever she felt Wilhelmina had made a particularly good point.

Dipper didn't react at all, which Wilhelmina surmised might mirror the audience's reaction, so that was helpful as well.

She knew he spoke, he gestured to her, and she made appropriate reaction expressions, she thought.

At least she assumed so, since nobody gave her odd looks.

And then it was over.

"Now we have the question period," Mr. Muller said, rising from his chair and turning to address the audience. "What is the first question?"

A gentleman raised his hand.

"Yes, Mr. Congreve?"

The man rose. "If the SAS agrees to accept ladies, does Lady Wilhelmina intend to join?"

Wilhelmina frowned. "If the SAS believes the society will be improved with the addition of female members, I will join." She spread her hands out wide. "I trust this membership to do what is right for the society in specific, and that means if the society votes to allow ladies to be admitted, I will not deny the society the opportunity to learn from my knowledge."

The man grunted his displeasure, sitting back down again.

Aunt Flora rose, and Wilhelmina felt her breath hitch. Her aunt was not accustomed to being with other people, much less speaking to them.

"I would be interested to hear what Lady Wilhelmina thinks should happen if a lady is wealthy in her own right."

Bram's friends all cheered as Aunt Flora sat again.

"The question should be directed toward Mr. Townsend," Mr. Muller said. "It is not appropriate to ask two questions in a row to one of the two presenters."

"Let her answer," Bram said. "If there are two questions for me, I will be happy to respond."

Wilhelmina met her aunt's gaze. "Well. The circumstance you describe would be quite unusual"—*unless it was six months hence, and it was Wilhelmina herself*—"but in that case, I would want the society to do what is best for the study of astronomy."

"Are there questions for Mr. Townsend?" Mr. Muller asked.

Mr. Osborne rose, and Wilhelmina heard Bram mutter something unintelligible.

"Mr. Townsend, do you mean to tell me you would be in favor of a lady joining the society rather than, say, marrying you and taking care of your home?"

Mr. Townsend folded his arms over his impressive chest. "Why could a lady not do both?"

Was it her imagination, or had he just shot a quick look at her?

"A lady is clearly as capable as any gentleman. More, honestly, since they have to do whatever they do wearing all their layers of clothing and remaining polite in the face of all sorts of inequities. If a lady chooses to indulge her passion, why can't she have everything she wants?"

It was her turn to stare at him now.

Did he mean what he said? What had he said? Was he just idly debating, or was there anything more to his words?

And why didn't she know how she felt? Or *what* she felt?

BRAM DIDN'T KNOW whether to throttle Theo or hug him. Perhaps both.

Asking the question allowed him to say what he felt, what he hoped she could hear and understand— that if she could allow herself the possibility of a more traditional future that it could be a happy one.

If she dared.

Which seemed odd, of course—most young ladies who dared to do things were trying things that young ladies did not usually do. Things like flying in hot-air balloons, or mountaineering, or publishing scandalous novels under their own names.

She would have no qualms about doing any of those things, he imagined, if she had the inclination.

But to tie herself to one other person for the rest of her life?

She would decline, unless it was Dipper issuing the invitation.

"We will retire to the council room and vote," Mr. Muller was saying.

Right. No matter what happened here today, she had proven herself more than worthy of joining the society—if they didn't want her, more fools them.

And if they did—she would be able to realize her dream. Perhaps submit a paper for their journal, *The Stroke of Venus*, the title of which never failed to make him laugh, as though he was twelve years old again and just discovering the naughtiness of sex.

Now he was thirty years old, and still hadn't discovered all of the mysteries of sex, though he certainly knew a lot more than he did eighteen years ago.

From what she'd intimated—no, from what she'd actually *said*—he was suspecting that both of them would be discovering the mysteries of sex together, eventually.

And then what?

Lord, he hoped it wouldn't depend on whatever he did during—during that time. Because since he'd never done it before, he didn't know if it would be pleasurable. For her, at least; he was fairly certain he was going to enjoy the hell out of it.

"Mr. Townsend."

He blinked, seeing Wilhelmina was standing in front of him, a wry smile on her face. "What were you thinking of?" she asked. "It looked like you were a million miles away."

"Up with your stars," he replied, smiling.

She tilted her head as she gazed at him appraisingly. "I think you would fit right in with the Taurus constellation. The Pleiades are within that one, you know."

"What you were trying to see that first night?"

When he'd had no idea of how much his life, how much his perceptions, were changing. He'd only begrudged having to retrieve her off the bridge because it would delay his arrival to meet his friends.

"Yes." She nodded. "Taurus is traditionally a bull, you know, and I believe that would describe you quite well. Bullheaded, bullish, the type of person who would take a bull by the horns."

"Surely I'm not that argumentative," he protested, but he spoke in an amused tone.

"Oh, but you are. That is one of the things I like about you," she replied.

"What else do you like about me?"

He couldn't resist asking. He had to know if there was even a chance she felt a fraction of what he felt for her. If she did—well, he'd ensure his Taurus-like characteristics were on full display.

She gave him a wicked smile he felt all the way down to his toes. Though mostly in his cock, if he was being honest.

"I like your . . . intelligence," she said in a low tone, making it sound as though *intelligence* was an entirely salacious word. "I like your . . . curiosity, and your loyalty." She bit her lip, making his gaze go there, right where he wished he could kiss her. "I am also superficial enough to say I like how you look, and how tall you are."

"You know I had nothing to do with that," he said. "Unlike the first parts."

"Mmm-hmm," she agreed. "But the whole of you, all the parts of you, are entirely appealing, and it would be disingenuous for me to say I wasn't attracted to the outside as much as I am to the inside."

"Oh," he said, feeling his chest constrict. "When—"

But he had to stop speaking, because Mr. Muller was stepping back onto the stage, a notebook in his hand, a disgruntled expression on his face.

"The members have voted," he began, glancing from Bram to Wilhelmina, who had retreated to her side of the stage, "and Mr. Townsend has been declared the winner."

Wilhelmina's eyes widened, and Bram felt his heart sink. No matter what the outcome was his heart would have sunk, he knew that. But just—just having this aspect finished would bring them one step closer to the end, when they would part ways.

Unless they didn't.

Which meant he had to persuade her without persuading her. Because if he unleashed his full torrent of bullheadedness on her, he might prevail in the short term—his rhetoric was that excellent, he knew—but he would lose in the long run because she might not have all the information she'd need to make such a profound decision.

The audience was clapping now, and then his friends were swarming him, shaking his hand in congratulations and making sure to congratulate her as well.

And then she was once again in front of him, her eyes sparkling. "You did very well," she said, a smile tugging her lips. "It seems the SAS has some thinking to do now."

He took her hand, covering it with his other hand.

"I am pleased you will get to do what you have been yearning for."

She leaned in close to him. "Not yet I haven't. That will be tonight."

Tonight.

"Aunt Flora is going out with your friends. They've promised to take her to Vauxhall Gardens, which she used to go to when she was a debutante. It has changed substantially since then, I believe, but the four of them will keep her safe."

"And you and I?"

She gave an artful shrug. "We will have to go to your rooms, won't we? I mean, we cannot go to my house."

His rooms. Drat, why hadn't he thought of that when he'd left for the evening? He hoped it was tidy enough. Though she wasn't coming to his rooms to see to his personal cleanliness, was she?

She was coming over to his rooms to be ravished. And to ravish him, in equal and proportionate measure.

Was she going to do this?

She knew before she even asked herself the question that she was.

What other chance would she have? With someone as gloriously splendid as he? With that brain, and that body? She'd be a fool not to take advantage of it, and she was no fool.

Foolish, definitely. She'd proven that the first time they'd met when she'd—foolishly, now she could admit—got up on that parapet to stare at the stars. It wasn't that it was a foolish endeavor per se; but it hadn't gotten her any closer to what she wanted to see, not really, and she had been in some danger.

If he hadn't come along who knows what might have happened?

Likely nothing.

She would have gazed up at the stars, wished she could fly among them, and then gotten down and snuck home, never knowing someone as clever and opinionated as Mr. Townsend—Bram—existed.

And his friends as well.

She knew she would never have met any of the gentlemen under normal circumstances.

Although there was that auction—but likely if Alethea had bid on him without Wilhelmina having met him before, she would have kept herself locked down, not allowing herself to enjoy either the opera or his presence.

"Well," he said, glancing around the room, "since it seems everyone is otherwise occupied, shall we go?"

"Mmm-hmm," she said, not trusting herself to speak.

They walked quickly out of the hall, increasing her pace to match his long stride. He had hold of her hand, and was half tugging her down the hall, as though he was as eager to get to his rooms as she was.

Perhaps, she thought with a smile, he was.

After a mercifully short hackney ride they were in front of his house, rooms he rented from a woman whose late husband had been a law clerk. He pushed open the door, which led into a dark hallway, and guided her up two flights of stairs to where he lived. Other members of the legal profession also rented rooms there, he explained, and she had to bite her tongue to tell him she didn't give a tinker's damn who else lived there—all she cared about was him, and what would happen tonight.

"Here it is," he said, sounding oddly nervous. Was he nervous? Surely he had done this before—the skillful way he kissed her implied some expertise.

"This is my desk, and my chair, and where I slee—" he said, then stopped abruptly.

"What is it?" she asked.

He shook his head. "You don't care anything about my rooms, do you?"

"No," she said. "I only care about you."

And then she went to him, wrapped her arms around his neck, and brought his head down to kiss her.

Men I Do Not Wish to Marry:
A Not at All Comprehensive List by
Lady Wilhelmina Bettesford

Men who glare at you when you step on their toes. Yes, Lord Paskins, I mean you.

Chapter Twenty-Six

$\mathcal{B}$ram swallowed, all his hard-won confidence suddenly deserting him in the face of this.

In the face of *her*.

But now they were kissing, and everything felt right, and he knew this was the only place he wanted to be, and whatever happened—as happen it would, if she had her way—it would be excellent, because he loved her, and she was . . . what? Enamored of his brain and, by the way her hands were clutching him there, his shoulders?

Her mouth was so soft, and now she knew to slide her tongue into his mouth, pressing her body close against his as she explored and licked and sucked.

And he let her. He wanted her to lead this dance, at least right now; he presumed later that some baser instinct would take over, and he would be the one to guide what would happen. That he would know just how to slide his cock into her warmth, after he had taken pains to ensure she was ready for him.

He hadn't done anything himself, but he had spent enough time with Simeon and Theo to have more than a basic handle on the proceedings.

Even if he hadn't wanted to listen, their vociferous

and frequent conversations on the subject would have meant he learned something, just by being friends with them.

So he knew, for example, to slide his fingertips along her jaw, stroking the soft skin there. To move slowly, languorously, to her ear, touching it delicately as he concentrated on kissing her.

Everything in his entire being was focused on her, on every little sigh and movement she made.

They stood in the middle of his rooms, the small area that wasn't already covered by his bed, his wardrobe, his desk, and the small table where he prepared his tea. It was a space of only a few feet square, big enough to make the room seem spacious—if he was lying in bed at the time—and small enough to make him feel like he was all elbows and legs when he was late and rushing to get ready.

He broke the kiss, immediately placing his lips at the base of her throat, his tongue delving into the delicate hollow. He gripped her head with one hand, while the other moved to her waist, his fingers finding purchase in her pliable warmth.

He could hear her breath in his ear, and then she was speaking—at first he was too distracted by her, by her skin, by her scent, to comprehend what she was saying, and then when he did hear it was as though she'd exploded a grenade in his mind.

"I want to see you unclothed," she said in a low, husky voice. "And I presume you wish to see me the same?" she added, a hint of amusement lacing the passion in her tone.

"Mmph," he grunted, stepping back to undo his cravat with remarkable speed. Even Simeon would have been impressed.

When he stopped laughing, that was.

He yanked it away, flinging it to wherever it landed, then got out of his coat, tossing it onto the back of his chair.

He held her gaze as he leaned down to one booted foot, hopping on the other as he pulled it off, throwing it with a thud to the corner of the room. The other quickly followed, making an outsized noise as it clattered against the bucket of coals that fed his stove.

They both laughed at the noise, and then he wobbled, his stockings catching on a nail in the floor, and then before he knew it he'd lost his balance, ending up flat on his back, still laughing.

She gazed down at him with a look of pure appreciation, and he began to move to get up, but she gave a slow shake of her head. "Stay there. It's like when we first met and I landed on you. Do you remember?"

How could he forget?

"Does that mean—?" he began, but by the time he finished she was on the floor also, clambering on top of him, a wicked smile on her mouth.

"You are under my control, Mr. Townsend," she said, her eyes sliding down his body. She put her hands to the opening of his shirt and shot him a taunting look. "We're not in public. So does that mean I can tear this?" she asked.

His cock was so hard it strained against his trousers, pressing up against her warm bottom where it rested on him.

"Please," he said, his voice ragged.

Her smile widened, and then he heard the shred of fabric as she yanked the shirt apart. The material fluttered briefly in the air, then fell to either side of his chest.

"Oh my," she said, her eyes wide as she stared at his bared chest.

He tilted his head to see what she found so fascinating, but couldn't understand it—his upper body was much like his friends', firm skin over taut muscle, kept fit by frequent walking and the occasional boxing match.

But he couldn't analyze anything when her hands flattened themselves against him, and she slid her palms over his skin as though she was learning him by touch.

"What about you?" he said as she kept touching his chest, shifting her lower body as if she wasn't quite comfortable.

He wasn't comfortable either, but it was a sweet agony, the feeling of his hard cock separated from her by only a few layers of fabric. Or more than a few, given what he knew about ladies' garments. But still. Rather close.

"What about me?" she asked, stilling.

He jerked his chin toward her body. "Your clothes. Isn't there supposed to be a quid pro quo?"

She rolled her eyes. "Leave it to a barrister to quote Latin to me at such a time."

He grinned. "You love it," he asserted.

"I do," she said, twisting around so her back was to him. She turned her head to speak over her shoulder. "You're going to have to undo me. I can't reach those buttons."

His hands were sliding button from buttonhole before she had finished speaking, until there was enough of a separation for her to slide the fabric down over her shoulders, leaving the gown in a bunch at her waist.

She turned back and stood up, shoving the material down as she shimmied out, leaving her in her chemise, corset, and stockings.

His mouth went dry.

For a moment, she looked shy, but then she took a deep breath as she flung her head back, her glorious hair spilling down her back.

He hadn't realized she'd removed her hairpins, and her hair hung down around her face in disordered curls, making her look as free in appearance as she was in spirit.

"I suppose these should come off too," she said, gesturing to her chemise and corset.

"Only if you want to show me your bare breasts so I can put my mouth on them," he said, hoping it was the right thing to say.

She shuddered, and her fingers fairly flew at the laces of her corset, and then her chemise was off, and she was naked except for her white stockings caressing the round firmness of her legs.

Apparently it was the right thing to say.

She bent as if to roll one down, and he made a noise of protestation. "Not those—leave those on, please."

There was something so erotic about seeing her completely bared except for those sheer, delicate pieces of fabric that covered her lower legs.

His gaze traveled up her body, from where the stockings cut into her thighs to the dark patch of curls at her entrance, on up to the soft roundness of her belly, to her full, gorgeous breasts.

He hadn't realized it, but he was already undoing his trousers, shucking them as he lay on the floor.

"Excellent," she said, her eyes following the movement of his hands. "And then those—what are those anyway?" she asked, furrowing her brow.

"Smallclothes," he replied, removing the offending garment.

She knelt on the floor beside him, her knees folded, and she leaned forward to touch—

"Aah," he said as her fingers made contact with his cock.

She snatched them away, her expression altering from one of passion to one of dismay. "I'm sorry, did I hurt you?"

He grabbed her hand and put it back on himself, squeezing his fingers around hers. "No, that was a very satisfied groan. If you recall, I made a very different noise when you fell on top of me," he added, a wry smile creeping onto his face.

She rolled her eyes, then clambered back onto him, still holding his shaft. "Show me how," she said.

He put his hand over hers again, and showed her how to slide her hand up and down, tightly gripping him, until she had him groaning and arching his back.

"You're going to—you've got to stop," he said at last. "We haven't even made it to the bed, and you'll have me spending on my floor. This night is supposed to be for you, remember?"

"For both of us," she asserted, but she gradually slowed her movement, then arched her eyebrow toward him, jerking her chin to the bed. "You want us to go there?" She sounded skeptical.

He craned his head to look at his bed—narrow,

built just barely for him—and then looked back at her. "Absolutely."

She huffed out an exasperated breath. "Fine. If you insist."

She rose and scampered to the bed, flinging herself under the covers so vigorously it felt as though the whole room shook. "Hurry up," she said. "I want you to speak Latin to me as we explore one another," she said.

"Interrogabo vos et ego operor," he replied, tucking himself next to her.

Men I Do Not Wish to Marry:
A Not at All Comprehensive List by
Lady Wilhelmina Bettesford

Samuel Thompson, the "Confidence Man." (First of all, isn't "Confidence Man" redundant?)

Thompson convinced naïve people to show their confidence in them by giving him watches or money. That is not a sustainable profession, never mind that it is inherently wrong.

Chapter Twenty-Seven

Wilhelmina wriggled with delight in his tiny bed, made even tinier when he joined her in it.

She was bare save her stockings, which he'd wanted her to keep on, for some reason—and once she'd seen his expression as he gazed at her, she'd wanted to keep them on, too. If it kept that look that mingled desire, passion, want, and something very hungry, she would wear stockings all the time. In the bath, under her nightdress, and—well, she couldn't think of another time she wouldn't be wearing stockings, but if any such occasion occurred, she would take pains to wear them even so.

His skin was warm, his body pressed against hers. He lay next to her, his face turned into her shoulder, his hand resting on her stomach. She felt her breath hitch, and then his fingers were making their way to her breast, and it was already aching for his touch, her nipple stiffening. His fingers just barely grazed the sensitive flesh, and she gasped as he chuckled against her skin.

"I suppose you have this effect on everyone," she said, making an attempt at lightness. Not wanting to reveal just how much all of this meant to her.

"I've never been with anyone like this," he said simply.

She froze. "What? Never?"

His hand continued to stroke her skin, his palm brushing her nipple as he bestowed a soft bite on her shoulder. "Never."

"You mean—you mean you've never done this before?"

He raised his head, meeting her gaze. The shocking blue of his eyes struck her as they always did, as if he was the human embodiment of a star and she was able to see all the burning, pulsating gases.

Which, if she were to say that to him, would sound a lot less complimentary than she meant it.

"I've never done this before," he confirmed. "Do you want to stop and find someone who has?"

His tone was mild, but she could hear the fierce passion underneath his question.

"Of course not," she replied, huffing out a breath. "This will be even more fun because we will learn together. And you know," she said in a confidential tone, "if you hadn't told me I would never have known. You are very . . . competent."

"Just what every gentleman wants to hear during an intimate moment," he said dryly, his eyes twinkling with delight.

She felt something in her chest ease, and she returned his smile, and then took his hand, placing it on the spot that ached the most.

"I want you to touch me, Bram," she said. "Explore. I imagine it will feel differently with your fingers than with my own."

He raised a brow. "You mean you have done this yourself?"

She snorted. "Of course. I am a scientist. That means that I like to learn things."

His fingers slid down, down toward where she was wet and aching, and she shivered. "I like to learn things as well. Like what will make you scream my name," he said, suddenly thrusting a finger inside, making her gasp.

"What will have you begging for me to put my cock inside you, inside that sweet quim." His voice was a low, powerful rumble, and it felt as though her whole body reacted to its timbre.

"I thought you didn't know anything?" she said, her voice sounding breathier than usual. Meanwhile, his fingers had begun to stroke her nub, and she let out a moan.

"Just because I haven't done anything doesn't mean I don't know anything," he said sternly. "You haven't been to the stars, but you know what they're made of, right?"

"Ye-yes," she said, "though we're not entirely certain. Gas, and dust, and some—some other things," she said, unable to parse coherent thoughts because of what his fingers were doing.

She was on her back, with him curled around her, his hand working its magic down there while he kissed various parts of her upper body. And then he had eased over her, half on top of her, half still on the bed, and his mouth had found her breast while his fingers continued, and she was writhing under him, feeling the building pressure there, the combined effects of his hand and his mouth almost unbearably painful—he'd called it a "sweet agony," and that described it perfectly.

And then she was arching up, the crescendo

building to a peak, and she was crying out, saying his name, and sobbing as she climaxed, her whole body awash in bliss.

"Quod esset bonum?" he said.

"What does that mean?" she asked, barely able to concentrate on her own words, much less his.

"That was good?"

She smacked him lightly on the back—as much energy as she was able to muster at the moment. "You know it was. Not bad for a first time," she added in a mischievous tone. "Only now I believe it is your turn."

"Do your worst," Bram said, stroking her skin idly.

He'd just brought her to pleasure, and he honestly didn't care if he didn't find his own—her reaction was so satisfying, so wonderful to see, that it would be enough.

But he knew her, and her sense of justice and fairness, and he knew it wouldn't be enough for her.

Which meant, he thought wryly, she was going to make this as good for him as he had made it for her. He couldn't deny he was looking forward to it.

"Do my worst?" she said, giving him a disbelieving look. "If I did that, I'd lock your hands to your bedposts—not that you have bedposts, mind you— and leave without letting you touch yourself at all."

She did not do her worst, however, given that her hand was even now sliding to his cock, which was at attention waiting for her.

She wrapped her hand around him and slid her palm up and down again, not as quickly as before, while she propped herself up on one elbow and lowered her face to his to kiss him.

He arched up to meet her mouth, and then she was clambering across him, tossing his covers to the floor.

She straddled him, her bottom resting on his lower abdomen, her hand reaching behind her to keep her grasp on him.

"You are quite flexib—" he observed, stopping when she gave his penis a tug that sent sensation flooding through his entire body.

And then she was raising herself up on her knees, holding his cock as she positioned herself above him.

He peered down at what was happening. "Do you think—?" he began.

"Hush," she said, her sharp tone indicating she was concentrating elsewhere.

And then she lowered herself so his cock was touching her wet, soft warmth, and he gasped as she gave a little moan.

And then she lowered herself a bit more, and he could feel her soft folds, and wanted nothing more than to have her take him entirely, all the way to the hilt. Their bodies joined as his cock found her heat.

She bit her lip as she lowered herself another inch or so, and now he was inside, his hands on her hips, holding her as she kept sliding down.

"Oh," she said, wiggling as she took the last bit of him.

"Aagh," he said, closing his eyes from the sheer bliss of it.

He hadn't known. He'd suspected, true, but he hadn't *known*.

It felt like he'd entered heaven, only better—it was

her quim, her cunt, her lovely intimate spot that held him tight within her.

"And now what?" she asked, pushing forward a bit.

"Now I believe you ride me, love," he said.

Her eyes widened in delight, and he wanted to freeze this moment, capture it in a box so he could bring it out and replay it again and again when she was no longer in his life.

"Ride you? That sounds fun," she said. "Like—?"

"Well, I don't know for certain," he said, speaking through gritted teeth, the exquisite feeling almost too much and too sweetly painful to stand, "but I think it's like when you post on a horse."

"Ah!" she said, sounding as though she understood.

And, oh God, he thought, she did.

She raised herself up again, not so much he slid out, but enough so he felt the difference, then moved back down again. "This is like my hand, only now it's my—" And he could have sworn she blushed, his deliciously sexy scientist, even though she was bold enough to do all of this even though she'd never done it before.

"It's your . . ." he said, flashing her a wicked grin before groaning again.

It felt too good.

Too good to only happen once. And that was what he was contemplating, wasn't it? There would be this night, and then she would figure out how to resolve her problem with her father and stepmother, and she would have no need of him anymore.

Unless he somehow was able to get her to persuade herself that he might be the better future.

But he'd have to trust her to do that—he couldn't

have anything to do with it, beyond showing her, as much as he dared, that he loved her.

"Aah," he gasped as she began to ride him more quickly. "You are very good at this," he was able to say, before digging his fingers into her hips as she kept up her unrelenting rhythm, the slap of their bodies an aural augmentation of the lewd and wonderful thing they were doing.

She had her hands on his chest, her palms flat against his skin, and her skin was flushed, and her hair was a riotous, glorious mess around her shoulders. Her breasts bounced with each movement, and it was all too much, and not enough, and then—and then—he tilted his head back as the feeling overpowered him, spilling his seed inside her as she kept riding through every last pulse of his orgasm.

Minutes later—or was it hours?—he was finally able to meet her gaze. "That was incredible," he said, his voice low and rough.

"It was, wasn't it?" she said, looking smug. "And to think neither one of us had ever done it before. We are both very smart."

"Or very attracted to one another," he added as she slid off him and lay on her side, her body still pressed up against his.

"That, too. Smart and attracted," she said, sounding as though she was making a closing argument.

**Men I Do Not Wish to Marry:
A Not at All Comprehensive List by
Lady Wilhelmina Bettesford**

A man who does not stand up for what he believes in.

Chapter Twenty-Eight

Wilhelmina was delightfully sore the next day as she let Jones get her dressed for the day.

Bram had helped her sneak back into her house in the middle of the night, giving her a quick, hard kiss before easing the door open to let her in.

She'd held her breath for a few moments, but nobody was waiting for her in the foyer, thank goodness—she'd wondered if Alethea's inerrant sense might have led her to wake up in the middle of the night to catch her, but her stepmother did not make an appearance.

Only Dipper trotted down to greet her, twirling in a circle as he yipped his delight.

She had scooped him up and hastened to her bedroom, where she was able to manage a few hours' sleep before morning.

"What a glorious morning," she sighed as Jones put pins in her hair.

Her maid darted a look out the window, then frowned in confusion. It was raining, the dreary, unending rain that was rare in summer, turning the skies as gray as a December day.

"That is, a glorious morning to sit and have tea," Wilhelmina amended.

"Yes, my lady," Jones replied. "I heard that Lord Paskins is coming to take tea with your father today."

Wilhelmina stiffened. "Take tea?" A euphemism, no doubt, for something far worse than the ingestion of a hot beverage. "Drat, do you think—?"

"I do, my lady. That is, that is what you will be saying at the altar with Lord Paskins!" Jones said, sounding proud of her own wit.

Wilhelmina would have been proud as well if she wasn't so appalled.

The whole point had been to dissuade anyone from taking the step to ask for her hand—she had thought Lord Paskins might have figured out that Mr. Townsend had the lead, but apparently he was oblivious. Or desperate.

Which didn't say a lot about Wilhelmina's appeal, but that wasn't the point.

Why had she even agreed to the whole pretend courtship arrangement?

Oh, right, she had *not* agreed. It had been forced on her, like so many other decisions: where to go in the evening, who to spend time with, what she was allowed to speak about in public, what she could wear.

Who she might spend the rest of her life with.

She wanted to make her own decisions, which was one of the reasons she had done what she had with Bram the night before—if her virginity was regarded as some sort of golden chalice of womanhood, she wanted to be the one to manage it, not anybody else.

She wanted to make all of her own decisions.

She wanted to study with the Earl of Rosse and his telescope in Ireland, she wanted to have gentleman friends without being judged for it, she wanted to move to the country with Aunt Flora and spend the rest of her days in solitude as she gazed at the stars at night.

Only—did she?

Perhaps you want friends, friends like Maude Chalmers. Friends like the ones he had, people who would listen to you, tease you, tell you when you were wrong about fiction, and the opera, and tell you it was absolutely not a frivolous idea to take pride in your appearance, and your ability not to step on anybody's toes when dancing. But still remain friends when you did step on toes.

"Are you all right, my lady?" Jones asked, sounding concerned.

Only realizing all my premises about myself are faulty, Wilhelmina wanted to say.

Because she didn't want to live in solitude in the country.

She'd only resorted to that because her aunt was in need of companionship, and because the alternatives were far more unpleasant. She'd taken the most manageable option, and decided it was what she wanted, when it wasn't what she wanted at all.

Because she knew what she wanted.

The man she'd fallen in love with.

The life she thought she never wanted—to be with someone for the rest of her life.

To her utter and total chagrin, she realized she'd gone and fallen in love with Bram. The man she'd specifically said she would not put under any kind of obligation.

And now she had to figure out what to do with all that.

"Jones, thank you," Wilhelmina said, rising from her chair. "I just need to go speak with my aunt for a moment." *Because I am a flibbertigibbet, as it happens, and I have to do something about that.*

"So early, my lady?" Jones said. It was barely ten, and Aunt Flora often slept until well after two o'clock.

"It is too important to wait," Wilhelmina replied firmly. She walked to the door, flinging it open, Dipper on her heels as she made her way down to Aunt Flora's room.

BRAM FELT AS though something was pounding inside his head. He was in his bed, entirely naked, and he knew he hadn't had anything to drink the night before—unless he was drunk on her, which was entirely possible.

He blinked a few times as the pounding continued, and then he sat up suddenly, realizing the pounding was at his door, not inside his brain.

"Bram!" Simeon's voice called.

"We know you're in there," Theo added.

"Because your landlady told us," Benedict's voice said dryly.

Fenton must have been out there as well, only too engrossed in a book or something to add his opinion to the fray.

"I want to get your opinion on this mathematical argument."

There was Fenton.

"Just a minute, you louts," Bram shouted, hopping out of bed. His clothes hung on the back of his chair where he'd left them after returning in the wee hours of the night. He'd walked Wilhelmina home, painfully aware that this interlude in his life was drawing to a close.

Unless he could do something about it, which he simply couldn't see.

But this wasn't getting him dressed.

He shook his thoughts away, and focused on getting enough clothing on so he could open the door.

When he did, his four friends all tumbled inside, Simeon and Theo looking as though they'd been raking their hands through their hair repeatedly, and even Benedict looked slightly ruffled.

Fenton, of course, looked just the same, which meant he could have been mistaken as either an eccentric aristocrat or a dustbin collector.

"It's noon already!" Theo said, giving Bram a sharp look. "Why are you still abed—? Ah," he said, his expression changing to one of smug satisfaction. "Our Bram got his Towns ended," he said.

"That doesn't mean anything, you idiot," Bram muttered, but apparently everyone else in the room guessed, correctly, what Theo had at least intimated.

"What are you going to do about her?" Simeon asked. "We're at our wits' end—we thought we had her when we staged the debate."

"Yes, so clever to ask her to debate marriage," Benedict remarked dryly. "She'd never have a clue that you actually wanted her to think about it."

"She didn't say anything?" Fenton pressed.

"What was she supposed to say?" Bram shot back. "'Oh, I know we met and both vehemently agreed we were marriage-averse, but I've had a think, and I'd like to change my mind'?"

"Particularly awkward given what happened here last night," Benedict observed.

Bram's cheeks flamed red as Simeon and Theo doubled over in laughter.

"How can we help?" Simeon said when the laughter had subsided.

Bram shook his head. "You've tried, I just—"

Another knock sounded at the door and all five of them looked in confusion at one another.

"Mr. Townsend?" a voice called.

Bram shrugged, walking over to open the door to reveal Wilhelmina's Aunt Flora.

"Well," she said brightly, "we're all here. That makes it easier."

"Umf?" Aunt Flora said as Wilhelmina tapped on her door.

Wilhelmina took a deep breath, pushing the door open and stepping inside, Dipper following.

Aunt Flora's room was filled with mismatched furniture, trunks with odd bits of material hanging out from them, gardening tools, and a small collection of gardening books.

Her bed was set in the middle of the room, an enormous item that was a vestige of her married life, since she'd specifically chosen, as she told Wilhelmina, a bed that would allow her a bit of privacy from her husband.

The only visible part of her aunt was her hair, which was fluffy and gray, resting on one of the many pillows strewn on the bed.

Wilhelmina saw the coverlet move, and then Aunt Flora's head appeared, her eyes blinking rapidly as she regarded Wilhelmina.

"Why are you here so early?" she asked. "It's just ten!"

Wilhelmina walked to Aunt Flora's bed and perched on its side, reaching for her aunt's hand.

"I came because I need to talk to you," she said.

Aunt Flora's expression sobered, and she sat up, leaning back against the headboard.

She wore a nightdress of faded ivory, which buttoned to her neck, its bodice threaded with lace at marked intervals. She looked older than usual, which made sense since she had just woken up, and hadn't done any of her ablutions prior to greeting the day yet.

Wilhelmina felt her heart constrict at what she might possibly be about to do.

"What is it?" Aunt Flora said, reaching out a hand to take Wilhelmina's.

"I don't know," Wilhelmina replied, which was the truth in many ways—she didn't know what she wanted, she didn't know what to do, and she didn't know how to figure anything out.

She did know, however, that she had to tell her aunt that the future her aunt wanted was not the future Wilhelmina wanted. Though she didn't know what she did want.

Him, a voice whispered in her head.

No, it's not possible, the same voice contradicted.

But you wouldn't know unless you talk about it, the voice reasoned.

"What is it you don't know?" Aunt Flora continued. "I don't know a lot of things—I don't know how cobblers make shoes. I don't know why the sky is blue or gray," she said, looking out the window at the rain. "I don't know if I like my green day gown or the yellow paisley one—both look nice, and each has their own appeal. I don't know—"

"I don't think I want to move to the country, after all," Wilhelmina blurted out, interrupting Aunt Flora's continuous stream of conversation.

Remarkable, really, given she had just woken up.

Aunt Flora's expression grew confused. "But we agreed," she said, and her voice trembled just a bit.

Wilhelmina bit her lip, then exhaled sharply. "We did. Or you did. I know you were deeply unhappy with your husband, and I saw how Mother faded, eventually, but that doesn't mean that Father will treat Alethea equally poorly, or that I have to give up the opportunity—the opportunity for happiness because of your life."

She winced after she spoke. The words sounded far harsher than she meant them, and she watched her aunt with concern, hoping the other woman would be able to parse out what she was trying to say.

Not that Wilhelmina quite knew herself, so that would be a remarkable feat. Even more remarkable, given Aunt Flora's usual inability to follow a topic for more than a minute or two.

"Oh," her aunt said softly, and Wilhelmina crumpled.

"No, I mean, never mind. I shouldn't have said anything." She spoke rapidly, pressing her aunt's hand for emphasis.

"What you are saying," Aunt Flora replied, ignoring Wilhelmina's attempt to take it back, "is that you have fallen in love?"

Wilhelmina's breath hitched, and she had to swallow before replying. "I have."

"With that tall dark-haired gentleman? The one who looks like a Greek god?"

Wilhelmina's lips twitched at Aunt Flora's description, an apt one, for sure; after all, she'd told him he had a "jaw like Adonis" when they'd first met, and that was when she had disliked him thoroughly.

"The same," she said. "Mr. Townsend. Bram."

"Well then," Aunt Flora said, clearly trying to process this new information. "I have no choice but to believe you, and to trust that this gentleman is everything you say he is."

Not that she'd said anything, but that wasn't the point, was it.

"Especially since you came to announce it at this godforsaken hour, so you must mean it." She twisted her mouth in concentration. "You are correct, also, that your life is not mine." Her gaze shifted away from Wilhelmina's. "Or your mother's, or your father's, or Alethea's. It is yours to do with as you choose. You have to do what you think is right, my dear."

"I wish I knew what that was," Wilhelmina said, feeling tears welling up in her eyes. "Can you help me?"

Aunt Flora met Wilhelmina's gaze, then gave a slow nod. Her eyes glistened as well. "Of course, my dear. I want you to be happy." She jerked her chin toward one of the wardrobes at the edge of the room. "But I'll need to get dressed first. Can you hand me whichever day gown you like the best?"

Wilhelmina rose, giving her aunt a grateful smile. "Thank you. I don't think it'll be easy to figure out," she said. "Not the choice of day gown—I know which one I will choose," she amended. "I mean my future and happiness and all of that."

Was she actually going to reject the future she'd been trying so hard to achieve? Possibly making her aunt unhappy as well?

"Oh, I imagine it will be easier than you think," Aunt Flora replied. "After all, love is a very powerful force."

Men I Do Not Wish to Marry:
A Not at All Comprehensive List by
Lady Wilhelmina Bettesford

A gentleman who does not read. He can read the newspaper, he can read fiction, he can read government reports detailing the minutiae of the Corn Laws, but he has to read.

Chapter Twenty-Nine

$\mathscr{M}$y lady," Bram said, starting to step toward her, but Benedict was faster, and reached the door sooner, escorting Lady Flora inside.

Simeon, Theo, and Bram quickly grabbed everything lying on Bram's desk, table, and chair: several legal documents, a few pens, his stockings, his waistcoat, and his copy of *Views of the Architecture of the Heavens*, which he'd been using for nighttime reading.

"Would you like to have a seat, my lady?" Benedict said as Bram whisked away one errant stocking from the back of the chair.

"Yes, please. I brought Wilhelmina's maid, Jones— she is in the carriage. I didn't know how much room there'd be here, and I thought it would be best if we speak privately." The lady frowned. "That is, as privately as one can among six people. Is that private? Or is that a closed conversation?" She shook her head. "One doesn't know. I did not bring Dipper," she continued, making everyone but Bram look confused, "because Wilhelmina is still at home trying to decide her future or something."

Bram nodded, as though everything she'd said made sense.

"Would you like a cup of tea, my lady?" Fenton asked suddenly.

Lady Bettesford smiled. "Yes, my dear Fenton, I would."

Bram glanced from one to the other in surprise. The last he'd seen of everyone, his friends had been escorting Lady Bettesford out for the evening while he—while he and Wilhelmina cavorted. In that bed over there.

Apparently they had all grown quite cozy with one another.

"And the reason for your visit—?" Bram prompted.

"Yes, of course," she replied. "You see, I spoke with Wilhelmina this morning. Dreadfully early, so I knew something was amiss." She turned a surprisingly piercing gaze at Bram. "I am aware that Wilhelmina did not return home until the middle of the night. She doesn't know I know, but I do." She turned her gaze back to the others. "And then this morning my niece woke me saying something about her future."

Bram felt his chest tighten. Her future. Did that mean—?

"Does that mean she is reconsidering what it is she wants to do with her life?"

Thank God Fenton was here, and thank God he was unrivaled in his ability to ask direct, if often awkward, questions.

"Yes," she replied. "That is it entirely. And I believe, Mr. Townsend, that her future belongs with you." She returned that gaze to him, and he felt unsettled. "That is," she continued, the intensity of her gaze increasing, "if you wish to be with her."

"He does," his friends all chimed in.

"He's besotted with her," Simeon remarked. "He only finished this month's book club selection on time, not two weeks early, because he was otherwise preoccupied. Besotted," he repeated, shooting Bram a warm smile.

"He agreed to go into Society without having to be threatened with bodily harm," Theo added.

"He has changed his mind," Fenton said, sounding incredulous.

"And we've never seen him so happy," Benedict added.

"We want him to be happy," Fenton said simply.

There was a moment of silence as Bram absorbed everything his friends had said. All of it was true, of course, but he wouldn't have had the capacity to love as he did without having them as friends, whether from watching Simeon and Theo have any number of dramatic relationships, or Fenton cutting to the heart of the matter with his scientific analysis, or Benedict just being Benedict, which meant being wiser and more solemn than everyone else.

"Well," Lady Bettesford said, her voice trembling as though she was on the verge of tears, "that is lovely to hear. I only want the best for my niece, and I thought the best would be to stay unmarried because some gentlemen"—and then she stopped, and Benedict patted her hand—"but I can see that you are not one of those, Mr. Townsend."

"And if he were, we'd murder him," Simeon said in a conversational tone.

"Slowly and painfully," Theo added.

"So let us plan what we will do to make this happen," Lady Bettesford said.

"MINA!"

Wilhelmina groaned as she heard Alethea's voice. She'd returned to her room after speaking with Aunt Flora, and had spent the next two hours trying to figure out what she wanted.

Who she wanted.

Well, she knew that, but she didn't know how to tell him that was what she wanted.

Because if she did an about-face in terms of what she'd said she intended, she'd be putting him in a completely awkward position; he'd entered into their fake courtship under the assumption it was, indeed, fake. To then have her say she'd actually like it to be real would be duplicitous.

And hadn't he prided himself on always telling her the truth? Who would she be if she didn't do the same to him?

"Mina!"

"But I love him," she said aloud, startling Dipper, who was snoozing on her bed. "I have gone and fallen in love with the interfering baboon, which means that I—that I am truly a flibbertigibbet."

But she wasn't ashamed of that. She *was* a flibbertigibbet; she was also, she knew, a smart woman who had so much to give, and so much she wanted to do, and he was just the man she could give and do things to. And he would support her whatever she wanted. He wouldn't try to stifle any of her scientific interests, although he might make her read fiction more often.

He would love her, and protect her, and champion her. And she would do the same for him.

But only if she could figure out how to tell him. How to persuade him to change his mind about marriage. Specifically, change his mind about marrying *her*.

"Mina!" Alethea's voice was just outside her door, and Wilhelmina scrambled toward her mirror, pretending she was seeing to her toilette.

If there was one thing that Alethea would allow, it was that one was so distracted with one's own appearance that one didn't hear one's name being called several times.

The door opened, and Alethea burst in, stopping short as she saw what Wilhelmina was doing—or pretending to do.

"I was calling you," she said. "Lord Paskins is here."

"Oh," Wilhelmina said, turning as she adopted an expression of surprise. "I knew he was on his way, which is why I was taking pains with my appear—"

"You look fine. Come down now," Alethea interrupted.

Alethea was truly desperate to get Wilhelmina married off if she was cutting short Wilhelmina's primping at the mirror.

The reality of it struck Wilhelmina like a cold punch to her gut. Yes, she'd known the whole point was to get her married off, and out of this house, but she hadn't realized just how serious it had all become.

She'd thought she'd have more time to sort it all out.

She'd thought she might be able to figure out a way to tell Bram she had fallen foolishly, helplessly, and wholeheartedly in love with him.

Instead, she'd have to do something to put Lord Paskins off her entirely as she stalled for even more time.

She took a deep breath and followed Alethea down the stairs. Hopefully not to her doom.

"IT TOOK YOU long enough," Wilhelmina's father grumbled as the two ladies walked into the formal receiving room.

Alethea had redecorated here as well, and Wilhelmina couldn't help but admire her stepmother's light touch with the wallpaper and draperies. Instead of the heavy fabric and overdone patterns from before, the walls were covered in a cream-colored paper with embossed flowers, while the drapes were a darker cream, made of an elegantly stiff fabric.

Her father had been sitting in the large chair facing the sofa, while Lord Paskins appeared to have been pacing. Both men rose and bowed as Wilhelmina and Alethea entered the room.

"We wanted to make certain we looked our best," Alethea said, offering a placating smile to her husband, who smiled in return.

"Lord Paskins has kindly come, Mina, to speak with you on a matter of great interest to all of us," her father proclaimed. As though he was discussing a general tax that would affect everyone equally, and not something that would irrevocably change her life while it would alter his somewhat.

"Yes, my lady," Lord Paskins said, rushing up to Wilhelmina, who took a step back without thinking. "I am hoping we can come to an agreement on terms."

I'm not a treaty to be negotiated or a scientific paper to edit, Wilhelmina thought bitterly.

"Alethea, let us leave the two young people in

peace," her father began, but then all four of them turned as they heard voices in the hallway.

Alethea and Wilhelmina's father looked at one another, and then both turned to stare at Wilhelmina, who shrugged. "I have no idea who that could—" she began, but then the door flung open, and Aunt Flora trotted in, followed by Bram and all four of his friends.

"Goodness," Aunt Flora said, blinking in surprise as she took in the scene, "I didn't realize Lord Paskins was here."

"Yes, he is," the earl replied, sounding annoyed.

"We were going to have a bit of refreshment," Alethea said, using her most gracious tone. "Would you care to join us? Mr. Townsend, Mr. Quintrell, Mr.— I'm sorry, I don't believe I know you," she continued, speaking to Mr. Ash, Mr. Osborne, and Mr. Jones.

"Fenton," Mr. Ash replied quickly. "And this is Theo and this is Simeon."

Alethea allowed a tiny furrowing of her brow to register her confusion.

"But we've got business with Lord Paskins here," Mr. Jones said, giving a wolfish grin toward the gentleman. "Can you just—?"

Mr. Osborne and Mr. Jones went to either side of Lord Paskins, and it seemed as though they picked him up by his elbows and carried him out of the room.

Wilhelmina, Alethea, and her father all gaped as the three moved out of sight. Within a few minutes, Mr. Osborne and Mr. Jones had returned, with Mr. Jones looking pleased with himself and slightly out of breath.

"See here," Wilhelmina's father said, "just what is the meaning of this?"

Aunt Flora stepped toward her brother, making a gesture that indicated she wished for quiet. "We are here to conduct a trial, dear brother."

The earl gave his sister a look that managed to combine indignance and incredulity all at once.

Remarkable feat, really, Wilhelmina mused.

"A trial? What are you even talking about?" He made a sputtering sound. "This is all nonsense, to be sure."

Aunt Flora met his gaze, her eyes sharp and clear. "A trial to determine your daughter's future."

And then she turned, giving her niece a warm, kind smile that made Wilhelmina think that, just maybe, it would all be all right.

BRAM DIDN'T THINK it would be possible to be even more nervous than he had been during the Stars Above Society's debate. But his mouth was dry, his palms were moist, and his whole body felt hot.

So basically he was a desert and a tropical rain forest all at once.

But if it meant he had a chance, he would embody the continents of Europe and Asia, respectively, all by himself.

"My lord, my lady," Benedict said, nodding to the earl and his wife, "you will be the jury." He gestured to the large sofa that faced the fireplace. "If you would take a seat?"

His general tone of authority made it impossible for either of the two to refuse, though the earl made a few more sputtering noises.

"Lady Flora is the judge," Benedict continued, while Simeon bowed low in front of her and then rose, indicating for her to take his arm. Simeon escorted her to a large chair that sat to the side of the sofa. "Bram—Mr. Townsend—is the barrister, arguing for the matter at hand."

"And just what is the matter at hand?" the earl demanded loudly.

"Whether or not Lady Wilhelmina should marry Mr. Townsend."

"I think not," the earl said, nearly exploding out of his seat. He turned to his wife, his face turning a shade of purple. "Is this your doing? You said he wasn't a real suitor, that he was just going to pretend so as to—"

"So as to get other gentlemen interested," Wilhelmina said flatly.

"And it worked, didn't it?" Lady Croyde replied. "Lord Paskins was here—where has he gone?" she said, turning to look around the room with a confused expression.

"He was called away unexpectedly," Benedict supplied.

"His chin had an urgent appointment with my fist," Theo murmured, and Wilhelmina's father and stepmother were too distracted to notice, Bram thought in relief.

"And now here is this—this—"

"This orphan?" Simeon said silkily, his tone a warning to anyone who knew him.

"Yes! We don't know who his parents are. We—"

"Excuse me, my lord." The housekeeper stood at the door, her posture rigid.

"We do not require refreshments now," the earl thundered, and Bram was impressed that she didn't flinch.

"I am not here for refreshments," she said tightly, stepping into the room.

"What is it?" the earl asked in exasperation. "Goodness only knows we have enough people in here spouting nonsense—we might as well add you to the fray."

The housekeeper—Bram couldn't recall her name—folded her hands in front of her and made a visible attempt to settle herself.

"You said you don't know who this gentleman's parents are," the housekeeper said, glancing quickly toward Bram and then back at the earl. "But I do." She took a deep breath.

"He is my son."

Men I Do Not Wish to Marry: A Not at All Comprehensive List by Lady Wilhelmina Bettesford

Nero, the Roman emperor.

He was a terrible ruler, but most pertinent to this discussion is that he murdered his entire family. Which, one presumes, would include a wife.

Chapter Thirty

Wilhelmina felt as though she had suddenly been thrust into a French farce, or perhaps a Punch and Judy show, only her father would never allow anything so vulgar as those two things to take place in his house.

But it appeared he'd lost control of everything, so perhaps this was a plebeian dream.

Or he had changed, as she had; after all, he had married Alethea, who was lower in status than he. Though he was as pedantic and judgmental as before, so perhaps she was just seeing him in a different light.

Lord Paskins had gone just after Bram and his friends arrived, and she couldn't help but think the swap was a vast improvement.

But she could not figure out why they were all here—they said it was to argue that she should marry Bram, but if he felt strongly about her, shouldn't he have just . . . told her?

Though she hadn't told him how she felt, so perhaps she was being hypocritical.

And now Mrs. Windham had made her startling

announcement, and Wilhelmina didn't know just what to feel.

"He is your son?" her father said, his eyes wide. "But . . . ?"

Alethea patted her husband's arm. "Perhaps we could let Mrs. Windham explain." Her brow furrowed. "You've just met him, haven't you? Just how did you know anyway?"

Mrs. Windham gave Bram a look so fond Wilhelmina felt her insides melt. "He looks just like his father. I couldn't believe it when I first saw him, but he is the spitting image of Vittorio. Vittorio Rossi, he was a traveling musician." Her expression grew dreamy. "He broke his leg while singing on a high wire, and he had to stay in the town after his companions left. We had plans to marry after he'd made enough money to support us." Her mouth tightened in pain. "But then I heard he was forced to leave England because his troupe ran into trouble with the authorities." She paused. "I never saw him again."

"Oh, how tragic!" Alethea exclaimed. She clasped Mrs. Windham's hands in sympathy. "Imagine not being able to be with the love of your life," she said, glancing toward her husband.

Wilhelmina felt her eyes prickling. To be in love, to believe you were going to be with someone for the rest of your life, only to lose them so unexpectedly—that was indeed tragic, as Alethea said.

And, she realized, a feeling of cold terror coursing down her spine, that would happen to her if she didn't say or do something.

Because she knew what she wanted. She could

have her scientific studies and him as well; she wouldn't have to compromise.

If her father approved, eventually, that would be lovely. But she wouldn't allow anybody but herself to dictate what she was going to do. Not anymore.

"Mrs.—" Mr. Jones said, hesitating.

"Windham," Mrs. Windham replied.

"Mrs. Windham, if you and Bram here would like to take a moment, perhaps talk—"

"No," Mrs. Windham interrupted. "I understand that you are all here to discuss whether or not Lady Wilhelmina should marry my—should marry Mr. Townsend." She took a deep breath. "And I have to say, if they love one another, then they should not delay, because you do not know what is going to happen." She nodded toward Bram. "Later we can talk about everything. But right now, I don't want to see another chance at love lost to circumstances beyond one's control."

Wilhelmina felt her chest constrict at the thought that she could lose Bram when she didn't even truly have him.

The night before didn't count, not really. Because she had had him in a very different way, and that shouldn't oblige people to commit themselves if that wasn't what they wanted.

"Allow me to assist you to a chair, then," Mr. Jones said, holding his arm out to the housekeeper. She took it, her eyes tremulous, and sat, giving an encouraging nod toward Wilhelmina.

"Well then," Mr. Quintrell said. "Shall we continue?"

Aunt Flora clapped her hands together excitedly. Wilhelmina had honestly forgotten her aunt was there, tucked into the corner of the room.

"I am the judge, and my brother and Lady Croyde
are—"

"Are the jury."

"I will be arguing for the defense," Bram said.

"Isn't that biased of you?" Aunt Flora asked.
"Given that you love my niece?"

That he loves her. He loved her?

Wilhelmina felt a warm rush of emotion course
through her at her aunt's words, and then she
frowned.

"Do you disagree, my lady?" Bram asked softly.
"You forget, I see you. Always."

"No, I was just wondering why my aunt knows
you love me before I do," Wilhelmina blurted.

Bram's eyebrows rose, while his friends tried to
stifle their laughter.

"Uh—" he began, but Wilhelmina waved her
hand in dismissal.

"Never mind," she said. "Let's just get on with it."

As romantic declarations went, it definitely
lacked something. But it spoke to her scientific
heart, since it was a process of testing, and was
a controlled experiment. There were only two of
them, after all, and the purpose of the test would
be to prove that both of them loved the other. It
was only through a series of rigorous tests that
each could be satisfied as to the feelings of the
other.

And last night did not count, since passion and
lust and desire were their own different elements.

"Well then," Bram said, clasping his hands be-
hind his back, "allow me to call my first witness."
He gave her a pointed look, and her eyes widened.
"Yes, you," he said, a sly grin tugging the corner of

his mouth. "I call Lady Wilhelmina Bettesford to the stand."

BRAM COULDN'T LET himself think about his mother's revelation, nor that he finally had a mother in the first place. There would be time to get to know her, but she wasn't wrong about the urgency—Lord Paskins would return, eventually, and Bram knew now was his best opportunity to persuade her.

And she would have to persuade him.

Because the truth of it was, he wouldn't do anything that she didn't want, even though his soul ached for her. Even though the night before had convinced him more than ever that she was the one he wanted in his life, and if he didn't have her, he wouldn't settle for anybody.

But questioning her about her feelings was the only way he could know for certain—she'd have to swear to tell the truth, wouldn't she?

She was too honest to lie anyway. She was bold, and brave, and fearless, and she would not lie. He'd seen it when he'd asked her opinion of the opera, when she'd kissed him for the first time, when she'd been so furious with him about the deception her father and stepmother proposed.

"I'll be the bailiff," Benedict said. He nodded to Wilhelmina, who had taken a seat in the chair next to the fireplace. "Do you swear to tell the truth, my lady?"

Her expression was solemn. "I do."

Benedict turned to Bram. "Your witness."

"See here," the earl said, "you have a barrister for one side, but not for the other."

"I'll represent the other side," Wilhelmina said, making Bram's blood turn cold. "After all," she continued, "who better to determine the truth of the matter than the other one of the two witnesses? Because of course I will have to call *you* to the stand, Mr. Townsend."

Bram's friends whooped, and cheered, and whistled, as he stared at her, his heart thudding in his chest.

Why was she—? But he knew the answer. It was because she was determined that there be fairness, whether it was to allow females into a scientific society, to give them the ability to determine their own fate, even to walk into a pub, if they wished it.

"Well," Bram said, clearing his throat, "let us begin."

Bram went to stand in front of her, trying not to get distracted by her lovely face, the fierce, reckless look in her eyes, or the memory of her smooth, warm skin under his hands.

"Mr. Townsend?" she prompted.

"Yes," he said, clasping his hands behind him again, because if he didn't, he might be tempted to catch her up and haul her out of the room in his arms, proving his love to her with his mouth, his hands, and his cock.

"Is it true, my lady, that you wish to study the stars?"

"Yes," she replied, her eyebrows furrowed as though in question.

"And is it also true that you believe that a husband of any sort would hamper your ability to do so?"

"Also yes," she said.

"But—"

"Hush, Charles," Lady Flora admonished. "This is a court of law. At least for the moment, and we do not allow interruptions."

The earl grumbled, but kept quiet.

"Do you think that if you were to marry me that I would impede your ability to study the stars?"

"No," was her quick response.

"And why is that?" he asked.

"Because," she began, biting her lip, "you care for me."

"And if you were given the opportunity to marry me, would you do so? Knowing that I would not interfere with your studies? With anything you wished to do, in fact?"

"Isn't that leading the witness?" Theo said.

Bram shot him a dark look, and Theo grinned in reply.

She took a very long time to answer, and Bram felt as though everyone in the room could hear his heart beating wildly in his chest.

"I would," she said at last, at which Bram exhaled a sigh of relief.

"And why is that, my lady?"

She lifted her chin to meet his gaze. "Because I love you."

THERE. SHE'D SAID it. She hadn't kept it a secret, and worried about it ruining his life if she told him—there was enough of that type of melodrama in the books he read, she imagined.

So she'd just said it.

His expression was relieved, as though there was any doubt before.

But of course there had been doubt. Because

she'd told him how important her freedom was to her, and for her to relinquish it was a very big step, and one he had to have been willing to give up, if it meant her happiness.

She was grateful to his ridiculous friends for forcing the issue, because she knew it had been them—concerned as they were for his well-being— who had concocted this spectacle in an attempt to prove beyond a shadow of a doubt that they were meant for one another.

Proving it also, she hoped, to her father and stepmother.

"I rest my case," Bram said, smiling at her. She returned the smile, feeling a heated spark burn through her at the very thought of spending the rest of her life with this man.

"It doesn't matter if they love one another," her father exploded, getting up out of his seat, Alethea's hand on his arm unable to restrain him. "My daughter cannot marry this man because—because you all know why."

"Because I'm a bastard?" Bram said in a low voice.

Her father's face reddened, and he didn't look at anyone as he spoke. "Yes."

BRAM IMAGINED IT wouldn't be proper etiquette to shake your potential father-in-law, but then again, he wasn't proper, so perhaps he should.

"We have not heard from the other side," Wilhelmina said in a mild tone. She'd risen from her chair, and beckoned him toward it. Bram went, sitting where she had, turning his face up to look at her.

He wouldn't dare think this would be the last

moment he'd get the chance to look at her—now that he knew she loved him, he would tear down anything to get at her—but he didn't dare to look away, in case her father engaged in some aristocratic hijinks to whisk her away in a second, before she or Bram had a chance to do anything.

"Mr. Townsend," she began, and he held his breath as he waited for her question. "Mr. Townsend," she said again, "is it true you love me?" she asked, smiling so widely he knew it would be all right. Somehow, she would make it all right.

"It is," he confirmed, exhaling. They shared a smile, and then she began to speak again, nearly shocking him out of his seat.

"And is it also true that last night we engaged in activities normally and conventionally restricted to married couples?"

Bram felt his face heat, and heard the low appreciative murmurs from his friends. "Also true, yes."

"These activities—if they were known more widely than just between the two participants, what would be the result of that?"

"It would depend entirely on the two participants, and what their status was in life."

"Explain," she directed.

"Well, if the two participants were of the same class, they would likely marry."

"And if, for example, one of the participants was of a higher class?" she said.

"Again, it would depend on which party was which." He went on at her questioning expression. "If the higher class person was the male of the two participants, he might not have to do anything about his, um, activities." His face must be tomato-red by now, he thought. He didn't like talking about these things with his closest friends, much less in a room with all of his closest friends plus the relatives of the woman he'd actually done the act with.

He didn't dare look at Simeon or Theo; he knew both of them were likely enjoying this hugely.

"Is that fair?" she asked.

"Of course not," he shot back. "A person should always be responsible for his or her actions, regardless of their gender."

"Is that why you entered the law profession, Mr. Townsend?"

He nodded. "Yes."

"So you are an honorable person, is that right?"

"I try to be."

"So if you were to have done something that would require an action—say, getting married to another person to rescue their reputation or simply to do the right thing—you would do it?"

His lips curled into a smile. "I would."

"Therefore, Mr. Townsend," she said, dropping down to one knee, "since I have compromised you, would you do me the honor of marrying me?"

His smile widened to a grin as he spoke. "I would."

"Thank you," she said softly, gazing up at him.

She rose, and turned to address her father, but her aunt spoke first.

"As the judge of this trial, I am announcing that this unexpected new piece of evidence is proof that these two love one another, and should be together for the rest of their lives." She banged her hand on the arm of her chair. "And so it is ordered."

There was silence for a moment, and everyone looked at the earl, whose lips had tightened, but he didn't say a word.

Eventually, Lady Alethea spoke. "My love, these two have a very similar story to us, if you recall."

Bram felt his eyes widen, and saw Wilhelmina jerk in surprise.

"At the time, I asked if my birth would be an impediment, and you assured me that nothing would stand in the way of true love," she continued. She patted his arm. "I am so delighted that your daughter has found the truest love she could, and we should be so happy for her." A pause. "Shouldn't we?"

And then the earl rose, slowly, and advanced toward Wilhelmina, opening his arms as she stepped into them, giving her a warm embrace before releasing her to turn to Bram.

"You'll take good care of my daughter," he said.

"I will," Bram promised.

**Men I Do Not Wish to Marry:
A Not at All Comprehensive List by
Lady Wilhelmina Bettesford**

Any man who does not at least acknowledge that there are certain advantages they hold over the opposite sex.

Chapter Thirty-One

After that, it was chaos; Aunt Flora rang for refreshments, and Bram's friends began to ply Mrs. Windham with questions, treating her as an equal and not at all a fallen woman.

Her father and Alethea sat together, holding hands, Alethea giving Wilhelmina an encouraging look every so often.

When the refreshments arrived, Aunt Flora took charge, ordering where they were to go, and then asking that the furniture be pushed to the corners of the room.

Apparently, Aunt Flora had a long-held desire to dance, and she thought that this was the perfect opportunity, even though there was no music.

But Mr. Jones could hum quite well, and soon the gentlemen were dancing with Aunt Flora and Mrs. Windham, the two who were not dancing at the time merely waiting for their turn.

"Should we go?" Wilhelmina said, tugging on Bram's sleeve. "It seems everyone is busy, so I don't think we'll be missed."

Bram looked down at her, a smile tugging his lips. "Yes, please. I would like to be alone with you."

"To make a scientific study to prove last night's delirious pleasure wasn't an anomaly? I like the way you think, Mr. Townsend," she said with a grin.

"To be able to kiss you and treat you as you should be treated, Lady Luminous," he replied.

She took his hand and led him out of the room, meeting Mr. Quintrell's gaze for a moment before they slipped out the door.

They ran up the stairs, their laughter hushed, until she brought him to her room, shooing Dipper out and shutting the door behind them.

It was odd to see him in her bedroom, but it also felt perfectly right.

He stood as though waiting for her to take the lead, making her keenly aware of the power she held.

She walked to him, sliding her arms around his neck and raising her face to his.

"Kiss me, Mr. Helpful," she said.

He did. And it was as glorious as before—or even more so, because she knew she would be kissing him, and he would be kissing her, for the rest of their lives. Because he would give her the freedom to do what she wanted, and she would love him with all the ferocity in her heart. Because he had given her not only himself, but his brothers in spirit, and she was so grateful to have a newfound family as well.

And then she shoved his coat off his shoulders, yanked his shirt apart, and pressed herself against him as his fingers undid the buttons at the back of her gown.

Soon they were naked, on her bed, and they were experimenting with another position, one that made his entering her feel different from before.

"I might have to write a paper on the results from

each position," she mused as his mouth found her breast, and then moved lower, until all thoughts fell away from her mind, and she was gasping in delight as he brought her to climax.

Only when she felt once again in control of her faculties did she look down at him. Into those piercing blue eyes, now lit with an unholy passion that thrilled her.

"You make me see stars," she said softly.

"And you carry me to them," he replied.

Epilogue

Wilhelmina shifted in the gown Alethea had chosen—a gorgeous confection made of layers and layers of tulle, ribbon, ruffles, and silk. She wore a headpiece of stiff satin, embroidered stars dancing over its surface. In the weeks following Wilhelmina's proposal, Bram had achieved a position as a judge, and had purchased a cozy house at the outskirts of his jurisdiction, decorating it with pieces Wilhelmina had retrieved from the attic where Alethea had stored them.

But first they were headed to Ireland, to Lord Rosse's estate, along with the enormous telescope Bram had bought for her as a wedding gift. She far preferred that gift to what most young ladies received on accepting a proposal.

And besides, she was the one who had proposed.

Aunt Flora had moved out of her brother's house and in with Fenton, who had suddenly decided he wanted his own aunt, since he'd never had one. Wilhelmina suspected that Fenton didn't actually want an aunt, but he did want Aunt Flora to be able to do what she wished when she wished. Fenton had

resumed his calculations on who the Home's benefactor could be, and Aunt Flora was helping in that
endeavor as well. If by helping one meant interrupting at odd times to inquire about puddings and
mathematical equations in equal measure.

"You look lovely," Alethea said, her tone proud. "I
do believe you will be the most beautiful woman at
your wedding, Mina, and I will be attending!"

Wilhelmina bit back a laugh at Alethea's uncon-
scious self-absorption. "Thank you, Alethea. I owe
a great deal of this to you," she said, gesturing to
the gown.

"You do," her stepmother replied simply. "Now
let's go, your father does not like to be kept waiting."

No, he does not, Wilhelmina thought. That, at least,
hadn't changed.

She and Alethea walked out of the small room
they'd been preparing in, and stepped into the large
ballroom in the Croyde town house. It was unusual
to marry in a private home, but Wilhelmina hadn't
wanted all the attention a large church wedding
would engender, and she also did not want anybody to muse on Bram's parentage, especially since
he'd asked Mrs. Windham to stand up with him
during the ceremony.

That was even more unusual, but Wilhelmina was
grateful he and his mother were forging a much be-
lated bond. Mrs. Windham was training Jones as
a housekeeper, and when that was complete, was
going to come live with the newly married couple, even though she'd tried to demur, saying they
needed time alone.

Wilhelmina had argued as vehemently as Bram

against this, detailing all the ways a strong family was much better than a couple, no matter how in love the two were.

The earl waited for her, and tucked her arm into his as they began to walk down the aisle to where Bram and his mother stood.

Bram's friends were the only other attendees, and Wilhelmina smiled at each of them in turn, knowing they all had a hand in her happily-ever-after. Hoping they, too, would get their happily-ever-afters.

"Will you take this man to be your lawfully wedded husband?" the officiant said. "To have and to hold, in sickness and health, to love and honor, in good times and woe, for richer or poorer, keeping yourself solely unto him for as long as you both shall live?"

She'd asked him to omit the "obey" part, since she had no intention of obeying him, nor he her. That was how both of them wanted it, since they'd agreed they would prefer to debate any potential disagreement rather than insist on their way.

"I do," Wilhelmina said.

"I now pronounce you husband and wife," the officiant said as Bram's friends erupted into cheers.

Wilhelmina smiled up into Bram's face. "I'm so glad I fell on you," she said softly.

"And I'm so glad I was there to be fallen onto," he replied, lowering his mouth to hers.

Keep reading for a sneak peek at

HIS STUDY
in
SCANDAL

the next book in Megan Frampton's
School for Scoundrels series

Chapter One

Two years and one day.

Two years and one day more than she would have wanted to mourn her husband, but Society insisted the widow of a duke must spend that long in sad contemplation of her loss.

Every so often, Alexandra wanted to ask Society just how one was supposed to contemplate sadly. She imagined it would involve many hours of sitting in a mountain of black, staring at the seat he used to sit in. Perhaps choking on a few silent sobs when Cook served his favorite dish of boiled ham and potatoes.

She hadn't done any of that. And she loathed boiled ham and potatoes.

Instead, Alexandra had ordered a few black gowns and had taken to doing all the things her husband had frowned on her doing while he was alive. Things like tending the garden, reading novels, taking afternoon naps, and having a second biscuit at tea. Talking to her daughter about nothing, rather than instructing her in proper deportment. Things that a duchess shouldn't deign to do—according to her late husband—regardless of how the duchess in question felt.

All while waiting until the day she didn't have to wear black and pretend things she didn't feel. Vowing not to waste a minute once she was safely past the time she might scandalize Society with her flagrant weed-pulling.

Which was why, two years and one day after her husband had died, she was standing on a small platform in the middle of a fitting room in a London dress shop, about to destroy her mourning clothing.

Preparing to order an entire new wardrobe so she could chaperone her daughter's delayed debut into Society.

"Hand me the scissors, please?" Alexandra said, turning her head to address one of the two seamstresses in the fitting room.

"You're actually going to—" her stepdaughter, Edith, said in an admiring tone. A tone Alexandra appreciated, since Edith was by far the most adventurous person Alexandra had ever met—so adventurous, in fact, that Edith's father, Alexandra's husband, had always gotten a peculiar expression on his face when her name was mentioned.

Which was probably why Edith spent most of her time traveling, far away from her father's judgment.

"I am," Alexandra said firmly.

They were in Madame Lucille's Fine Millinery, a shop just off Bond Street that Alexandra had learned about from her late husband. Before he died, of course.

The duke had been adamantly opposed to creating laws that would improve working conditions for seamstresses, saying they would embolden female workers, and had disdainfully cited Madame

Lucille's establishment because Madame Lucille offered close to a living wage for ten hours of work a day, not far less for far more hours.

Madame Lucille herself had welcomed Alexandra and Edith, at first with trepidation as though anticipating the dowager duchess had arrived to continue the work her husband had begun, then with glee as Alexandra explained what she wanted, accompanied by Edith's whoops of encouragement. The shop was small but immaculately clean, and Madame Lucille had given the two ladies a tour, where Alexandra was relieved to see cheery seamstresses in the back work areas, all talking amongst themselves as they plied their needles.

Madame Lucille had then shown them into the small fitting room, far smaller than the shops that the duke had insisted Alexandra patronize, then excused herself to locate the bolts of fabric she wanted in order to make up Alexandra's new post-mourning wardrobe.

The wardrobe she would wear, all the while hoping her daughter would find a man—eventually—with whom she would fall in love, not make a strategic dynastic pairing. When Harriet spoke about her Season, she talked about meeting new people, and seeing as much of London as she could, and didn't seem to want to get married right away.

Alexandra felt a fizzing awareness of her future, something she hadn't had since before she was married. She'd wear as many colors as possible, drink champagne with insouciance—or souciance, if she felt like it—and generally behave as she wished to, not as others wished her to. Perhaps even take a *third* biscuit, if the biscuits were particularly delicious and she was feeling decidedly peckish.

Once her daughter was safely and well taken care of, of course. Until then, she would have to maintain her duchess façade. But clad in colors and fabrics *she* chose.

Two of the young seamstresses remained in the room, on hand for any assistance if needed. Both of them seemed overwhelmed by having an actual duchess in their midst, even if Alexandra was now just a dowager duchess.

Alexandra took the scissors the shorter of the two workers handed her, then directed her attention to putting her fingers in the appropriate places, pointing the sharp edge of the shears at her neckline, which caused one of the two workers to emit a startled squeak. The neckline was uncomfortably high, and the black bombazine fabric was stiff and unyielding.

Rather like my late husband, Alexandra thought. She nearly shared the quip with Edith, but she didn't want to scandalize the seamstresses.

The metal of the scissors was cool against her heated skin, and she uttered an involuntary gasp before positioning herself awkwardly so she could cut.

The first close of the scissors wasn't the triumphant action Alexandra was hoping for; the fabric of her gown was apparently too determined to withstand the scissors' onslaught.

But then she clamped her jaw and readjusted her grip, and the scissors bit into the unforgiving material, the two sides falling away as Alexandra continued the downward motion.

She was strong enough to overcome the obstacle of something that was stiff and unyielding.

The snap of the scissors and the whispered shush of the fabric was the only sound in the room.

Until, finally, she reached the bottom, cutting through the ruffled hem and sighing in satisfaction as the two halves of the gown fell apart, revealing her undergarments, a stark white against the dull black of her outer garment. Still holding the scissors in one hand, she straightened, tugging the two sides of the gown apart until they were on her body only because of the sleeves encasing her arms. She turned to hand the scissors back to the worker, then began to slide the sleeves off, biting her lip in anticipation.

No more black. No more mourning.

"Bravo!" Edith cheered. Alexandra looked at her stepdaughter's face and grinned in response. "This calls for a celebration," Edith added, a mischievous look on her face. "You've got one night before the rest of the family arrives and the Season starts. Let's have some fun."

THEOPHILUS OSBORNE PLUCKED the last sheet of paper that lay on the left of his desk, laid it directly in front of him, scanned it, then picked up his pen and signed his name with a flourish. Then he picked up the paper and perched it atop the enormous stack on the right, emitting a sigh of satisfaction.

He leaned back in his chair, folding his hands behind his head.

It was done. For today, at least.

And when he married the Duke of Chelmswich's

sister, he would have accomplished all his late father wished for him.

The duke had paid a call earlier that day, suggesting an arrangement that would suit both parties. Theo would marry Lady Harriet, and in exchange for the family's impeccable bloodlines, Theo would make several strategic investments into the duke's struggling interests. That the duke could also wield certain legal tactics to Theo's advantage might have been mentioned as well.

It was the kind of cold-hearted bargain that only the most aristocratic families engaged in. Theo was willing to forgo the opportunity of marrying for love if it meant he could both improve his business and fulfill his late father's dream.

Osborne and Son had grown, over the course of Theo's stewardship, to include one shipping line, various wholesale industries, a railroad, several London shops, and a pleasure garden.

It was the last item he was thinking of now; he'd purchased it a few years ago, when he'd found himself returning for, well, *pleasure* over the course of a month.

Unlike Vauxhall Gardens, which had been wildly popular in his father's youth, and still offered a variety of familial entertainments, the more discreet Garden of Hedon was for adults who wished to indulge their desires. Any and everything was permitted, as long as everyone involved agreed.

And Theo often found himself there agreeing wholeheartedly. It was a place where he could forget, for a few hours, that he carried the weight of hundreds of people's livelihoods on his back. Forget that most of the gentlemen he met during the course of his business were just as likely to look down on him for his low birth as they were to take his money.

Fucking for forgetfulness was his second favorite hobby. His first was his monthly meetings with his friends, four fellow orphans he'd met at the Devenaugh Home for Destitute Boys.

Each of the five had been placed with good families. In his case, he'd been placed with a gentleman who'd never married but who longed for a family of his own. Theo and Mr. Osborne had been as close as any actual father and son, and Mr. Osborne had taught Theo everything he knew about the business.

Theo had stayed close with his fellow orphans through the years, and they'd been his solace when Mr. Osborne had finally succumbed to a nasty cold. The monthly meetings were his only regularly scheduled time away from work.

But since the next meeting wasn't for a few days—he hadn't even bought the book they were to discuss, Charlotte Lennox's *The Female Quixote*—he'd take himself to the Garden of H, where he hoped to find a likeminded female for some mindless mutual enjoyment.

It would be the last time he would allow himself to go there. As a patron, at least; he was to meet his intended at her debut, and he wouldn't continue his usual activities once he'd met her. It was something aristocrats likely would scoff at, but Theo intended to be faithful to his wife, regardless of how he came to marry her.

So tonight would be very special.

"Good evening, Mr. Osborne," the guard said as Theo alit from the hackney.

Theo leaned in and spoke in a low tone. "Remember, no names. We take pride in our discretion."

The guard's eyes widened, and he snapped to attention. "Of course, Mr. Os—that is, Mr. Mysterious Gentleman."

Theo smothered a grin at the guard's attempt at subterfuge, then strolled through the gates, glancing around at the medium-sized crowd already in attendance.

"Theo!" a voice called. So much for keeping his identity secret.

He swung around, seeing his friend Lucy. Lucy owned a millinery, and she rented the space for her business from him. Much later, they'd run into one another at the Garden, spending a few hours together several months ago. They had both agreed it was enjoyable, but that they'd rather stay friends than try it again.

Theo was just as happy, since he didn't want a commitment with anyone. Not even anyone he'd fucked to exhaustion. His business took up enough time as it was; he didn't have time for any kind of relationship, no matter how mutually beneficial it would be.

Which did rather beg the question of what introducing a wife into his life would look like. But that was the whole point, wasn't it? To marry, and utilize the duke's connections to ensure he could step away from his business interests and live the life of a gentleman of leisure. It would take some doing, but he wasn't scared of hard work.

Tomorrow, he promised himself, he would plan all of it. *Not tonight.*

"How are you?" he said, kissing her cheek.

As always, she was garbed impeccably, a walking advertisement for the excellence of her shop.

"I'm wonderful. I'm dressing a duchess now, if you can believe it. A dowager duchess, to be sure, but a duchess nonetheless."

"Excellent! Am I going to have to raise your rent?" he asked, accompanying his words with a wink.

She poked him in the chest. "No, she hasn't paid her bill yet." She gave him an assessing look. "And you, you're here because you've been working too hard?"

"How did you know that?" he asked.

She rolled her eyes. "Because you're always working too hard." She gave him a gentle push toward the middle of the Garden. "Go have fun, heaven knows you deserve it."

"Thanks, Lucy."

"And make sure to tell the lady how fortunate she is to get you," she called over her shoulder, waving a goodbye.

"I shouldn't have to tell her," Theo murmured. "I'll have already shown her. Preferably a few times at least."

He surveyed the crowd, most of whom were watching a contortionist twist herself into a pretzel on stage. While the Garden was a place for anonymous couplings, it also hosted a variety of other entertainments, most of which weren't salacious at all.

The guiding ethos of the Garden is that whatever anyone chose to do it should be fun. Whether that meant sexual exploration or a sprightly game of chess, it didn't matter.

Theo believed strongly that if one worked hard, one should also play hard. The Garden was for the hard-working people of London, people who had a few spare pence to afford the admittance fee. Some of the patrons—the ones from the best families—had expressed surprise that they were elbow-to-elbow with the merchants they purchased pottery from, or the bankers they did business with. Theo would then strongly suggest those complainers leave the Garden never to return.

"What are we doing here?" he heard a woman say somewhere behind him.

"We're here," another woman replied, "so that you can know what it feels like to have fun." The second woman spoke firmly.

"I know what it feels like—" the first woman began, then trailed off. "Never mind. You are absolutely right. There's fun, and then there is *fun*. What kind of fun are we talking about? Oh, I see a chess game over there! And look, some people are riding donkeys! I've never ridden a donkey. That seems fun!"

Theo smothered a smile at the woman's excited tone.

"We are not here for you to ride a donkey, for heaven's sake," the second woman said, sounding aggrieved. "Look, there is a gentleman up ahead. Why don't you ask him what he likes to do here?"

"You mean go up to a stranger and begin talking?" the woman said. From the way she spoke, she might have been suggesting standing on her head while reciting poetry, it was such an outlandish idea.

"Why not?"

Silence as the first woman seemed to process the idea. "Fine. But if I do not have fun, it is your fault."

"Go," the second woman said. "I'll meet you back here in two hours. I'm going to find my own type of fun."

Theo turned to look at the two women, nearly stumbling into one of them, who was heading directly for him.

This must be the first woman, the one who had never had fun.

She was striking, if not necessarily traditionally beautiful; her eyes were wide-set, and dark, with strong eyebrows set above. Her nose was strong as well, giving her an almost haughty appearance. Her wide mouth curled up into a smile, and her lips were full and rose-colored and eminently bitable. Her hair was a medium blond, at least in the flickering light, and looked as though it tended to waviness. She had it pulled back into a practical chignon, a few strands falling out from her coiffure.

"Good evening," he said as she opened her mouth to speak. "Are you here for the entertainment?" he said, gesturing vaguely toward the main area of the Garden.

"I don't know what I'm here for," she muttered, but Theo heard her.

He held his arm out for her. "Allow me to show you," he said, as she took his arm. "And you can tell me what you want."